Also in this series:

USBORNE
SANDY LANE STABLES
OMNIBUS

A Horse for the Summer

The Runaway Pony

Strangers at the Stables

First published in 1997 by Usborne Publishing Ltd, Usborne
House, 83-85 Saffron Hill, London EC1N 8RT, England.

Copyright © 1997 Usborne Publishing Ltd.

The name Usborne and the device 🎈 are Trade Marks of
Usborne Publishing Ltd.

ISBN 0 7460 3153 X

Typeset in Times

Printed in Great Britain

Series Editor: Gaby Waters
Designer: Lucy Parris
Cover photograph supplied by:
Bob Langrish
Map illustrations by John Woodcock

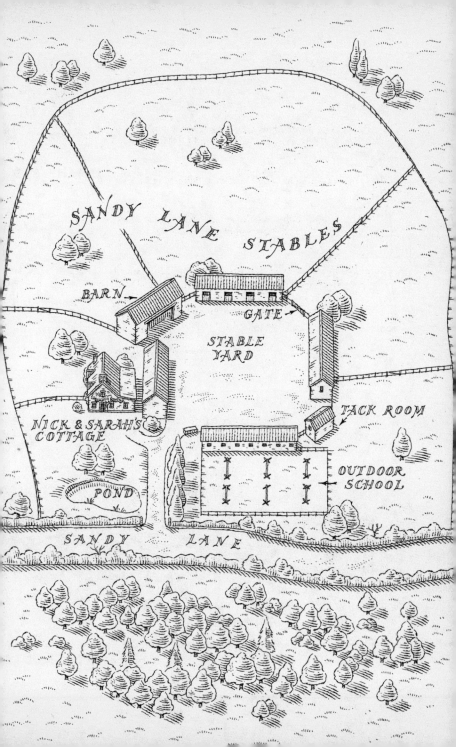

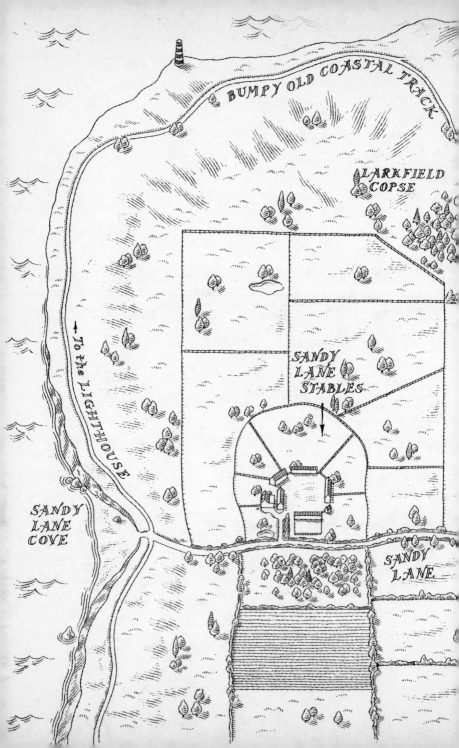

SANDY
BAY

BUCKNELL
WOODS

TO ASH HILL

To
COLCOTT

PIG
FARM

A HORSE
FOR THE
SUMMER

Michelle Bates

CONTENTS

1

EXCITING NEWS

Tom Buchanan pedalled furiously down the drive to Sandy Lane Stables and rattled into the yard. He couldn't believe it had been two years since he'd started riding there. Two whole years... it seemed like only yesterday that he'd first arrived. Time had flown. Yet today was very different from any other day, deliciously different, for Tom had some very exciting news to share. The early morning mist was rising from the fields as a hazy glow filled the air. Tom jumped off his bike and, throwing it to the ground, charged into the tack room.

"Nick, Sarah, where are you?" he cried, hardly able to contain his excitement. "You're never going to believe my luck." Silence.

Tom called again, only louder this time, but there was still no answer. That was unusual. Nick Brooks and his wife Sarah, the owners of Sandy Lane, could normally be found in the tack room on the dot of eight, carefully planning the day ahead after the early morning feeds.

Tom stood in the doorway and scratched his head. Where was everyone? Twisting slowly around, he scanned the yard. Ah, there was Nick now, coming out of Feather's stable followed by the vet, a burly man with a florid, weather-beaten complexion. Feather had been having trouble with her leg for ages. Tom hoped it wasn't anything serious.

"A sprain in the suspensory ligament... plenty of rest... that's the only thing I can prescribe for her."

Tom could just catch snippets of what the vet was saying.

"Hose her down for the next forty-eight hours to reduce the inflammation," the vet continued, "and add a support bandage to the opposite leg. That should help it take the extra weight without becoming too strained."

"Well, that settles that then," Nick replied gloomily. "Feather isn't rideable for at least two months."

Tom sighed despondently. An injured horse was the last thing that Sandy Lane needed. Since Nick and Sarah had bought the stables three years ago, they had faced constant financial difficulties. It was hard enough already to compete with the more established stables in the area – every one of the horses needed to pull its weight if Sandy Lane was to survive. A horse eating its head off and not working didn't bring in the money, even if the horse was very beautiful. And no one could dispute Feather's beauty. She was enchanting. A grey Arab with a coat so ghostly-white that she could have been mistaken for a phantom.

Tom knew that Feather wasn't really white, even if he liked to think she was. Everybody knew that there wasn't really such a thing as a white horse. On paper, they could be classified as light grey, iron grey, dappled grey or even flea-bitten grey... never white. Not one of the descriptions was right for Feather. Flea-bitten came the closest, for she had little black hairs over her coat giving her a slightly mottled appearance. But this struck Tom as a rather unflattering way to describe something as wonderful as a horse, especially a horse like Feather.

As Tom gazed across the yard, Feather looked out over her door. It was heartbreaking to see her confined to the stable. She was one of Nick and Sarah's most valuable animals and very popular with the older riders. There wasn't a horse at the stables to replace her.

Now where had Nick disappeared to? Tom thought to himself. Everywhere was deadly quiet this morning. Normally the hustle and bustle of the yard was well under way by now. Tom shrugged his shoulders. Nick must have gone to discuss things with Sarah at the cottage. Should he go and look for him there? He didn't want to disturb them, but at the same time he felt he would burst if he didn't tell someone his news.

The cottage lay to the left of the stables, near enough to be a part of it yet detached enough to be a separate home. Rambling wild roses covered the walls, hiding the crumbling brickwork. It was desperately in need of a lick of paint. Like everything at Sandy Lane it was slightly antiquated, still Tom couldn't help feeling that both Nick and Sarah preferred it that way.

Both Nick and Sarah rode, although Sarah was

rarely in the yard nowadays. What with sorting out the mountain of bills and paperwork that kept flooding in, she simply didn't have the time. Nick however, couldn't be kept away from the horses. He'd been a jockey once upon a time, but had given it all up, vowed never to race again on the day that his steeplechaser, Golden Fleece, had fallen to her death. For a while, Sarah had thought that he would never even *ride* again, then they had bought Sandy Lane. Now Nick was trying to put the tragedy behind him.

Tom hurried over to the cottage and knocked on the back door. Nick and Sarah were deep in conversation as he walked into the kitchen, almost tripping over Ebony, the black Labrador who lay sprawled across the floor.

"I've been looking for you everywhere," Tom said.

"What's up?" Sarah asked, peering over her tortoiseshell glasses and looking intently at Tom. "I can't take any more bad news."

"No, no," said Tom. "It's good news actually."

"Well go on then. Fire away," Sarah said gloomily. "It'll make a change from all these figures."

"It's Georgina and Chancey you see," Tom started. "She's going abroad with her parents and she's left *me* to look after him... to do anything I want with. Isn't it the most fantastic news? She's not coming back for ages. Not for two and a half months... yippee. So I've got him all to myself and Horton Chancellor is ready to collect whenever I want." The words spilled out as Tom stopped to draw breath.

"Whoa, now slow down," said Sarah. "I can't understand a word you're saying. Who on earth are Georgina and Chancey and what is Horton Chancellor?"

"Sorry," said Tom, blushing furiously. "Georgina is my awful cousin, Georgina Thompson, and Chancey is short for Horton Chancellor. You remember, the horse that took the showjumping circuit by storm last season when ridden by Emily Manners. He was bought for Georgina by my Uncle Bob," Tom added, beaming.

"Hmm. Let me think. Yes, I do remember that horse." Nick wrinkled up his forehead. "An absolute star... 14.2 hands, chestnut gelding, cleared everything in sight. Jumped like a dream if I remember rightly."

"That's the one," Tom replied. "Well, I've been lent him for the summer and I was wondering. Well, hoping really, that I might be able to keep him at Sandy Lane."

Nick and Sarah looked at each other. They knew what a chance this was for Tom, but it couldn't have come at a worse time for them. With Feather injured, they could ill-afford another horse, certainly not one that wasn't going to earn his keep. But Tom had been indispensable to them in the two years they had known him. How could they refuse his plea?

Sarah gazed fondly at Tom, remembering when he had first arrived at Sandy Lane, a shy, reserved eleven year old. How much he had changed since that day. He had told them then that he had wanted to ride for as long as he could remember. But his parents weren't horsey people and he had never been able to afford it. Then his Great Aunt Flo had died, leaving the family some money and his parents had thought it only fair that everyone should benefit. Tom, of course, had asked for the long-awaited riding lessons and been allowed to book twelve of them at Sandy Lane. Sarah had been touched by his story.

By the time the lessons were at an end, Tom was

totally hooked on riding and had started to spend more time than ever just helping out down at the stables. Nick and Sarah were more than happy to give him a free lesson in return for his work. Tom was to become the first of the helpers down at Sandy Lane – the regulars, as Nick and Sarah liked to call them. For that, they were especially attached to him. And there was no disputing his talent. He was a true horseman, born not made.

Nevertheless, an extra horse meant extra costs and Nick and Sarah had a business to run. Sarah also knew that Tom would never be able to afford a livery fee and there was no way his mother would let him keep the horse in her prized garden.

"Stabling a horse isn't cheap Tom," Nick said thoughtfully. "You of all people know how much they cost and how much looking after they need."

"I know. I know all that. But term ends in two weeks, so I would be down here all summer anyway. I could give you my pocket money. I'd work extra hard... and... and..."

"We're not trying to be mean," Sarah went on. "It's just that now we've lost the use of Feather, that would make two horses eating and not paying their way."

"That's just it though," said Tom. "Horton Chancellor could pay his way. You could use him in lessons for the more experienced riders instead of Feather. I don't mind if it helps you out and I could ride him when he's not booked up. He wouldn't be any bother because I'd look after him."

Nick looked uncertain and sighed.

Tom took a deep breath.

"Well," Nick began hesitantly, "since you put it like

that." He smiled. Sarah raised her eyes to heaven. Tom knew that the battle was almost won.

"All right then," Nick finished. "Bring Chancey to Sandy Lane and we'll see how it goes."

"Thank you, oh thank you," Tom gasped. "I can't believe it. We won't let you down, I promise. Wait till I tell the others."

2

SANDY LANE FRIENDS

The others had been as excited as Tom when they heard his news. Alex, Kate, Jess and Rosie were all regulars at Sandy Lane. Of varying riding abilities, they all had two things in common – their passion for riding and their love of horses. In the week before Chancey's arrival, they could talk of little else but the prizewinning horse.

And Tom couldn't stop dreaming of the blissful days ahead of him. He was looking forward to a long summer filled with days upon days of riding. Tom told himself that he would work hard to become good enough to ride at Benbridge at the end of August – the show that everyone had set their hearts on. He could almost see it now... the breeze whipping past him as he flew around the course and rode through the finish to the sound of thunderous applause...

"That was Tom Buchanan on Horton Chancellor,

jumping clear with no time faults..."

Thud! Tom's vision was rudely interrupted as Napoleon kicked over his water bucket.

"Oh, you stupid animal. Look what you've done now," Tom said crossly, as the water seeped across the floor of the stable. "I don't know. I'm always having to tidy up after you, aren't I?"

Automatically, Tom started to clean away the mess but his mind was elsewhere. He could barely contain his excitement. If someone had told him a month ago he would be lent a horse for the whole summer, he would never have believed it. And Chancey was due to arrive tomorrow.

Walking across the yard, Tom refilled Napoleon's water bucket from the old trough. Water sprayed everywhere as he turned the taps on full blast. He could see Rosie and Jess in the outdoor school from where he was standing.

"Heels down, toes in, look straight ahead of you. What on earth has happened to the pair of you?" Nick bellowed. "Your hands and forearms should form a straight line with the reins. If you're not going to concentrate, Jess, you may as well not be here."

Rosie and Jess were in the same year at school... best of friends and yet complete opposites. Where Rosie was careful, quiet and rational, Jess was impulsive, daring... and often in trouble.

As their lesson came to an end, the two best friends wandered into the yard, chattering loudly. Quickly tethering their ponies to the rails, they set about sponging them down.

"Hey," cried Rosie, as Jess dipped her body brush into the bucket and doused her with water. "We're supposed to be grooming the ponies, not each other."

"Well, I've been trying to attract your attention for ages," laughed Jess. "I've been splashing you for the last five minutes and you've only just noticed. You must have gone over Pepper's withers at least a dozen times. You'll rub him away if you're not careful."

Tom wandered away, smiling to himself. He was small for his thirteen years with tousled brown hair and a round, cheerful face. As the star pupil at Sandy Lane, he could have been arrogant and impossible, yet he wasn't. Always willing to help with whatever needed to be done, Tom was well-liked. There was no horse he couldn't handle, or so Jess and Rosie thought. They secretly admired him and hoped that one day they would be as good as him.

"Jess, have you got time to tack up Napoleon?" Tom called from the tack room. "I've got to get Hector ready, and then I think Nick is just about set to take the 4 o'clock class."

"Sure," said Jess. "Rosie, can you keep an eye on Minstrel for me? I'll be back in a minute."

Quickly, Jess slipped into Napoleon's box. Slipping the head collar down the bay neck, she put the bridle on. She was a dab hand at tacking up now, still she hadn't always found it that easy. Many tears of frustration had been shed when she was still learning the basics. Now however, without hesitation, she slid the saddle smoothly down Napoleon's back and tightened the girth. Heading out into the blazing sunshine, she took him to the mounting block as Tom led out Hector.

Hector was a big sturdy bay hack, with a coat of polished mahogany, that Sarah had inherited from a woman looking for a good home for him. He was Alex's favourite at the stables, and everyone was very fond of him. He was twenty years old – an old man in horse years – but a solid ride and ideal for beginners. He was the first horse that Tom had ever ridden and at 16.2 hands, Tom had felt as small as a sparrow on top of an elephant!

Soon everyone was mounted and the ride was ready. As Nick led the class out of the yard, Tom thought how tired he looked. He hoped that Nick and Sarah would have more luck this year. Sandy Lane was such a fantastic stables, it seemed so unfair that they were continually struggling. As Tom walked back into the yard, he saw the last two of his friends arrive.

"Aha! Alex, Kate, you're here at last, you lazy sloths," he yelled. Alex and Kate were brother and sister and usually went everywhere as a pair.

"Ugh. We were forced to go to our Aunt June's fortieth birthday party," groaned Alex. "Total nightmare. Loads of relatives telling us how much we'd grown. We got here as quickly as we could. Hopefully we won't have to do any more family gatherings for a while, not till Christmas anyway."

"Well, you've arrived bang on time to help turn out the horses for the evening anyway."

"Great," Alex groaned, lazily. "Is that all you've got to say to me? I haven't seen my best mate for a couple of days and he sets me to work straight away."

"There's a lot to be done and I am supposed to be coming round to your house later anyway," said Tom, grinning.

"Well, what's the news on Chancey?" Alex asked.

"He's arriving tomorrow at eleven, so make sure

you're here to greet him," Tom said, looking around him at his friends. "Personally, I don't know how I'll ever get to sleep tonight. Come on Alex," he said, turning to his friend. "I'll help you turn out those horses..."

3

A BAD BEGINNING

Tom did manage to get to sleep and woke early the next morning. Too early. By seven, he'd been awake for what seemed like ages and could stand it no longer. Getting out of bed, he walked over to the window and looked outside. He smiled. It was going to be a very hot day.

Pulling on his jodhpurs, Tom hurried down the stairs and strode out into the morning air. Narrowly escaping his mother's breakfast call, he set off for the stables. It was a good fifteen minute cycle ride to Sandy Lane from where Tom lived, on the outskirts of nearby Colcott, but one that he didn't mind too much. Whistling to himself as he past the old tannery, he sped down the hill.

Not far now. Out of breath as he reached the last stretch, he zoomed passed the duck pond at the corner of the stables and hurtled into the yard. The horses had already been brought in from the fields and the stables were buzzing with activity.

"Tom, chuck us a dandy brush will you?" Jess called. She was going to have her work cut out grooming Minstrel. He was a skewbald and the white parts of him got extremely muddy. Tom handed her the dandy brush and headed off to make a start on Napoleon. Cheerfully, they chatted together as they busied themselves around the yard.

By a quarter to eleven, Nick had taken two classes and a hack. The day was fully under way. As usual, Alex and Kate were late and didn't get to the stables until five to eleven, when most of the work had already been done. As they arrived, an approaching engine could be heard rounding the corner to Sandy Lane and they had to jump out of the way as a large horse box juddered to a halt beside them. This was the moment everyone had been waiting for. Chancey had arrived.

Everyone was quiet as a disgruntled-looking man stepped down from the cab, alone.

Where's Georgina? Tom thought to himself. Surely she would have come with Chancey to settle him in and say goodbye.

"I don't know what you've got in there," said the man, hunching his shoulders. "Supposed to be a horse... well, he was when I loaded him anyway. A right handful. Only just managed to get him in the box and that was nothing compared to the journey. Thought he was going to kick the box down. Rather you than me, lad," he said, climbing into the box before Tom had a chance to reply.

There was a frantic whinny and the sound of drumming hooves reverberated around the yard as

Chancey pranced down the ramp. He was certainly on his toes, but he didn't look like the sleek, well turned-out horse that Tom remembered seeing last season. He was still unclipped and his shabby winter coat was flecked with foam as, feverishly, he pawed the ground. No one knew what to say.

Eventually, Rosie managed to pipe up with: "Are you sure it's the same horse?"

"Of course it is," Tom snapped, unable to keep the disappointment out of his voice. "He only needs to be clipped and he'll look fine."

"I wouldn't be so sure," Jess muttered under her breath.

"Shouldn't he have been clipped already?" said Rosie. She was always looking things up in her Pony Club manual and was sure that she had read that horses should be clipped before January, or their summer coat would be spoiled.

"He probably should have been, still that won't be too much of a problem," said Nick kindly. "Now come on everyone, stop crowding him and get back to what you were doing. Take him to his new home, Tom."

Tom approached the horse and took the head collar that the man offered him. Chancey jumped skittishly from side to side, rolling his eyes and flicking his tail as Tom led him off.

"Poor Tom," said Rosie. "He was so excited about that horse. Still, even though Chancey isn't very good-looking, I'm sure he'll be an absolute dream to ride."

Tom didn't know what to think. When he had seen Chancey last season, he had been one hundred percent fit, his muscles rippling under his glossy chestnut coat. Tom was sure that he hadn't been mistaken, he was definitely the same horse.

Tom picked up the things that the box driver had left in the middle of the yard. There was a saddle and bridle, a dark blue New Zealand rug and a box full of smart grooming brushes that looked as though they had never been used. Putting them in the tack room, he grabbed an old body brush and curry comb, and hurried back to Chancey's stable. He would have to be quick if he was going to be able to give Chancey a quick groom and get home in time for lunch. Tom opened the door slowly, taking care not to startle him.

"Come on, my boy. Let's get you cleaned up and give you your lunch. I bet you're hungry after that awful journey," he crooned.

Chancey seemed to have settled down a little and nuzzled Tom's pockets inquisitively. Tom fumbled around for a mint. The horse's lips were as soft as crushed velvet as he gratefully accepted the offering.

"That's better," said Tom. "I thought you'd taken an instant dislike to me, and it's very important that we're friends if we're going to spend the whole summer together."

"Hey, now hang on a minute," said Tom, as the nuzzling turned into a frantic chewing. "I'm sure my jacket doesn't taste that great and I won't be getting a new one if you eat it either." Gently, Tom pushed Chancey's nose away.

"I've got to go home for lunch in a minute," Tom went on, giving him a quick rubdown. "I'll be back at two. Nick has said that we can join the 3 o'clock class. Are you listening?"

Chancey wasn't paying the slightest bit of notice. Already bored of all the attention, his head was buried deep in a bucket of pony nuts as Tom bolted the door of the stable and set off for home.

Lunch was something that Tom's mother insisted upon. If he was going to be at the stables all day, she said that he must at least come back at one to eat. He was careful to obey her, if only to stop her from going on about the amount of time he spent at Sandy Lane.

It was already ten to one. He was going to be late again. Brilliant. He would have to get going, and fast.

Tom got home at five past one. Rushing inside, he headed straight for the bathroom to wash his hands. The rest of his family were already starting lunch when Tom stumbled to the table and sat himself down before anything could be said. His little sister, Sophie, was reading.

"Put that away, Sophie," her mother said sternly. "How many times do I have to tell you it's rude to read at the table?"

"Well, Dad does it," Sophie answered back. "He's always reading the paper and eating at the same time."

"Well, that's different. When you're your father's age, you'll be allowed to do it too," she said, as Sophie surreptitiously slid the book onto her lap.

"Come on David, we really ought to set an example to the children," said Mrs. Buchanan, turning to her husband. Tom's father looked up from his paper.

"So, how was cousin Georgina then?" he asked Tom as he put away his paper. "Did you remember to thank her for lending you her horse?"

"Well, the odd thing is, she didn't come with Chancey," said Tom. "He was delivered by a stranger."

"What's so odd about that?" asked his mother. "Perhaps Georgina has got too much to do before she goes away. Packing can be a nightmare. It always takes me ages."

Tom shrugged his shoulders. He wasn't convinced that was the reason. If he was ever lucky enough to own his own horse, he knew he would simply make time to say goodbye. He didn't think he would even be able to leave his horse's side... not for a whole summer.

"What's the horse like though?" asked Sophie, looking up from her lap.

"OK," said Tom.

"Just OK?" said Mr. Buchanan. "But we've heard of nothing other than this horse for the last week. He must be better than OK."

"He will be, but I haven't tried him yet," Tom said tiredly. He didn't want to tell them how Chancey had come careering out of the horsebox – his mother would only worry.

Tom might have been having lunch with his family, but his mind was elsewhere.

"Oh Thomas, you haven't gulped down your food have you? You'll get indigestion if you're not careful."

Tom's mother only called him Thomas when she was really annoyed with him.

"Sorry," said Tom. "But I do have to get back to Sandy Lane. Nick has said that I can ride Chancey in the 3 o'clock class. May I get down from the table?"

"Hmm. All right then," said Mrs. Buchanan. "You mustn't be back late though, it isn't the summer holidays yet. You still have your homework to do..." Her voice tailed off as Tom dived for his riding hat and shot to the door.

"Thanks Mum," he said.

Tom scooted out of the house and threw himself onto his bike. The countryside sped past as he raced off to Sandy Lane. He hardly even noticed the uphill climb on the way back, and soon he was pedalling into the yard.

Scrambling off his bike, he went to find Nick. He didn't have to look far. Nick was sitting at the desk in the tack room, signing people in for the next ride and collecting the money.

"Who's in the 3 o'clock, Nick?" Tom asked.

"Anna, Mark, Claudine, Lydia and... someone I don't remember... oh, could it be you?" Nick smiled teasingly.

"Phew!" Tom gasped. They were all pretty good riders. He hoped that he was up to it, that he wouldn't let Chancey down.

"Do you want to go and tack up Chancey then, Tom? He seems to have settled in all right now. And we're almost ready to start."

"Sure," Tom smiled, hurrying off.

As he let himself into the stable, Chancey's brown face turned to look at him enquiringly. Tom patted his neck and tickled his nose, letting the horse smell his clothes to get used to him. Then, deftly, he tacked him up and led him out of his stable, down the lane and into the outdoor school. Rosie, Jess, Alex and Kate gathered to watch.

"He looks much better now that he's been groomed and rested," said Rosie.

"Yes, and he doesn't have that mad glint in his eye any more," said Jess encouragingly. "He was probably just a bit unsettled by the journey."

Tom felt proud as he walked round the school and

thought back to how well Chancey had performed on the circuit last season. He knew that he was on a good horse and trembled with anticipation at the power beneath him.

Chancey arched his neck and let out a loud whinny. He was well proportioned, with shoulders that sloped smoothly up to his withers and wide, muscular flanks.

"Is this the new horse that you were telling us about Nick?" asked Anna. She normally rode Feather, but since the little mare had gone lame, had been riding Hector and was looking for a smaller replacement.

"Yes," said Nick. "As I said, he's Tom's, but other people will be able to ride him if they like."

Loosening up their horses, the riders started at a rising trot and then, one by one, began to canter around the track. Chancey wanted to take the lead and Tom found it hard to keep him behind the others.

"Can you all return to the walk and shorten your stirrups. We're going to try some jumping," Nick called, sending everybody off to the other end of the outdoor school.

They were going to start with a pair of cross poles and jump from the trot. Anna trotted Hector round, and popped him neatly over the jump, as did the other riders. Tom watched intently as Mark took off too early with Jester. Tom felt uneasy as Chancey jogged on the spot, fighting for his head.

"Mark, I'll put a pole on the ground in front of the jump to mark the take-off and then you can try it again," Nick called from the middle of the school. This time, Jester jumped successfully.

Looking back, Tom couldn't remember when it all began to go so desperately wrong. Chancey had already started shying at imaginary creatures in the hedgerow and Tom was finding it increasingly difficult to hold him. As the pair approached the jump, Chancey threw his head in the air and dashed towards it.

"Try not to check him too much Tom," Nick shouted. "I know it's hard, but he's fighting with you for control. If you try to alter his strides, he's going to lose his balance."

Tom and Chancey headed for the jump. With a loud snort and a flash of his tail, Chancey ducked out from the jump and swerved to the right. And then he was off, charging around the paddock. Three circuits later, an ashen-faced Tom had managed to pull him up.

"Right Tom," Nick called. "I think that's enough excitement for one day."

"That horse looks crazy," said Anna. " He's certainly not another Feather."

Nick stared silently. "Tom, don't worry, I'll talk to you about it later."

It was easy for Nick to sound confident, but Tom knew Anna was right. Chancey had looked mad, and Nick had been banking on being able to use him as a replacement for Feather.

Back in Chancey's stable, Tom started to untack the horse. He ran the stirrups up the leathers on the saddle before sliding it off. Then, in a trance, he slipped the strap of the head collar over the chestnut neck and took off the bridle.

"Why, oh why, did you have to show me up like that?" he sighed, burying his head in Chancey's mane. "You totally humiliated me and in front of everyone... all of my friends at Sandy Lane. No one will want to ride you now, and then what will happen? It's only because of Nick and Sarah's kindness that you're here anyway. You were supposed to be looking after me today."

Chancey stared balefully at Tom. There was not a hint of apology in his dark eyes.

"I'm not going to cry," Tom said through gritted teeth. "I'm not going to let you win. I know how good you can be. I've seen how good you can be. I'm going to make you that good again. I'm going to take you to the top. I swear it."

4

BACK TO SQUARE ONE

It was dark when Tom got home. His parents had been starting to worry. But when he pushed open the back door and walked headlong into his mother, she could see he was upset and let him skip supper.

Alone in his room, he sat down on his bed and let out a loud sigh. It was so easy to feel determined about Chancey at Sandy Lane, but when he was away from the yard, doubts crowded his mind. He looked around his room. Every wall was covered with posters of horses and famous riders – riders on whom he had modelled himself. How stupid he had been. What had made him think he could ever be as good as any of them? He simply didn't have it in him.

"It was me who was at fault today, not Chancey," he said aloud. "If I was any good, I would have been able to control him."

Despondently, he put his head in his hands. What

should he do? Clearly the horse wasn't suitable for lessons and he couldn't really expect Nick and Sarah to keep Chancey on at Sandy Lane for free.

At the same time, Nick and Sarah were talking along similar lines in the cottage at Sandy Lane.

"We've got to be realistic. We can't use him in the school. What if he went crazy with one of our clients? It would ruin our reputation," said Sarah.

"You're right," Nick said glumly.

"We'll have to buy another horse to replace Feather. You'll need to tell Tom that he can't keep Chancey with us any more," said Sarah.

"What!" said Nick. "We can't do that, Sarah. You know that Tom has set his heart on having him."

"Still, we only agreed to it on the understanding that we would be able to use the horse in lessons," said Sarah, "and now that's clearly impossible. It was bad enough supporting one horse that wasn't pulling its weight but *two*."

Nick looked downcast. "But Chancey is a magnificent animal. If we can get him back to his old self, we could use him in lessons. And if he's seen performing well at shows, it'll do Sandy Lane's reputation no end of good."

"What if we can't?" Sarah had put Nick's worst fears into words. "He's obviously been ruined somewhere along the line. Oh, if only you weren't so impetuous, Nick Brooks."

"Well, if it comes to it, I suppose we could sell Whispering Silver," Nick said tentatively. "We'd get a good price for her. She'd make an excellent hunter and then we could afford to buy a replacement for Feather and have some money left over to buy another horse too."

Sarah gazed at him fondly. He really meant it. He was willing to give up the horse he valued most in the world – Whispering Silver, the retired racehorse he had nursed back to health. No one else had thought that Nick could do it. Sarah thought back to the day he had bought her at the sale, saving her from the knacker's yard. It had turned out all right in the end, but for a while it had been touch and go as to whether she would even live.

"No, Nick. I don't want you to do that. You need Whisp to take lessons on," Sarah continued, breaking the silence. "Besides, she's yours. She couldn't possibly belong to anyone else. You were the one who saved her life." Sarah took a deep breath. "No, we'll find the extra money somehow. If we start scouting through the horse magazines we'll get something, only we won't be able to aim as high as Feather."

"But horses are so much more expensive if you buy them privately. Couldn't we..."

"No, Nick," groaned Sarah. "Promise me one thing... no more sales. It's too much of a risk. You just don't know what you're going to end up with. We want guarantees, vets' certificates... no more gambles."

"You're right. I know you're right," said Nick.

Sarah smiled.

"Now, are you going to be the one to tell Tom of our decision?" she asked quietly.

"Yes, I'll go and have a word with him now."

"Now?" said Sarah, looking at her watch. "But Mrs. Buchanan will freak. It's so late to turn up on someone's doorstep uninvited."

"I know. But this can't wait until the morning. He

was so disappointed."

"OK," said Sarah. "And make sure you sort out some sort of training programme..."

Sarah didn't have a chance to finish her sentence as Nick hurried out of the cottage and climbed into their battered old Land Rover. Revving up the engine, he headed out of Sandy Lane. Tom lived on a new estate about four miles away. It was as far removed from the world of Sandy Lane as you could get – neat paths, smart lawns, clipped hedges. Nick couldn't imagine Tom being allowed in the kitchen in his dirty riding boots.

Even though Mrs. Buchanan was surprised to see Nick when she opened the door, she didn't ask any questions. She knew Tom was upset but was careful not to pry into his other world.

"Tom, you have a visitor," she called up the stairs.

Tom looked up as Nick stuck his head around the door.

"Can I come in, Tom?" he asked gently. Tom nodded. He knew what Nick had come to say, knew that it was unfair of him to expect otherwise. After all, Nick and Sarah did have a business to run.

"Don't say anything. You don't have to explain. I know he's no use." Tom blurted out the words.

"Hey, now hold on a minute," said Nick looking surprised. "I didn't come here to say that." He smiled.

"I know things this afternoon weren't that great. But it's not the end of the world. Chancey was and could still be a champion. We can't use him in lessons at the moment, and Sarah and I will have to think about buying a horse to replace Feather..."

"I know and I'm so sorry, Nick," Tom interrupted.

"Hang on," said Nick. "That's not for you to worry about. It's our problem." Tom listened desperately as Nick continued.

"Sarah and I have decided to take a chance with the horse, if you'll excuse the pun," he grinned. "If you're prepared to put in the work, we'll let you keep him on at the stables. What do you say?"

"Oh yes," Tom breathed, hardly able to believe what he was hearing.

"Right. Well, first things first," said Nick. "We'll have to take him back to the beginning and school him again. I don't want to guess what your cousin's been doing with him. All I know is that if Chancey was once a champion, which he clearly was, then he can be made a champion again. We've got just under eight weeks if he's to be fit and ready for the Benbridge show at the end of August," Nick finished. "Do you want to take on the challenge?"

"You bet," said Tom, grinning from under the strand of hair that had fallen over his face. "What do you want me to do?"

"Well, he'll have to be clipped. I'll organize that this week while you're at school. And he'll need to be shod and have his teeth checked. They'll probably have to be rasped. Then we'll have to discuss a schedule for training and getting him fit, and carefully monitor his eating habits."

"I can do that," said Tom, eagerly.

"I'm not going to have a great deal of time to help you straight away. There's lots going on at Sandy Lane at the moment, so you must be patient," Nick continued. "Oh and most important of all. You must swear that you won't take Chancey out on your own.

Not until I think you're both ready for it anyway. We just can't trust him at the moment. He's dangerous. Sarah would never forgive me if anything was to happen to you," he chuckled. "Besides, I don't want people thinking we're not safe at Sandy Lane. So, do I have your word?"

"Of course, Nick. I promise."

"Well, that's about it then. You could come down to Sandy Lane after school on Wednesday if you like. I should have had a chance to do a bit of work with him by then. I've got a spare hour at five. We could spend it in the outdoor school. What do you say?"

"Fantastic." Tom beamed.

"When does term end by the way?" asked Nick.

"Next Friday," Tom answered.

"Good," said Nick. "Well, see you Wednesday evening then."

It was a statement rather than a question. Everything had been decided so quickly. Tom looked up half-embarrassed.

"Will you thank Sarah for me? And, I... I... well... thank you."

Nick smiled and closed the door behind him.

* * * * * * * * * * * * * * * *

Time went so slowly over the next three days. Tom could hardly believe it when on Wednesday the bell sounded around the school as the day ended. He was the first to get to the classroom door and bolted out of the building before anyone could stop him.

"Another day over, two more to go," he chanted to himself.

Turning out of the school drive, Tom sprinted to the stables. When he reached Sandy Lane, Tom hurried straight to the outdoor school. Nick was as good as his word and already had Chancey on a lunge rein. The saddle on Chancey's back looked funny without any stirrups. As he trotted around the school, he looked altogether like a different horse. He was calm for a start.

"I've been lungeing him since Monday. He's been getting better and better. Come into the middle here," said Nick, clicking Chancey on into a canter, flicking the whip lightly towards his hock. "He hasn't forgotten his paces."

Nick slowed Chancey down to a trot with the word 'ter-rot'. Tom walked into the school and took the lunge rein that Nick offered him. Nick stood next to Tom and guided him through the horse's paces. Tom only needed to use the whip very lightly as Chancey started to respond to the sound of his voice.

"Very good," said Nick. "Let's try him with some loose jumping. I think Georgina must have been fighting with him for control before a jump, that's why he's so nervy. Every horse likes to find his own natural take-off point." Nick put up some cross poles and got Tom to lunge Chancey over them.

"You see. He jumps perfectly on his own. And because the poles are crossed, it gets him to take off in the middle of the jump. Give him another five minutes and then we'll put him away for the night," said Nick.

"He's been so well-behaved. I don't think we want to push him too hard. We could try riding him out at the weekend. It's just a matter of building up mutual trust. He's not really a problem horse and he's certainly not too old to learn..." Nick's voice tailed off as the ring of the telephone sounded from the tack room.

"Oh blast," Nick said. "I'll speak to you later," he called, running for the phone.

"You see, there's hope for you yet," Tom said, turning to lead Chancey up the drive. "Now, you listen here. I won't see you for a while now. Well, not until Saturday anyway, so you'd better be on your best behaviour."

The yard was still as Tom and Chancey crunched across the gravel. Tom led the horse to his box and gave him a quick rub down. Tenderly, he pulled Chancey's ears before bolting him in for the night. Slinging the bridle over his shoulder and carrying the saddle on his arm, he crossed the yard to return them to the tack room.

"Do you fancy going to the Ash Hill horse sale with me on Saturday morning, Tom?" Nick's voiced echoed around the yard. "Just to have a look around."

"Isn't Sarah always telling us how risky it is to buy at a sale?" Tom called back, confused. But Nick was out of earshot and there was no reply. Tom shrugged his shoulders. He knew he should be pleased that out of everyone, Nick had asked him to go with him. But he couldn't help feeling that it would be a waste of time and he had really wanted to ride Chancey on Saturday morning. Oh well, perhaps they could do some work with him in the afternoon.

Tom shivered as he strolled over to his bike and headed off into the still evening. He was exhausted, but at last he felt he was getting somewhere with Chancey. It had been a long day, and yet one that marked a turning point for Tom... one he wouldn't forget in a hurry.

5

STORM CLOUD

Saturday arrived quicker than Tom could have imagined. Rolling over in bed, he looked out of the window and smiled. He would be able to spend the whole day with Chancey. Then he groaned... the Ash Hill sale, and he'd said to Nick that he would go with him. He'd have to get a move on, it started at nine. Hurriedly, he threw on some clothes, grabbed a slice of bread and rushed outside to his bike.

He got to the bottom of Clee Hill in record time and cycled hard to the top. Taking his feet out of the pedals as he reached the summit, he zoomed down the other side and into Sandy Lane. Nick was already waiting when Tom reached the yard.

"All set Tom?" he smiled. "Now, we'll just look at the horses that are fully warranted. I want to see what's around at the moment but we're not going to buy anything."

"Well, shouldn't we take the horse box just in case?" Tom asked.

"No," said Nick rather too quickly. "If we don't take it, we won't be tempted."

Tom smiled to himself. He'd heard it all before. If Nick got carried away, nothing would stop him from being tempted.

Jumping into the Land Rover, they jolted out of the yard, down Sandy Lane and onto the road to Ash Hill. The engine groaned as Nick changed gear and they chugged along. It didn't take them long to drive the two miles.

Tom frowned as he got out at the sale and stared in despair at the long rows of horses. It was the most depressing place on earth. Why had he agreed to come? All of these horses and ponies – creatures from good homes and once well-loved, now standing alone awaiting their fate.

"Have a look at the catalogue, Tom. I've marked a couple of possibles."

Tom looked at the entries Nick had put a cross by – a registered bay mare of 14.2 hands, and a grey hunter.

"What about this one too, Nick?" Tom asked, pointing to a lot in the catalogue.

"Registered yellow Dun working pony, rising four, two white socks, 13.2 hands without shoes. Fully warranted. Sounds good," Nick said.

"Come on, let's go and have a look."

But they didn't get that far. As they made their way down the lines of horses, Tom could see that Nick's eye was immediately caught by a fragile, dappled-grey pony in the corner. Tied to a muddy piece of rope, her head downcast, she didn't even look up as they approached. She was so thin. Tom knew from that moment that Nick was caught. He couldn't bear to drag himself away from the little pony. Gently Nick stroked her shoulder as she tilted her delicately dished face towards him, nuzzling his pockets for titbits. Quickly, he ran his hands down her legs.

"There isn't time to see her run up in hand. Look at the welts in her coat, Tom. She's been badly neglected. And she can't be any older than three. Her conformation is good."

And then they heard the bidding start.

"Come on, let's hurry," said Nick.

Swiftly, they made their way to the ringside. Nick turned to his catalogue.

"Lot number one, what will you give me for this bay cob here?" the auctioneer was saying.

"Who'll start me at three hundred? Three hundred. Am I bid three fifty? Three fifty, I'm bid. Four hundred?"

It was all happening so quickly, that Tom could hardly make out what was going on. Before he knew it, the cob had been sold to a man at the back.

"Knackers," said Nick. Tom felt tears well up in his eyes and blinked them away. He was going to have to be much tougher. If only he was rich, he would buy them all. He turned away, wanting to be apart from it.

"There are only ten more lots and then she's in," Nick whispered. "Probably about fifteen minutes if you want to go and grab a lemonade," he said, seeing Tom's pale face.

"I think that might be a good idea," Tom smiled weakly.

Tom squeezed through the crowd and headed for the refreshments tent. Joining the queue of people milling around, he felt as though he wasn't quite a part of it – like watching some sort of pantomime.

As he made his way back to Nick, he realized that the little grey pony was being led around the ring and Nick was in the bidding.

"I'll just go fifty more," Nick whispered as he raised his card in the air.

There was a deathly hush. Tom took a deep breath, praying that no one else would bid.

"Any advance on four hundred? Will anyone give me four fifty? All done at four hundred?" the auctioneer was saying.

Tom held his breath in anticipation.

"Four hundred I'm bid once. Four hundred twice. Going... going... gone."

With that the auctioneer banged his hammer on the desk.

"Sold to the man at the back," he said, staring straight at Nick. Tom turned to Nick and grinned. They had got her.

"Name?" he called.

"Nick Brooks," Nick answered.

"Address?" the man returned.

"Sandy Lane Stables, Sandy Lane, near Colcott."

It was all over, and without a second's thought, the auctioneer had turned his attention to the next lot.

"You have to pay in advance," a voice called from behind a counter at the side of the ring. Tom glanced over to see a woman sitting at a desk, looking quite out of place in a blue jumper with bright red nail varnish.

"I know," said Nick, reaching for his wallet.

Once they had paid and collected the relevant papers, Tom and Nick made their way over to where the little grey pony had been left. Quickly, Nick untethered her, talking to her all the time in a soft voice.

"We'll soon have you away from here my girl," he soothed.

"What's she called?" Tom asked quietly.

"Storm Cloud," Nick answered.

"Storm Cloud," Tom breathed. "It's perfect for her," he said, as the three of them walked slowly away from the sale.

"Why don't you hop up on her and I'll lead," Nick said quickly. "We'll come back later for the Land Rover."

"OK," said Tom, bending his knee for Nick to give him a leg-up. "What's Sarah going to say?"

"Well," Nick reddened, "that's not for you to worry about. I don't think she'll be too delighted, but when she sees Storm Cloud she'll feel differently. Sarah might pretend to be as hard as nails, but underneath it all, she's a bit of a softie."

"Well, at least Storm Cloud's fully warranted," said Tom. "That's one thing, so you won't have to pay any vet's bills. Fingers crossed. "

Slowly, they picked their way along the grass verge by the side of the road.

"She's got a nice long stride," Tom continued. "She just seems a bit tired."

"Oh, she only needs feeding up," said Nick. "There's plenty of summer grass for her to tuck into at home."

They walked along in silent contemplation as the

traffic sped past. Storm Cloud didn't even flinch at the cars.

"Could we do some training with Chancey this afternoon, Nick?" Tom asked, breaking the silence.

"I don't see why not. Sarah's taking out the hacks," he answered. "It'll be a good opportunity for us to get started with him."

"Great," said Tom, as Nick pulled Storm Cloud's head up from the grass.

"Come on. You'll have enough of that later," he said, "but we've got to get you home first and we're almost there."

Tom wrinkled up his nose as they passed the pig farm and neared the stables. They passed Bucknell Wood and were at the bottom of the drive in no time at all. Slowly, they strolled into the yard.

"Tom, do you think you could sort out Storm Cloud for me?" said Nick. "Put her in the loose box by the tack room. I'd better go and tell Sarah about our latest acquisition," he said sheepishly.

"Sure," said Tom, jumping swiftly to the ground. "Come on, Stormy," he whispered, as he led her to the stable. She was sweating slightly, tired after the long walk home. Tom rubbed her shivering body with a wisp of straw.

Moments later, Nick appeared with Sarah. Tom led Storm Cloud out and circled her as a group gathered to see the latest addition, waiting to hear if she was given the Sandy Lane seal of approval. Quickly, Sarah ran her hands down the horse's legs.

"Well, she's sound, and she's got kind eyes, even if she doesn't look in great shape." She patted her on the shoulder. "She'll soon fill out," she smiled, turning to

Nick, "even if she was from a sale." Everyone breathed a sigh of relief. Sarah did know her stuff.

"Come on Tom," said Nick as everyone dispersed. "Come and help, and then we could take Chancey out for that ride I promised you."

"Well, if you think he's ready for it," Tom stammered nervously.

"He'll be all right if we take it slowly," said Nick.

Tom hurried off to prepare a quick bran mash for Storm Cloud as Nick led the dejected horse back to her new home. It didn't take them long to get her rugged up and give her a quick rub down. And then Tom rushed to get Chancey ready. Feeling guilty that his beloved horse had taken a back seat, so enthralled had he been with the dappled grey pony, Tom determined to make an extra good job of grooming him.

And sure enough, Tom didn't rest content until he could have sworn he saw his reflection in Chancey's coat. Putting the bit into the horse's mouth, Tom slipped the bridle on and did up the throat lash. Carefully, he slid the saddle down Chancey's back and tightened the girth. Adjusting his riding hat, he led the horse out of his stable.

"Wow," said Nick. "Tom, you've done an amazing job on him. Chancey looks wonderful."

Tom glowed at Nick's words of praise. Climbing into their saddles, they strolled out of the yard and through the gate at the back. Tom hummed happily to himself. Neither of them said a word as they lengthened their reins and rode across the fields. It was a beautiful July day, the aquamarine sky was intense and the smell of the country engulfed them.

Chancey's coat shone a burnished red as the sun beat down on their backs and they entered Larkfield Copse. Tom didn't think he could ever feel happier, certainly never as content, as he lost himself in his riding and he and his horse became as one. And suddenly, they were out of the trees and crossing the old coastal track, over to the open fields that led to the cliff tops. Tom could smell the salt in the air. Chancey snorted excitedly, swishing his tail with a determined air.

"Come on, let's have a canter," Nick said mischievously. "Make sure you stay behind me and try to let me go for a few strides before you let Chancey follow on. I don't want you forcing me into a gallop," he laughed. "Luckily Whisp won't panic, she's too much of an old lady for that, she'll hold you back."

Tom crouched low in the saddle and urged Chancey on after Nick. They rode like the wind and, as they pounded across the springy turf, it seemed as though they were covering miles. All at once, there was a fallen tree in their path. For a moment, Tom was startled. What would Chancey do? They were going at quite a speed. And then he remembered all that Nick had told him – let the horse do the work and don't interfere. Scornfully, Chancey soared three feet above the log. Nick looked under his arm in amazement, as he slowed down to a trot and then to a walk.

"That was magnificent Tom," he said breathlessly. "He jumps like a stag. I haven't seen a horse like him in a long time."

Tom smiled to himself as they made their way back to the stables. Winding their way through the little copse of trees, they let their horses stretch their heads after their exertions. Slowly ambling back the way that they had come less than an hour ago, they picked their way through the fields, back through the gate to Sandy Lane and clattered noisily into the yard.

6

TOM'S SECRET

It was a wet, muggy, Wednesday morning. Tom was fed up as he sat in the tack room watching the summer rain splatter down the window pane. Chancey hadn't been ridden for well over a week.

Pitter... patter... pitter... patter. The rain hammered rhythmically against the outside of the building. Tracing patterns in the condensation, Tom outlined the horse's head that he had become so good at drawing.

Nick hurried in out of the rain, holding his waterproof jacket over his head as an umbrella. He had been caught in the summer shower unawares and the tack room had been his nearest shelter.

"I've been lungeing Storm Cloud. She's got so much potential. If she continues the way she's going, it won't be long before I'll be able to use her in lessons," Nick said proudly. "What's up with you?" he asked, seeing Tom's glum face.

"Oh, nothing really. I was just wondering if you might have some time to look at Chancey and me today?" Tom said quietly.

"Not today, Tom. I haven't a spare moment," Nick answered. "I'm giving two classes, maybe even three and then I really need to do another hour with Storm Cloud. You could lead him around the school for half an hour if you like."

"Couldn't I ride Chancey in the hack, Nick?" Tom pleaded.

"I don't think it's a very good idea, Tom. He's not ready for it yet. You know how agitated he gets if he's with more than one horse. He tried to kick Jester last time he was out."

Tom sighed impatiently. He knew what Nick was saying was true, but at this rate, Chancey was never going to be ready for the Benbridge show. He felt mean complaining. Nick and Sarah had done so much for him. If it wasn't for them, he wouldn't even have had a home for the horse. Nevertheless, Chancey did need to be schooled if he was going to get fit. And if Nick didn't have the time to help, there wasn't a great deal that Tom could do about it. Or was there?

And suddenly it came to him. Perhaps he could do something to help. Perhaps *he* could train Chancey. Nick didn't need to know anything about it. After all, Chancey had gone so well for him the last time he had ridden him and he hadn't really needed Nick there, had he?

Tom sighed. He knew that it wasn't quite true. He did need Nick, and Nick had expressly forbidden him to take Chancey out on his own.

Tom put his head around the tack room door and

stepped outside. He held out his hands. It was still spitting as he crossed the yard to Chancey's stable.

"If I got up early in the mornings and trained you, nobody would even notice," Tom whispered, trying to convince himself as much as Chancey that he wouldn't be doing anything wrong.

"You'd like that too," he murmured. "You'd get out more then. We'd have to be very careful that we weren't caught, that's all."

Chancey snorted, as if in response, a piece of straw hanging from his mouth.

"You shouldn't be chewing on that either," said Tom crossly. "If you eat too much of it, you'll find you end up with colic."

That was what made Tom's mind up. If Chancey was eating his bed, he must be more bored than Tom had imagined.

"We'll start training tomorrow, then. I'll get here early to tack you up."

"What are you doing in there, Tom?" asked Alex, poking his head over the stable door. "You're not talking to yourself are you?"

"No," said Tom, turning bright red. "Just Chancey."

"You're mad!" Alex chuckled. "What are you saying to him anyway?"

The thought of letting Alex in on his plans passed fleetingly through Tom's mind. He opened his mouth to tell him, and then closed it firmly again. No, it wasn't fair. It wasn't fair to expect Alex to lie for him. This was something he had decided to undertake. He had to bear the full responsibility.

"Are you reading me?" said Alex. "Come in Tom. Are you going out on the 12 o'clock hack?"

Tom pulled himself together as he realized that Alex had asked him the same question twice.

"N-No," Tom stuttered. "I'm going home. Can you say goodbye to the others for me?"

"Sure," said Alex, puzzled at Tom's strange behaviour. It was most unlike him to spend any time away from Sandy Lane.

Thoughtfully, Tom wandered over to his bike. He wanted the afternoon to think about how he could put his plan into action. He also couldn't bear the thought of being around Nick and having to lie to him at the same time. It would be better once he had started the training. Once Chancey had started to improve, it would all seem worth it.

Back at home, Tom slid into the sitting room clutching a pad of note paper. He felt like a criminal.

"Come on, get a grip," he muttered to himself, thinking aloud. "Nick brings the other horses in from the fields at seven thirty, which means we'll have to start at six to be finished in time."

He wrote it all down, chewing the end of his pencil as he worked out his plan. That meant he would have to be up at the stables at half past five. Tom groaned to himself. It was a very early start. And how long would he have to do it for? Should he make up a training programme? Tom churned these thoughts over in his mind for the rest of the day.

* * * * * * * * * * * * * * * *

Tom's alarm went off at a quarter past five the next morning. Fumbling under his pillow, he switched it off and sat bolt upright. He rubbed his eyes. It was already light outside. Pulling on his jodhpurs, he stole down the stairs and out of the sleepy house. Quickly, he unchained his bike from the drainpipe. His heart was beating fast and there was a knot in his stomach. There would be such trouble if he was caught.

Nothing stirred, nothing rustled, as Tom cycled along. The stables were silent as Tom reached the yard... unnervingly still and quiet as he crept to Chancey's stable.

"Sshh," said Tom, stifling Chancey's whinny with a sugar lump as he hurriedly tacked him up. Tom was sure that Nick would hear the clatter of Chancey's shoes on the gravel as he led him out of his stable and through the gate at the back. Nervously, Tom looked up at the bedroom windows of the cottage. No one seemed to be up yet. The curtains were tightly drawn and Tom breathed a sigh of relief. Everyone must still be fast asleep. It was only when Tom was in the last of the fields behind the yard that he felt safe... safe away from prying eyes. Tom sprang into the saddle and gathered up the reins.

"Come on Chancey. We've only got an hour and there's a lot to fit in."

Chancey responded promptly to the light squeeze from Tom's calves and went forward into a trot. Automatically, Tom turned him in the direction of Larkfield Copse. They were headed for the beach. Gently, Chancey cantered along, over the fields, through the trees and soon they were on the open stretches beyond. Tom started to relax. This was fun.

As they reached the top of the cliffs, Tom could just make out the distant shape of a ship on the bleak horizon. The tide was out and the beach was deserted at this time of the morning. The wind was whipping up the waves, billowing the water into clouds of spray. Gently, Tom leant back, putting his hand on Chancey's rump to steady himself as they picked their way down the path from the cliff.

Then they were down on the beach and suddenly they were galloping as though nothing else mattered... along the sand, through the waves and past the caves that he and Alex had discovered only last summer. It was glorious. Tom found it hard to pull Chancey up when there was nothing to stop them from going on and on forever.

"Whoa boy, calm down," said Tom, clapping his hand to Chancey's neck and slowly pulling him up. Chancey snatched at the bit.

"That was just to warm you up," Tom laughed. "We'll have to do some proper exercise now – serpentines. Ready?"

Chancey was jumpy as Tom tried to get him to make the 's' shape in the sand. But soon they had perfected the movement, bending from right to left, leaving a trail in the sand like a snake. Tom was miles away, when suddenly he realized the time.

"Oh help!" he cried, looking at his watch. "We'll have to hurry back. We'll ride in the outdoor school tomorrow," he told Chancey. "It's all well and good going fast, but we'll have to go through your paces and practise some jumping too."

Quietly, they wound their way back to Sandy Lane and stealthily crept into the yard. It was already twenty past seven. Luckily no one was around this time, still they would have to be more careful about timing in future. Quickly, Tom put Chancey away in his stable.

"You'll have to wait for your food, Chancey – well, until Nick comes round with the morning feeds anyway."

"You're here early, Tom," a voice boomed out from behind him. Tom nearly jumped out of his skin. "Couldn't keep yourself away from Chancey, eh?" It was Nick.

"Er-I didn't have a very good night's sleep, so I got up and thought I might as well head down here," Tom stuttered. Nick shook his head and smiled. He didn't seem to have noticed anything out of the ordinary. Tom breathed a sigh of relief that he hadn't been discovered. He was sure that his guilt must have been written all over his face.

"Well, you could get cracking with the feeds anyway," Nick suggested. "By the way, I put up the poster about the local show yesterday. Everyone's very excited about it. It's only three weeks away. Good practice for Benbridge. You could ride Napoleon if you like. No one dared sign up for him. I think they're all scared of you." Nick laughed.

Tom felt a sudden pang of guilt. Napoleon had always been his favourite horse at the stables. Everyone said they went like a bomb. But since Chancey had arrived... well, Tom couldn't feel the same about any other horse.

"Thanks Nick, I'll go and check it out," said Tom. He didn't dare ask if he could ride Chancey at the local show – he couldn't bear to hear Nick's refusal.

Nick looked puzzled. Normally Tom would have

been rushing to sign up by Napoleon.

"I'm sorry, Tom. I don't think I'm going to have a minute to spare to spend with you and Chancey today. It'll have to be tomorrow," he said.

"Oh, don't worry," said Tom. He turned away rather too quickly, hoping that Nick hadn't noticed him reddening. Tom hated going behind Nick's back. He hoped he would be able to live with his conscience over the next few weeks.

7

A NARROW ESCAPE

As the date of the local show drew nearer, Tom proved to be right about Nick – there simply weren't enough hours in the day for him to take lessons, school Storm Cloud *and* help out with Chancey too. So Tom continued his secret outings, not just to the beach, but in the outdoor school as well. It was more risky there, as anyone coming early to Sandy Lane would be sure to see them, but Chancey had to get used to an enclosed area. Tom told himself it was worth taking the risk.

Leading Chancey out of his stable that morning, Tom was careful to avoid taking the drive down to the outdoor school. Although it was the quickest way there, they would be sure to be heard from the cottage. Tom felt guilty as he rode the long way round through the fields but he told himself it had to be done. His heart started to beat faster. It was only when they had reached the outdoor school that he started to calm down.

Quickly, he climbed into the saddle and started to limber up. After a quarter of an hour of basic exercise, Chancey was clearly bored.

"Come on," Tom cried impatiently as he tried to drive Chancey into the corners. Chancey wouldn't respond.

"OK. I know you've had enough of that," Tom said. "We'll try some jumping." He dismounted and tethered Chancey to the railings.

"Now, what height had we got to?" he asked the horse. "Here?"

Tom raised the post and rails by two feet. Chancey snorted.

"Ah, so you want it higher do you? OK then." Tom grinned as he moved on to the next fence.

It took him a while to raise the jumps, and he would only have to knock them down again once they had finished. It was a nuisance, but better that than risk getting caught. Nick had finished off with a class of beginners yesterday, and there was no way they would have been jumping three and a half feet. It would look highly suspicious if Tom left the jumps as they were.

"Come on, my boy," he said.

Chancey danced on the spot as Tom showed him the course he had prepared for them.

"Come on, let's go, or it'll be back to lessons for you and I know that you don't want that."

Chancey shook his head and neighed impatiently as he waited for the signal to start. Slowly, Tom nudged him on with his heels and they approached the first. Carefully, they eased their way around the course, clearing each of the jumps in easy succession.

"One more time, Chancey," Tom whispered, turning

the horse back to the start without stopping for a break.

Flying over the post and rails, Chancey went on to soar over the parallel bars. Landing lightly, Tom spun him on the spot for the treble on the far side of the school. Chancey didn't hesitate as Tom drove him forward. He jumped fluently, his tail swishing as he touched down after the first and went on to clear the next two jumps.

It never failed to amaze Tom how high Chancey could go. Sometimes he thought that he was asking too much of his horse. But Chancey never refused. He was a gutsy creature.

After what seemed like no more than half an hour of jumping, Tom looked at his watch.

"It's already ten past seven," he groaned. "We'll have to stop or we might find we have company."

Dismounting in the drive, Tom led Chancey to his stable and untacked him. Then he hurried back to the school to knock down the fences. Hurtling around the course, he kicked down the poles as he went. Opening the gate, Tom let himself out as the alarm on his watch started to beep. He had taken to setting it at seven fifteen – the final warning.

"Just in time," Tom said to himself, striding into the yard.

"Morning Tom," Nick called from Hector's stable.

"Morning Nick," Tom replied breezily as he strolled over to Chancey's stable. He wondered how long Nick had been there. A moment longer and they would have been caught red-handed.

"I've got a free hour at nine. We could do some work with Chancey then if you like," said Nick.

"Brilliant," said Tom, trying to muster up some

energy. He wished he hadn't pushed Chancey so hard and hoped he wouldn't be too tired.

"Hi Tom," Jess called cheerfully from across the yard. "Do you think you might find time to help me with the feeds?"

"OK," Tom laughed. Jess wasn't one for hanging about. Together they set to work and by quarter to ten they had mucked out five stables, filled eight haynets and groomed the horses that were going to be used that morning. They reckoned they had done more than their fair share of work.

"Do you want to go and get Chancey ready?" Nick called.

"Sure," Tom answered, hurrying off.

Chancey looked puzzled when Tom started to tack him up again.

"You're not to give the game away, Chancey," Tom whispered in his horse's ear as he led him down to the school. Chancey snickered softly.

"Right then, Tom. Let's see what you can do," said Nick, opening the gate to the outdoor school. "That's funny," he called. "I could have sworn the jumps were all standing yesterday. Someone's been mucking around in here."

Tom felt embarrassed as Nick went around the course putting the jumps back up.

"Right, are you ready? Pop him over the cross poles a couple of times to warm him up and then try this combination, Tom," said Nick. "You shouldn't find it difficult."

It was all the encouragement that Tom needed. With a little nudge of his heels, he urged Chancey on. Chancey cantered forward with long, easy strides, holding his head high, as he cleared the poles. Nick was mesmerised as he watched them moving gracefully around the paddock.

"I can't believe how well you're both going together," Nick called out from the railings. "It's a pleasure to watch. Each time that I've seen you both, there seems to be an overnight improvement. It's almost as though Chancey goes away after one of our sessions, thinks it all through and puts it into practice the next time round," Nick beamed.

"Yes, yes, I suppose you're right," Tom spluttered.

"Well, he's certainly perfected jumping that double anyway," Nick answered.

So Nick had started to notice a difference. Tom reddened and turned away. They had been practising the double in secret for almost a week now. And it certainly hadn't been an overnight improvement for Tom. What would Nick say if he ever found out it wasn't just his training that was responsible?

Tom felt nervous. Nick wasn't the only one who had noticed some changes. His mother had been complaining that Tom was spending too much time down at Sandy Lane. Tom was scared that if he wasn't careful, she might say something to Nick and Sarah. He couldn't have that happening. And he didn't dare admit to his mother that the owners of Sandy Lane didn't even know he was down there so early in the mornings. His game would surely be up without a doubt. There was no alternative, he would have to limit the amount of time he was spending with Chancey.

As Tom led Chancey back to the yard, he thought how complicated it was all getting. He didn't know how much longer he could go on with it all. Training Chancey and trying to keep it a secret was completely exhausting him. Nevertheless, Chancey was getting better. Tom tried to tell himself it would all be worth it in the end. Little did he know how close that end would be... that his plans were soon to be brought to an abrupt halt.

8

THE WARNING

Over a week had passed and Chancey was playing up yet again. When Tom asked him to canter, he trotted faster. When Tom wanted him to halt, he just carried on walking. It was as though he was being obstreperous on purpose, trying to tell Tom that he was bored and would rather be doing something he enjoyed more. He would never make a dressage horse, Tom knew that. So Tom decided to give up the schooling and jump him instead. And he was jumping beautifully.

"I'm not going to give in to you every time you misbehave, Chancey. Only this once. I like jumping as much as you do, but you've got to learn the ground rules too."

Tom raised the treble. Was it asking too much? Taking a deep breath, he faced Chancey at the spread.

It was a difficult combination, with only one horse stride between each of the jumps, but Chancey didn't hesitate as he approached the first. Sitting back on his hocks, he rocked backwards and released himself through the air like a coil. Springing over the jumps, he cleared them one by one with at least a foot to spare. Tom couldn't remember ever feeling so exhilarated.

"Wait till Nick next trains us," he whispered, slapping Chancey's neck so hard that it echoed like thunder around the school. "He'll be so pleased." And then Tom stopped and sighed. How long would it be before Nick could train them again? Certainly it wouldn't be that day. Nick had already told Tom that he was going to be busy taking lessons.

Tom knew that he shouldn't grumble. In the summer months there were so many holiday makers around... business was booming. It was exactly what Nick and Sarah needed and at least it made Tom feel less guilty that Chancey wasn't bringing in any money.

Tom was miles away when he felt conscious that they weren't alone. Someone was watching them. A solitary figure stood leaning against the railings. Tom's heart skipped a beat. He knew immediately who it was. They had been rumbled. What could he say? Tentatively, Tom walked Chancey over to the gate and took a deep breath.

"Hello Tom," said Nick. There was a strained silence between them.

"How long has this been going on then?" he continued calmly. There was no inflexion in Nick's voice for Tom to decide how to play things.

That was Nick all over, no words of reproach, just a composed question. It would have been easier if there had been angry words. Tom could have handled that. But Nick's restraint made it even worse. Tom tried to summon up courage.

"Nearly three weeks now. I didn't want to go behind your back, Nick. I had to." Tom swallowed hard. "We just weren't going to be ready for Benbridge otherwise. Chancey's going so well. Wait until you see him. You can't be angry then," he said nervously.

"There will be no seeing him," replied Nick in a quiet rage. "What do you think you're playing at? I can't have you setting this sort of example to the others. You could have been hurt. Who would get the blame then?" Tom had never seen Nick this angry before.

"I was only trying to help. I didn't mean any harm," Tom gasped, tears welling in his eyes. He rubbed them away with his sleeve, annoyed that he hadn't been able to stop himself.

"Please look at him, Nick. He's brilliant. I only wanted to get him started. We just weren't getting anywhere. I know that you've been busy but... but..."

There was an uncomfortable pause. Nick knew it was true. He had been too tied up with other things to help Tom and Chancey and he had said that he would. He did feel a little guilty, but a promise was a promise. Tom had overstepped the mark this time. Nick looked long and hard. Should he let them show him what they could do?

"I shouldn't, Tom. But I'll give you one last chance," he said quickly, softening a little. "Eleven o'clock this morning. I'll see you after the class of little ones. We'll take it from there." He turned on his heels.

Tom was left clutching Chancey's reins, his riding hat sliding down over his eyes. Trudging off to Chancey's stable, there was a faint glimmer of hope.

"We'll show them. We'll show them all." Tom

gritted his teeth. He untacked Chancey and put some food in the corner. When Chancey had finished eating, Tom began to groom him, starting with the legs and working up.

It didn't take long before the others knew what had happened. News spread quickly at Sandy Lane. They all felt sorry for Tom, but at the same time couldn't quite believe what he had done. None of them would have been as daring themselves.

"I'd never have guessed," said Jess, turning her back to Rosie as she gave a little girl a leg-up onto Blackjack.

"Poor Tom," said Rosie.

"I half suspected something was up," said Alex. "He's been really strange... so secretive."

The others all nodded in agreement.

"We normally do so much together," Alex went on in a hurt voice. "And we just haven't lately."

"I wonder what Chancey will be like this time," said Jess. "Tom must be pretty confident if he's prepared to show Nick."

Tom did feel confident. Only that morning, Chancey had jumped the treble with ease. Nick would be so impressed, he simply couldn't be angry. He would let Tom enter the local show on Chancey; they would be able to use Chancey for lessons; things would all be all right.

Tom busied himself around the yard, desperately trying to keep out of Nick's way until the allotted time. At ten to eleven, he went to get ready. Chancey was on his toes as Tom tacked him up.

"Come on, my boy. Calm down," Tom soothed.

"Where do you want to try him, Tom?" Nick asked, peering over the door.

"Oh, anywhere really," said Tom.

"We'll try him in the school then," Nick said.

Tom led Chancey out of his stable and sprang confidently into the saddle. As they headed down the drive, Chancey pirouetted, snorting as Tom gathered up the reins.

As Nick opened the gate, they entered the outdoor school. Tom felt uneasy. Nick frowned. There was a sense of foreboding in the air. Suddenly Tom didn't feel quite so confident.

Tom didn't even have a chance to show Nick what they could do. As the engine of a car roared in the distance, Chancey's ears flashed back and he started bucking like a maniac. Tom hadn't seen it coming. Before he knew it, he was flung to the ground and Chancey was tearing towards the gate. He looked as though he was going to cannon straight into it. But without hesitating, he launched himself over it and charged down the road at a cracking pace.

"Did you see that?" Alex cried excitedly. "Never mind him being mad. That was a five-barred gate he cleared and with miles to spare. I can't believe it."

Tom had landed heavily but the sand in the outdoor school had acted as a cushion. He sat rooted to the spot. His head was in his hands, his face was ashen, white with shock. Panic rose in his throat.

"What if he falls? He'll break his knees and then he'll be ruined. He'll have to be put down, and it will be all my fault. We've got to catch him," he said, struggling to his feet.

"We'll take the Land Rover, Tom," Nick said angrily. "I knew something like this would happen. He'll be miles away by now. This was the very reason

I didn't want you riding him."

"He's been going so well for me though," said Tom. "I don't know what's got into him. Maybe the noise of the cars on the road startled him."

"Maybe he just wasn't ready to be handled by a novice."

Nick's heated words stung Tom to the core as he realized the enormity of what had happened.

"Come on. Let's go," said Nick. "We have to try and catch him. If he's actually on the road, who knows what could happen. If he causes an accident, Sandy Lane could lose its licence."

"Grab a head collar, Tom. I'll go and tell Sarah," he said, hurrying off towards the cottage.

Moments later he reappeared. Climbing into the Land Rover, they rattled off down the drive and out of the yard.

"Keep your eyes peeled, Tom," said Nick. "I'll drive slowly past Bucknell Wood and you look in."

Tom couldn't see any movement in the thicket of pines. Chancey was nowhere to be seen. Nick drove on and on... past miles and miles of hedgerow, but although there were plenty of horses in the surrounding fields, Chancey was not among them. Tom's heart missed a beat as he saw a chestnut horse, but his hopes sank as the horse's white face turned to look at him.

Two hours of solid driving, down every road and through every field that Nick could think of, and still they hadn't found him. Tom was almost in despair.

"Where can he be? We've tried practically everywhere," he wailed, his voice rising into hysteria.

"Calm down, Tom. He'll have to stop somewhere. Let's go back to the stables and see if there's any news, do some phoning around. Someone may have rung in to the police by now," Nick said despondently.

As they rounded the corner to Sandy Lane, Rosie came rushing out to meet them.

"It's all right, Chancey's been found. He's safe. Alex managed to catch him. He was grazing in the fields behind the stables. He must have found his own way home."

Tom rushed forward to Chancey's stable to see for himself. Sure enough, there was Chancey, peacefully munching from a haynet as if nothing had happened. He looked up as Tom approached and whinnied softly. His eyes were bright and clear as his head cradled forward and his lips nuzzled Tom for a titbit.

"Not today, Chancey. You're not having a reward today," Tom said furiously. "You've done it this time." The others crowded anxiously around Tom.

"Tom, Tom, he was amazing," said Alex breathlessly, his eyes glinting with excitement. "I can't believe how he cleared that gate. He was born to jump. You were right, he has got it in him."

A hush fell over the group as Nick approached. No one dared breathe as they waited to hear what he had to say.

"Well Tom," said Nick. "There's nothing more for it. I forbade you to ride him before and I am forbidding you again. He's dangerous. If you go against my word this time, then you'll not only be forbidden to ride Chancey, you'll be out of Sandy Lane... for good."

9

THE LOCAL SHOW

Tom was at a loose end in the days following the warning. It was so unfair. Chancey had been going so well for him in secret. It must have been the noise of the car that had startled him. What bad luck for it to happen in front of Nick. And now, how could Tom ever prove that Chancey wasn't the crazed animal everyone thought he was, if he wasn't even allowed to ride him? In the end, it was Alex who came up with the solution... the perfect solution.

They were sitting in the dark in the tack room. It was late in the day and dusk had just started to set in. Nick was out with a class and the others had all gone home, leaving only Tom and Alex to clean the tack. Tom was polishing Chancey's saddle so hard that he could almost see his reflection in it.

"Look I'm sorry Alex," said Tom. "I know I should have told you what I was up to. It's just that I felt bad enough having to go behind Nick's back. I didn't want you to have to do it as well."

"I could have helped you though," said Alex in a hurt voice. "We could have done things together. I could have covered for you until you were one hundred percent ready to show Chancey to Nick."

"That's the trouble," said Tom gloomily. "I thought we were one hundred percent ready. I've been training him for weeks now and he's been getting better and better. It's the first spot of trouble I've had... typical that it had to be then of all times." Tom sighed. "What can I do?"

"There's only one thing to do Tom," said Alex. "You've got to prove to Nick that all your training was worth it, that he is the horse you know he is."

"How am I going to be able to do that now?" asked Tom.

"Well." Alex took a deep breath. "Ride him at the local show."

"That's impossible," Tom spluttered. "I've been forbidden to go near him. You heard what Nick said – I'd be out of Sandy Lane."

"Yes, but if Chancey matters that much, and you know you're right... you're down to ride Napoleon at the moment aren't you?"

"Yes," said Tom.

"So why not switch mounts and ride Chancey instead? By the time Nick realizes what's happened, it'll be too late for him to stop you. And when you've won, you'll have proved your point and he won't be angry any more."

"What if he is still angry?" said Tom. "And suppose Chancey and I can't do it? What if he plays up again?

It's risking everything."

"It's all you can do though. It's a gamble I know. But it's a gamble you have to take. I'll help you," Alex continued encouragingly. "I'm not riding in the open jumping which will give me the perfect opportunity to go and switch Napoleon's name for Chancey's at the show secretary's tent."

"Would you do that for me?" asked Tom.

"Yes, but we must keep it a secret. If anyone finds out, our plan will be ruined."

"OK," said Tom.

Tom was hesitant at first. But as the days passed, he started to feel more and more sure that Alex was right, that it was the only way.

* * * * * * * * * * * * * * * *

The day of the local show dawned cool and clear. The yard seethed with excitement as the horses were washed, groomed and plaited. Tom groomed Chancey in secret and doubled back to collect him once everyone had left Sandy Lane. The show was only two miles away, so it didn't take Tom long to hack him over there.

There was no going back now. The open jumping class had started an hour ago and there were only ten minutes until Tom was due in the ring. Nervously, he paced up and down in the woods. No doubt the others would be running around looking for him, panicking as Napoleon stood tied to the horse box, unattended and riderless. Tom felt a stab of guilt. Napoleon was a good horse and loved these shows, but Tom told himself he had to do it, for Chancey's sake.

Meanwhile, all he could do was wait. The hubbub of the crowd filled the showground and the smell of hot dogs hung in the air. Tom felt sick to the bottom of his stomach as he thought of what lay ahead of him. He had gone over the course again and again in his mind. It was fairly straightforward, Chancey should be able to walk it. But as they hadn't had time to practise since Nick's warning, Tom had little niggles of doubt. What if he was the one to muck up and let them down?

Tom's shoulders felt stiff and wooden, his hands clammy, as he mounted and started to loosen Chancey up in the woods away from the showground. He mustn't let Chancey sense he was nervous. He had to stay calm and collected if they were to stand a chance. Tom buttoned up his jacket and secured his chin strap. And then he heard his name being called.

"Number sixty-five... Tom Buchanan on Horton Chancellor," the voice called over the tannoy.

On the other side of the ring, Nick raised his head in astonishment at the announcement.

Tom cantered over to the ring and acknowledged the judges. He rode a circle, waiting for the bell.

R-r-ring. Tom was off. Nothing else was important. Nobody else mattered. His mind was focused on one thing, and one thing only – to jump clear. Chancey looked magnificent as he headed for the first jump in a collected canter. His nostrils flared and his eyes flashed amber as he gathered his pace.

"Go on, Tom, you can do it," Alex muttered as Tom pushed Chancey forward.

Tom couldn't hear him though. His mind was fixed on the course ahead. Concentration flickered across his face as the crowd became a blur of faces for him.

They were over the first and on to the gate. Tom felt Chancey speed up and tried to steady him. Soaring over the gate, they approached the stile. They were clear. Turning back on themselves, they raced up the middle to jump the treble.

"One, two, three," Alex muttered as Chancey bounded over the fences. One more turn to come, then the parallel bars and finally the huge wall. Chancey leapt over the parallel bars nimbly and went on to fly over the wall, clearing it with ease. And then they were cantering through the finish to the sound of applause, as the voice announced the result.

"Tom Buchanan on Horton Chancellor, jumping clear with no time faults and into the jump-off."

Tom grinned to himself. They were through to the next round.

"Well done my boy. You were brilliant." He patted Chancey proudly as the admiring spectators looked on at him. And then he saw Nick.

Tom looked at him pleadingly. Nick's eyes flashed angrily.

"What do you think you're doing, Tom?" he said. "Finish the jump-off and see me afterwards."

Tom felt sick again. They must win.

There were four competitors through to the jump-off, and Tom was third in the ring. Not a bad place, he thought to himself. He watched the other competitors from behind the rails, carefully weighing up the opposition. The first competitor had a bad round and sent everything crashing to the floor. The second competitor, a girl in immaculate cream jodhpurs and navy hacking jacket, set a better standard. She looked incredibly professional and for a moment Tom doubted that he should really be competing against her. She jumped clear.

Then it was Tom's turn. He cantered the obligatory circle, looked determinedly straight ahead and approached the first.

There was a loud bang as Chancey rapped the top of the rails. Tom's heart sank. He looked under his arm. But it was all right, the pole was still hanging there – how, he didn't know but it was still there. The near miss at the first fence had startled Chancey and he went on to clear the gate by miles, careful to pick his feet up as they flew over it. Collecting his stride, Tom faced Chancey at the stile, leaning forward to take his weight off his back. Tucking his legs up under him, Chancey sailed neatly over the jump.

Almost turning on the spot, Tom swung him round and they raced up the middle for the treble. Chancey cleared the three jumps with ease. Tom knew his horse, knew how far he could push him and with another sharp turn, Chancey sprang gracefully over the parallel bars and again there was only the wall. The crowd held their breath as horse and rider rose to the challenge. They were over it!

Everyone cheered madly as the voice announced that Tom Buchanan and Horton Chancellor had taken the lead with a time of three minutes and sixteen seconds.

"What a speed. No one will be able to beat that,"

Alex said excitedly to a stranger standing next to him. And sure enough, the last rider wasn't able to beat Tom's time and it seemed only moments later that Tom was galloping around the ring, a red rosette attached to Chancey's bridle.

Nick was the first to meet him as he came out of the ring. Tom looked shamefaced. Nick smiled. He had hardly been able to contain himself at the jump-off. And there was something else too. Tom reminded Nick of how he had been as a boy. If he was totally honest with himself, he knew that he would have done exactly the same thing.

"Well done, Tom. You were both magnificent," he grinned.

Tom felt jubilant. It was to be a good day for all of them. Alex went on to win a second in the novice jumping, Kate a third in the show class, Jess a second in the pole race and Rosie a first in the potato race.

"OK, Tom. You've proved your point," Nick said on the way home. "We're going to have to step up the Benbridge campaign now. After all, you'll be representing Sandy Lane there. And don't think I don't know who put you up to this." He turned and grinned at Alex.

Tom smiled wearily. It had been an exhausting day, both mentally and physically. All the worry about how Nick would react had taken its toll and the early morning outings had finally caught up with him.

"Everyone was talking about you, Tom," said Kate. "Everybody wanted to know who Chancey was. I wouldn't be surprised if you had quite a few offers for him after that amazing performance."

Kate was trying to be friendly, but her words rang

alarm bells in Tom's head. Of course people would be interested in Chancey – he was wonderful. At the end of the day though, Chancey wasn't his. Tom's heart felt heavy at the thought. He sighed. He couldn't be anything but a loser, for Benbridge meant the end of the summer, the return of Georgina and the loss of the horse to whom he had become so deeply attached.

10

AN UNWANTED VISITOR

Life at Sandy Lane was rather an anticlimax after the drama of the show. The only stir of excitement was caused by the arrival of entry forms for Benbridge. Tom was well aware that he would face much stiffer competition there than at the local show. Chancey would have to be at his very best if they were to have any hope of winning.

And there was something that was preying on Tom's mind – something he had been putting off doing. Four days had already passed since the local show, if he didn't say something soon, he never would.

"Nick, I was wondering if you would like to use Chancey in lessons now," Tom said hesitantly.

"That's a very generous offer, Tom," Nick said thoughtfully.

Tom's face dropped. Although he knew it was about time Chancey paid his way at Sandy Lane, Tom couldn't bear the thought of anyone else riding him.

"But I think it would be better if you alone rode him now that he's grown used to you," Nick continued, "until Benbridge anyway. Besides, we don't really need him. You could say we're overloaded with horses now that Feather's back in action and Storm Cloud wasn't such a disaster buy."

Tom breathed a sigh of relief and strolled over to the hay bales by the old barn to join Alex and Jess. He took out the packed lunch that his mother now allowed him to take to Sandy Lane. It had been a long battle, until finally she had agreed that there was no point in him coming all the way home at lunch time only to wolf down his food and hurry back again. Tom was also quick to point out that the other children had their lunches at Sandy Lane. Tom knew that his mother wouldn't want to seem less reasonable than other mothers.

Tom spread out the Benbridge entry form in front of him and munched happily on his sandwiches.

"Which classes are you going to enter, Tom?" asked Kate, as she joined him on the bales.

"Oh, only the open jumping. Chancey would hate the show classes. He'd never manage to stand still for long enough," Tom laughed.

"Well, I've entered absolutely everything," said Kate. "I don't care which classes I win, just as long as Minstrel's plastered with rosettes – though we've probably got the best chance in the showing," she said, blinking in the brilliant sunshine. "It's so bright out here. I can hardly see this entry form. Where do you put your name?"

"Here, silly," said Rosie, who had wandered across

the yard and was looking over Kate's shoulder. They were all together now, all of the Sandy Lane regulars. Nick had selected Tom, Kate and Alex to ride at Benbridge after their successes at the local show but both Rosie and Jess intended to go as well to support their friends.

"Well, I'm still pretty excited about my first in the potato race," said Rosie smiling. "Although I'd rather it had been in something a bit more graceful. My brothers howled with laughter when I told them."

Tom looked at his watch. Half past two. He had work to do with Chancey. Sarah was taking the others down to the beach for a ride.

As much as Tom loved the beach, Nick had said that he would train them for an hour in the school. And with Benbridge less than two weeks away, it was an offer he couldn't refuse. He packed away what was left of his lunch and headed, sandwich in mouth, to Chancey's stable.

Chancey's head appeared over the door as Tom held out the carrot that his mother had packed. He smiled to himself. Perhaps she was starting to feel some affection for his four-legged friend. Chancey stretched out his neck and sniffed apprehensively at the offering.

"It's not going to bite, silly," Tom laughed.

Once Chancey was sure that it was edible, his silky lips mumbled over Tom's flat hand, and in an instant the carrot disappeared. It made Tom laugh to see Chancey so careful with his food yet so bold when he jumped. Slipping into the stable, Tom tacked him up and led him out into the yard. The others were making a racket getting their mounts ready for their beach ride. Tom had to muster up all his will power to stop himself from turning around and going too. It would be wonderful on the beach at this time of day.

"See you later, Tom," Sarah called. "Tell Nick we'll be back by four. Certainly no later anyway as it's high tide at four."

"OK, I'll tell him," Tom answered.

At low tide, the wide expanse of beach at Sandy Bay was clear, but when the tide came in, the sand was flooded. If you weren't careful, you could find yourself cut off from land. Nick was careful to post a monthly copy of tide times on the tack room door and insisted that everyone check it before planning a ride to the beach. It was one of the first things that Tom had learnt about when he had started at Sandy Lane.

"Right, Tom," said Nick, stepping out of the tack room. "Let's go. I've set up a course for you in the outdoor school. See what you make of it. There's one tricky jump. But I think you should find it all right."

"OK," said Tom. Forgetting the beach ride in an instant, he headed off to the outdoor school. The white railings looked crisp in the bright sunshine, contrasting sharply with the gaily painted fences. Nick had erected a figure of eight jumps for them to practise over. Chancey eyed the course suspiciously. The tricky jump proved to be a square oxer.

"Parallel bars – difficult for a horse to judge the stretch and clear," Tom muttered to himself.

"I'll watch you for a while, Tom," said Nick, jumping up onto the railings. "Then I've got to go and take a private hack."

Tom trotted Chancey around the school and pushed him on into an easy canter.

"Take him round once more, Tom," said Nick. "It'll

make him more balanced when he starts jumping and it'll settle his rhythm too."

"OK," said Tom and swiftly they cantered around the circuit.

"Ready? You could take him over the course now, Tom," Nick called. "I want you to approach the first two jumps at a trot. It's good training for him."

Tom circled Chancey one more time and then popped him over the post and rails. Trotting him over the stile, he turned him wide at the corner of the school to give him enough time to see the square oxer. Chancey had been paying attention and, with a little encouragement from Tom, stepped up his pace to leap over the jump, clearing it easily. Collectedly, Tom rode across the school on a diagonal for the double.

"Be careful that you don't anticipate the jump and lean forward too early, Tom," Nick's voice boomed from the side of the school. "Let Chancey find his natural take-off point, otherwise you'll unbalance him and he'll try to put in an extra stride. Then you'll be the one who's unbalanced," he said laughing. "Otherwise, pretty good. It's as though he's a different horse."

"He's always like this with me now, Nick," Tom shouted back. "I think he's got used to me. He trusts me."

"I think you're right. Try him again," said Nick. "Then I really will have to go and get ready for this lesson."

Tom and Chancey soared around the course, unaware that Nick had crept away, leaving them to it. Jump after jump was cleared in swift succession until eventually Tom pulled Chancey to a halt. Leaping nimbly to the ground, he tethered him to the railings.

"That was just for practice," he said mischievously, as he went round the course raising the jumps. "Now this should wake you up."

Tom never had any sense of time when he jumped Chancey. Now, he was so involved with his riding, that he didn't notice the girl watching them from the shade of the cedar tree. Sulkily, she stared out at them, screwing up her sallow face as she took it all in.

All that could be heard was the sound of Chancey's hooves pounding against the ground as Tom and Chancey sailed over the jumps. Soon the others would be returning from their ride, and the stables would be buzzing with activity whilst everyone set about clearing up the yard for the evening. Little did Tom know of what lay ahead of him. Happily, he jumped off Chancey to raise the jumps again, not satisfied until he had stretched them both to the limit.

"Right. That's it for now, my boy," he said tiredly, as they knocked down a jump in the last round. "You're exhausted." Chancey's sides were puffing in and out like bellows. "You've had quite enough for one day. I don't want to push you too far."

Idly, he made his way to the gate and slid off the horse as the girl stepped out from the shadow of the tree. Tom was startled. The sun shone in his eyes as he returned the stony gaze of the girl who stood opposite him.

"Georgina," he gasped. "What are you doing back?"

11

FROM BAD TO WORSE

Tom couldn't believe his eyes. His cousin Georgina was standing right in front of him. Her cold blue eyes stared out at him from her pallid face. What was she doing here? She wasn't due back for another three weeks. Tom blinked, anxiously.

"I've come back early so I can ride Horton Chancellor at the Benbridge show," Georgina said quickly.

Tom's heart skipped a beat as he stared at the defiant face of his cousin. His worst nightmare was coming true. He felt a lump rising in his throat, almost choking him.

"Are you taking him home today then?" Tom asked, stumbling over the words.

"Oh no," Georgina said haughtily. "Change of plan. Daddy's tired of having him at home, says it's too much work for him. I've to arrange with the owners of Sandy

Lane to keep him on here at half-livery or something. Do you know them?"

"Of course I do," Tom said. Thoughts raced through his mind. Benbridge... keeping him at Sandy Lane... half-livery. Tom dismounted and, taking the reins in his right hand, led Chancey off to his stable.

"You'd better come with me," he said. "I'll take you to meet Nick. Do you want to take Chancey to his stable?"

"No, that's all right, you can do it," said Georgina breezily. "There'll be plenty of time for me to spend with him."

"All right then. Here's Nick now," he said as Nick strode towards them.

"What's going on?" Nick asked, as Tom hurriedly tried to explain the situation, holding on to a rather jumpy Chancey.

"This is my cousin, Georgina," said Tom, "the owner of Horton Chancellor. She would like to talk to you about the possibility of keeping him at livery with you."

"Oh, I see," said Nick thoughtfully. "Well, you'd better come and discuss things at the cottage with my wife Sarah, then." He tried to catch Tom's eye, but Tom had already turned away.

"So this is it then, boy," said Tom when he was alone with Chancey. "Your owner has come back to claim you, although rather earlier than expected."

Tom felt numb. He didn't know what he had thought would happen when Georgina returned. He had put it to the back of his mind for so long, half-hoping that she would never come back, half-hoping that she would forget about the horse altogether. Unrealistic dreams. He sighed.

"What's going on, Tom?" asked Rosie, leaning over the stable door and looking into Chancey's box.

"It's my cousin, Georgina," Tom said sadly. "She's back."

"Oh," said Rosie. "That's a bit early isn't it?" The words tumbled from her mouth before she had a chance to stop them.

"Yes it is," said Tom, turning away. Rosie could have kicked herself for being so thoughtless. She could see the hurt in Tom's eyes and wished she knew what to say to make him feel better.

"Er, I'm off home," she mumbled feebly. "What are you going to do now?"

"I don't know," said Tom. "Hang around here I suppose. I want to wait and see what Nick has to say."

"Oh," she said awkwardly. "Well, I'll see you tomorrow then."

"Yes, see you tomorrow," Tom said quietly as Rosie scuttled away.

Tom didn't have to wait long. He was the first person that Nick wanted to see before he made any decisions. He was well aware how attached Tom had become to the horse.

"Are you OK, Tom? I suppose you knew that she would be back at some point. Still, it doesn't make it any less of a shock, does it? I could say that there isn't any room for her to stable him here if it would make it easier for you."

"No, don't do that Nick," said Tom quickly. "That would make it so much worse. At least if he's here I can see him, even if he isn't really mine."

"I suppose you know that they're only asking to

keep him on at half-livery," said Nick. "That would mean you could at least ride him when Georgina isn't here. Although I've got some bad news. She's insisting that she rides him at Benbridge."

"I know, she was quick to tell me that," Tom said bitterly.

"I did try telling her about all the work you'd put in and about the rights and wrongs of it, but she wasn't interested," said Nick. "Look Tom, if it's any consolation, I'm entered on Feather for the open jumping at Benbridge. And I would be far happier if you rode her in my place. You know I don't like competitions much."

"But..."

"No buts," said Nick. "You would be representing Sandy Lane." Tom smiled and nodded in hesitant acceptance as he turned for home.

Tom's mother knew immediately that something was wrong when he trudged into the kitchen where she was washing up.

"What is it? What is it, darling? You look as though you've seen a ghost," she said.

"You could say that," said Tom. "It's Georgina, you see. She's... she's back." He could hardly get the words out. "She wants to ride Chancey at Benbridge."

"What do you mean?" asked his mother. "She's not due back for another three weeks."

"Sh-she's come back early to ride at Benbridge," he stammered.

Mrs. Buchanan didn't know what to say. She couldn't bear to see the look of disappointment on her son's face. Benbridge was all that he had talked about for weeks. She knew her niece though. If Georgina had her mind set on something, she would never be made to change it.

"Well, perhaps Nick would let you ride one of the other horses," she said half-heartedly, knowing that her solution offered no real consolation.

"He has," said Tom. "But it's not the same."

* * * * * * * * * * * * * * * *

When Tom woke the next day, he did so with a heavy heart. The sky was a deep cobalt blue. It was going to be a scorching summer's day. But Tom was in no hurry to get up. He couldn't face the thought of putting on a brave face and going down to Sandy Lane. Tom sighed. There were only ten days until Benbridge now. He owed it to Feather. On the count of ten, he forced himself out of bed.

Tom didn't get to the stables until 10 o'clock and when he did, he was furious to find Chancey still waiting to be groomed.

"What's going on Nick?" asked Tom. "Why isn't Chancey ready?"

"Hmm, I was wondering about that myself. I was under strict instructions from Georgina to leave him. She said that she would be down here to look after him. Looks as though she might have overslept."

"Might have guessed," said Tom. "I suppose I'd better get on with it then."

Tom was just getting the last pieces of straw out of

Chancey's tail when Georgina sauntered into the yard.

"Where do you think you've been?" said Tom angrily. "You can't just turn up when you feel like it if you've got a horse to look after."

"Now hang on a minute, Tom," Georgina crowed. "I don't have to answer to you. You're not my mother." Her blue eyes flashed scornfully at him. "Nick, I'm still booked in for the beach ride this morning, aren't I?" she asked, grabbing the brush from Tom as Nick passed by.

"That's right," he replied.

Tom groaned. He was booked to ride Feather on that very ride. Kate was on Jester, Jess had signed up for Minstrel, Rosie was riding Pepper and Alex was on Hector – all on their favourite horses. As it was such a beautiful day, Tom certainly wasn't going to give it up because Georgina would be there. Besides, he needed to make the most of his time with Feather if they were going to be ready for Benbridge.

"Now," said Nick, as everyone gathered round. "For those who are new to Sandy Lane... Georgina, are you listening? I'm only going to say it once."

"Yes Nick," she said sulkily, pulling her blonde hair into a pony tail as her reins trailed by Chancey's side.

Nick started again. "For all of you who don't know, there are strict rules about riding on the beach. First, always keep behind the horse in front of you. And secondly, although it's not applicable this morning, always check the tide sheet on the tack room door when planning a ride to the beach. The tide rolls in very quickly on this part of the coast and you could find yourselves cut off. At the very latest, you must be at the path to the cliffs by the time the water reaches

Gull Rock, which is half an hour before high tide. Sandy Lane won't accept responsibility for anyone disobeying the ground rules. Is that clear?"

"Yes Nick," came back a chorus of voices.

"Right then. Now that's out of the way, let's go."

Turning Whispering Silver to the gate, Nick led the riders out of the yard. In single file, they made their way around the outside of the first field and trotted on to the field of stubble beyond. They chattered excitedly as they made their way to Larkfield Copse. It was a track that Tom knew well. It was the first place he had ridden Chancey properly... really properly. He sighed. It seemed so long ago now. Tom cringed as he saw Georgina jab Chancey in the mouth as they entered the woods. He wanted to tell her that she didn't need a riding crop, but knew that it would only be causing trouble for himself. Now she was pulling on the reins and yet driving him on with her heels. No wonder Chancey was confused. Tom had to look away.

A gentle breeze flurried through the trees. Tom looked up, but couldn't see the blue of the sky, hidden as it was by a blanket of leaves.

As they emerged from the shade of the copse, the August sun bore down on their backs. Tom looked behind him at the line of trotting horses as they crossed the old coastal track to the open stretches. It was a lovely sight. Tom could smell the salt in the air as they cantered along the cliff tops.

Tom gazed down at the beach below as Feather sniffed the air. Slowly, the horses picked their way down the cliff path. Once on the sand, Chancey seemed even more edgy and looked as though he might launch himself forward at any moment. Georgina yanked at his head as they trotted along the shoreline.

"Try not to fight with him for his head, Georgina," Nick called out, seeing that she was having trouble. Georgina scowled.

Chancey's neck tightened as Georgina sawed furiously on the reins. He was beginning to foam at the mouth and the hollows of his nostrils were a blood red as he struggled against his leash. Tom looked on grimly.

"Right then everybody. Let's canter," said Nick. "Remember, it's not a race. Alex, you set off first and we'll follow on."

Alex pushed Hector on into a stiff canter, setting a pace for the others to follow. Soon they were streaming along behind him. Minstrel followed on Hector's toes, then came Kate, Rosie, Georgina and Tom. Nick brought up the rear with Whispering Silver.

Before Tom knew what was happening, he saw Georgina push Chancey on into a gallop. They had overtaken a rather startled looking Rosie and were wildly out of control as they overtook Kate and Jess and went neck and neck with Hector. Realizing that a race was on, the horses turned into a stampede as they bolted along the beach. Tom tried to pull Feather back gently but he couldn't stop her. His face felt taut as the wind whistled past.

Eventually, Chancey had had enough of racing and seemed to be tiring. He slowed down and soon he was gently cantering... trotting... walking. Tom breathed a sigh of relief. Nick was going to be furious but at least they had managed to stop. The others drew to a halt behind him. Rosie looked as white as a sheet.

"Georgina, did you listen to a word I said?" Nick

asked angrily.

"Yes," she replied insolently. "But I didn't want to go so slowly for all of the ride," she smiled, at what she thought were her new friends.

"As long as you ride at Sandy Lane, you ride under my rules," Nick roared. "Is that clear?"

"Yes Nick," said Georgina, pulling a face as he turned away.

With that, Nick led the riders on the route back to Sandy Lane. He didn't say a word, but it was obvious that he was livid. Tom himself was deep in thought as they rode back. He felt as though there was a black cloud hanging over him. It had really upset him to see Chancey egged on like that. He didn't want to sit by and watch the horse ruined. He would have to keep out of Chancey and Georgina's way, for the time being anyway. He would still go to visit Chancey with a daily titbit, only he would have to make sure that he wasn't in any classes with them.

There were nine days now to the Benbridge show. Tom wasn't going to be driven away from Sandy Lane because Georgina had come back. He would just spend more time with Feather. She might not have Chancey's strength, she might not have his all-encompassing courage, but she was a talented horse. And Tom was sure that they would go well at Benbridge.

12

BENBRIDGE!

The yard was busier than normal on the morning of the Benbridge show. Everyone was rushing around oiling hooves, searching for grooming kit, plaiting manes, putting studs in hooves, and so it went on. By nine o'clock, everyone was ready and the last of the horses had been boxed and bolted.

In spite of everything, Tom felt excited. Feather was easily the best of Nick and Sarah's horses. And at least Chancey was going to be at Benbridge, even if they wouldn't be sharing the same experience. He also had the added bonus that he didn't have to share the journey to Benbridge with Georgina. Tom smiled to himself.

Nick had thought that it would be too much to have Georgina in the horse box with Tom, so Sarah and the others had been lumbered with her in the Land Rover. She had already been complaining that she hadn't expected Chancey to have to share a horse box. Nick had soon shut her up by telling her that she didn't have to be taken to the show.

Of the Sandy Lane team, Kate had entered Jester for the 13.2 show class, Alex had entered Hector for the novice jumping and Tom and Georgina were down for the open jumping. Tom hoped that just because Georgina was arriving with them, people wouldn't think she was Sandy Lane trained. Her aggressive style of riding would do the stables' reputation no good whatsoever.

As they arrived, Tom's eyes widened. He had forgotten what it was like at a big show. It was all so official, so serious. Entries were being announced over a loudspeaker. Officials were running around. There was a stand for the judges. It even *smelled* important. Tom felt a knot in the pit of his stomach.

A steward glanced at their car park label and waved them on their way. Nick brought the horse box to a halt under the shade of a tree and Tom jumped out of the cab. Heading to the rear of the box, he put down the ramp to let out the horses. Tom was leading out Chancey when the Land Rover pulled up next to them and Georgina jumped out.

"Give him here," she cried, grabbing the head collar from Tom's hand. Chancey's eyes rolled as she yanked his head to the ring on the side of the horse box.

"I'd be careful with him if I were you, Georgina," said Alex. "You know how jumpy he can get."

"Nonsense. You've got to show them who's boss," Georgina argued.

"Well, let's not spoil such a wonderful day by squabbling anyway," said Kate sensibly. "Come on everyone, we should go and collect our entry numbers.

Tom, you and Georgina had better let them know of your change of horses."

"You're right," said Tom. Wandering over to the secretary's tent, they picked up their numbers and fastened them onto their backs importantly.

"They're huge," said Kate laughing. "It'll cover my whole back."

"That's the general idea," said Georgina.

"I'm going to throttle her if she doesn't shut up," Kate muttered under her breath. "She's such a know-all."

Tom smiled to himself. He was used to Georgina. He wasn't going to let her get to him... not today of all days.

"Can someone help me with my hair?" Kate mumbled, her mouth full of grips. "I can't seem to get it all in this hair net. I wish we didn't have to wear them." She scrabbled about on the ground for the hair tie she had dropped.

"I probably won't see you before the showing, Kate," Tom laughed, making a quick escape as Rosie went to the rescue. "It's on the other side of the ground to the jumping, so good luck."

"You too," she smiled.

Tom was eager to lose Georgina and quickly hurried away before she could tag along with him. Taking a deep breath, he looked at the jumps as they stretched out in front of him. It wasn't that they were enormous, it wasn't even that there were a lot of them, but it was a stiff course with so many difficult combinations – eleven jumps in all.

"Phew," Tom gasped, the adrenaline running through his body as he thought of what lay ahead.

Tom headed back to the horse box to find that his mother and father and Georgina's parents had arrived, and were gathered with the Sandy Lane group. Everyone was having lunch, even Georgina. Tom didn't know how she could eat anything. He felt quite sick with nerves.

"Hi Tom," said his Uncle Bob, holding out his hand. "Thanks for looking after Georgina's horse for us while we've been away. Apparently you've done a fantastic job with the brute."

Tom winced, hearing Chancey talked of in that way. Tom's mother looked at him sympathetically. She felt bad enough as it was that Georgina had taken Chancey away from him.

"You look so smart, Tom," she said, quickly changing the subject.

"Thanks Mum," he said looking down at his newly-pressed jodhpurs. He winced as he stretched his shoulders. Until that moment he had forgotten that his hacking jacket, though smart, was far too small for him and extremely uncomfortable. He'd rather be wearing his old mucking-out clothes any day.

"Georgina, have you walked the course yet?" he asked distractedly, staring into the distance.

"No, don't need to," said Georgina, her mouth crammed full of pork pie, "I've seen it. Looks fine."

"Right," said Tom, shrugging his shoulders. "Well, I'm off to loosen up Feather. I'll be at the collecting ring if anyone wants me. The jumping's started."

"Good luck, Tom," Mrs. Buchanan called, as Tom walked over to Chancey.

"Good luck, boy," he whispered to Chancey, pulling his ears gently. Chancey nudged him playfully, shifting his weight lazily from one foot to the other as he basked in the sun.

Then Tom made his way to Feather and carefully tacked her up. One of her plaits had come loose, so Tom quickly restitched it. Time was moving on and his butterflies were even worse now. He was sure that the horse would be able to feel the tension running through his body.

Quickly, he mounted and started to walk Feather towards the collecting ring where lots of professional-looking riders were limbering up their mounts. There were more than a hundred competitors in the open jumping class, the most popular event of the day. As Tom started to warm up Feather, Alex came riding past on Jester, a grin plastered on his face.

"Sixth," he called. Tom was pleased for him. Sixth was pretty good at a show of this standard and he felt encouraged by the result.

"There's hope for me yet then," Tom yelled back as Alex trotted on towards the gymkhana events.

And then there was an announcement over the speaker that brought Tom back to earth with a jolt.

"Name change... number sixty-two, Horton Chancellor, owned by Robert Thompson, will be ridden by Georgina Thompson and number sixty-eight, Feather, owned by Sandy Lane Stables, will be ridden by Tom Buchanan," rang out over the speaker.

Tom gritted his teeth and listened carefully to the numbers being announced. They were up to fifty-eight already. It would soon be Chancey's turn, and Georgina wasn't anywhere to be seen. Tom didn't usually like to watch anyone else riding the course. But he had to watch Chancey.

Jumping off Feather, he led her to the horse box and tied her to a ring before making his way to the stands. The crowd was quiet as competitor number sixty picked his way carefully around the course, finishing well within the three minute time limit. Tom stood away from his parents. He didn't want to hear any sympathetic noises when Georgina jumped Chancey. He was also in two minds about his feelings. He half-wanted Chancey to do well and yet he half-wanted Georgina to do badly.

Here they were now. Tom watched intently as Horton Chancellor was called into the ring and cantered a circle. Then they were off. Tom cringed as he heard the loud crack of the whip strike against Chancey's rump. Chancey looked equally displeased and almost leapt out of his skin with fright. He threw himself over the first jump, clearing it by miles. Georgina only just managed to regain her composure in time to sit still for the shark's teeth and the bank. They were over them, but at what a pace.

"Steady boy, steady," Tom breathed.

But it was too late, they were charging towards the combination, and now Georgina was kicking him on. Suddenly, she tried to check Chancey as he was about to jump the parallel. Tom closed his eyes as he heard the loud rap echo around the ring, but somehow the pole stayed up. They were rushing on to the treble. Georgina shortened her reins. Tom couldn't bear to look as Chancey struggled for his head and lurched over the three fences... clear.

She turned him stiffly towards the next jump. She wasn't going to be so lucky this time. There wasn't a moment for Chancey to gather impetus and, with a loud bang, he hit the gate which was sent crashing to the floor. Another loud whack resounded from Georgina's whip as Chancey headed for the last two jumps. Chancey lunged forward for the stile and staggered over it, his hooves just clipping the top. Then he reeled onto the gate. He was over it. But by the time he was through the finish, Chancey was foaming at the mouth and looked a nervous wreck. His body was drenched in sweat. Tom turned away in disgust at the sight of her parents congratulating her as the speaker announced that competitor number sixty-two had four faults.

Tom tried to compose himself as he collected Feather, eager to forget what he had seen. He worked out that they probably had about half an hour until it was their turn. Tom mounted and turned into the collecting ring. He trotted Feather around and then, with a light nudge, took her into a gentle canter. She had a lovely loping stride, a very easy canter to ride. Gently, she glided over the post and rails that was set up as a practice jump.

"It won't be long now," he told her, patting her shoulder as he slowed her down. Calmly, Tom walked Feather around the ring to settle her as they awaited their turn. He could see another competitor come trotting out of the ring. All too suddenly it was upon them.

Once Tom was called into the ring, he told himself to block everything else out. They were here to do their best, and that was all they could do.

The bell rang out and they cantered to the first. Tom eased Feather over the brush, and they approached the shark's teeth. Deftly, she sprang over it. And now it was the bank. Taking it all in her stride, she rode onto it and down the other side. Tom swung her round wide to the combination, giving her enough room to look at it. He sat tight to the saddle, determined not to make the same mistakes Georgina had. Gently, he rode Feather to the middle of the jumps, steadying her as she sailed over them. He was so light with his hands, she could hardly have known he was there. Tom was starting to enjoy himself.

Leisurely, he faced her at the treble and they soared over the three jumps in succession. Again, he swooped around in a large circle to take Feather over the gate, the stile, the wall. Touch down! There was a loud cheer from the crowd as they left the ring. Tom clapped his hand to Feather's shoulder and buried his head in her mane.

"You were brilliant," he mumbled.

The speaker announced the result.

"Tom Buchanan on Feather, jumping clear with no time faults."

"Well done," Rosie called, jumping up and down with excitement.

Tom was going to have to wait until the jump-off, so he wandered over to where his parents were watching the rest of the competitors.

"Well done, Tom," his mother cried. She couldn't believe how well he had ridden.

"You took your time, Tom," Georgina sneered spitefully. "It must be easy to jump clear if you go at that snail's pace. You'll have to be a bit faster next time if you don't want to be laughed out of the ring." Tom had to bite his tongue to stop himself from being very rude. Still Georgina went on.

"Horton Chancellor and I were rather unlucky to knock that gate, weren't we?" she said, not waiting for a reply. "He overran it rather. Still, less competition for you in the jump-off, eh?"

Tom was fuming, but he didn't have enough time to be angry, as the voice announced that there were ten riders through to the jump-off and the jumps were being raised that very moment. Tom rushed forward to watch.

The course was enormous now and speed was going to be crucial. He was the fifth one in. Not as good a position as he'd had at the local show, but still better than being first. The competition seemed pretty stiff. The other riders all looked as though they had been competing for years. Tom could hardly bear to watch, never mind listen, as the riders went into the ring and the results were announced. All of the times sounded very fast. Tom didn't have a clue what he needed to beat as he entered the ring for the second time. He would just have to go like the clappers.

"Good luck," Rosie and Jess called from behind the rails.

Tom couldn't hear them though. The crowd hushed as he circled Feather.

And then they were off... racing to the first as the clock began ticking its countdown. They sailed over the brush, and then raced over the shark's teeth and soared over the bank. Feather's black eyes gleamed and her ears were pricked as she arched her neck. Her Arab lines were clearly defined as she stretched out her stride and raced forward. All Tom could see were the fences ahead of him, all he could hear was the sound of pounding hooves. Tom turned Feather to the combination. There were no wide swoops this time. The crowd gasped at the sharpness of the turn, but Feather knew what was expected of her and didn't even hesitate at the combination. Tom rode her at the middle of the jump, propelling her forward with his legs and she tucked her feet up under her as if the poles were hot pokers.

Again, Tom turned her immediately they touched the ground, so that there was hardly enough time for them to gather momentum. But he had judged it just right and Feather surged forward for the treble. One, two, three. Tom leant forward in the saddle as the horse found her natural take-off and swiftly cleared the fences. Now there were only three more jumps. It was all happening so quickly. Feather cantered on the spot, preparing herself for the last turn. Tom steadied her as they approached the gate. Cleared. Then they were on to the stile. Cleared. Now they were approaching the huge wall. They were over, and at what a speed!

Tom could hardly contain himself as the voice from the speaker announced that he had taken the lead with a time of three minutes and four seconds. Tom clapped his hand to Feather's neck in excitement and neatly jumped to the floor.

"You were brilliant, Tom," called Jess, who had hardly been able to watch. "I bet you've won."

"No, someone's sure to beat me," he said. "There are still four competitors to go."

"I'm not so sure," said Nick, coming up behind them. "That will be a hard act to follow. Well done."

Tom walked Feather towards the trees to cool down for the result. He could hardly believe it, he had jumped clear. He didn't want to watch everyone else, it seemed unsportsmanlike to hope they wouldn't do well.

It seemed to take forever as the speaker called out the times and repeatedly announced that Tom held the lead. There were only two more riders to go. Tom held his breath at the gasps from the crowd as the competitors thundered around the course. But no one matched his time.

Tom couldn't quite believe it when his name was called as the winner. Somehow, he found himself trotting forward.

The next thing Tom knew, he was flying around the ring again, this time with a red rosette pinned to Feather's bridle and a huge silver cup in his hands. Beams of light sprang off it as it glinted in the sunlight and they galloped their lap of honour. This had to be the greatest moment of his life.

As he came out of the ring, all of his friends from Sandy Lane gathered around him. He couldn't believe it... he, Tom Buchanan, was the winner of the open jumping at Benbridge. And then his heart sank as he remembered who he should have been riding.

"But it wasn't with Chancey," he said sadly to himself.

13

TO THE RESCUE

"I can't believe that Georgina's parents were actually pleased with her performance at Benbridge. She might as well have been wearing spurs. Chancey would have won the open jumping if Tom had been riding him." It didn't sound mean coming from Alex who never had a bad word to say about anyone.

"And she's a show-off if you ask me," said Jess, wrinkling up her nose.

"Worse than that. She's going to be keeping Chancey on at Sandy Lane too. It's really rubbing Tom's face in it." Alex brushed the last traces of sawdust from Hector's tail.

"Well, at least he gets to see Chancey," said Jess. "It would have been awful if she had taken him away. Tom's completely devoted to that horse. He's done so much with him. Do you remember what he was like when he first arrived at Sandy Lane?"

Jess and Alex were still chatting away when Tom passed behind them. Oblivious to the fact that he had heard every word, they continued with their tasks.

They were right of course, but even so, Tom was finding it difficult. He couldn't stop thinking about Chancey at Benbridge. The horse had been driven into a complete frenzy and Tom wasn't even in a position where he could say anything. He shouldn't have let himself get so attached to the horse. He hadn't meant to. It had just happened that way and he hadn't realized how hard it would be to give him up.

As Tom untacked Feather, he glanced around the yard. Everything was in order, everything was in its correct place. Except Chancey's stable door was wide open and swinging in the wind!

Bang! Ominously, it slammed shut.

No doubt that wretched Georgina had forgotten to bolt it. Tom hurried over and stuck his head around the door. The stable was empty – neither Chancey nor his tack were there.

Tom was puzzled. Georgina couldn't be riding in the woods – he had just been there on his hack. She hated practising, so she wouldn't be in the outdoor school. Still, it was worth a try. Tom ran down the drive to the outdoor school. But there was no one there.

Then, as he turned back to the yard, it suddenly struck him. Georgina must have taken Chancey to the beach. Tom's heart sank as he remembered her impatience with the last coastal ride. She would love an opportunity to ride Chancey far out on the beach with no one to stop her. He looked at his watch and cringed. A quarter past four. He had a horrible feeling that it was high tide at five today. The beach would be almost covered by now.

Quickly, he ran to the tack room and looked at the tide sheet, breathlessly hoping that he was wrong. He felt the blood rushing to his head as he stared at the times before his eyes. Stupid girl.

"Nick, Nick," he cried, running to the cottage, desperately searching for help. But there was no one around. Where had Alex and Jess gone? There wasn't a moment to lose. Impulsively, he grabbed a bridle and ran to Feather's stable. He had no choice. He would have to go himself. Pulling the horse's head up out of her feed bowl, he put the bridle back on and led her out of the stable. There was no time for a saddle. He opened the gate and vaulted onto her back. Feather's neck was arched and her tail held high as she whinnied excitedly.

Tom turned her through the gate and pushed her on... faster and faster until they were galloping. Soon they were approaching the other side of the field. There wasn't time to stop and open the gate. He took a deep breath and prayed. Gritting his teeth as they went forward, he drove Feather towards the hedgerow. He grimaced as he heard the sharp twigs scratch her belly. He felt himself slipping and gripped harder with his knees. Feather took it as a command to go faster and started to gallop over the stubble at a cracking pace. Tom clung on for dear life as they raced through the woods, on and on to the open stretches beyond.

It was only when they were on the cliff tops that Tom drew Feather to a halt and looked down at the beach below. It was almost covered, except for a few remaining islands of sand left amidst the surging, swirling sea. The silver, shimmering expanse of water stretched out in front of him.

Tom listened carefully. All he could feel was his heart beating faster, all he could hear was the ominous cry of the gulls overhead. He squinted into the distance. Perhaps they weren't here after all, he thought hopefully.

And then he heard a pitiful cry coming from a sand bar some way beyond Gull Rock. Straining his eyes, he could just make out a person and a horse, the water seeping in around them. The horse was sweating up and frantically swishing his tail. It had to be Georgina and Chancey.

"Georgina,Georgina!" Tom cried. Why didn't she guide Chancey towards the shore? It was probably still within their depth. In any case, horses were good swimmers. They could still make it if they were quick. Tom felt completely hopeless. What could he do? If he and Feather swam out to them, the tide would be higher still. They would never make it back. And he knew that he wasn't strong enough to swim it alone.

Then it came to him. If he rode round towards the headland, he could climb down the blowhole into the caves that he and Alex had explored last summer, and then wade across the rocks to the sand bar. Without hesitating, he gathered up Feather's reins and pushed her forward. Deftly she raced along the cliff tops to the far side of the bay, picking her way through the loose stones as she went. Tom dismounted. There was nowhere to tie her. He took a deep breath and knotted her reins. Then he slapped her rump and sent her on her way, hoping that she would find her way back to Sandy Lane and raise the alarm.

Soon he had found what he was looking for. Tom

shuddered as he looked down into the inky black abyss below him.

"Here goes," he said to himself. He knew that he could get down. He'd done it loads of times with Alex. But this was different – he had to be quick. One slip and he would go crashing to the bottom of the hole.

Tom looked down at his hands as he clutched at the stumps of grass. His knuckles were white, and his breath was coming faster now. Trembling, he climbed into the hole. He knew there were foot holds cut out of the rock. He would have to feel for them. Think of it as a ladder, he said to himself and carefully he struggled down and down.

When his foot finally touched water, he couldn't believe he had made it. Stepping down from the hole, he looked around him. He would have to pick his way out of the cave very cautiously. Holding onto weed and rocks to steady himself, he waded out against the waves until he was up to his hips.

"Georgina, Georgina," he called again. And this time she heard him. Her face was contorted with fear.

"Hang on. I'm coming for you," he said, calmly. One moment, the water was up to his waist, the next a wave rolled in and he was up to his neck. But he was nearly there. He would just have to swim the last bit. It wasn't far. And then he reached the sand bar.

"Quickly, Georgina. There's not a moment to lose. The tide's still coming in. The sand bar will be covered before long."

"What do I do?" she wailed, the panic rising in her throat, her eyes white with fear. "Where did you come from?"

"Keep calm," said Tom. "I came from a cave over

there at the side of the cliff," he pointed. "If we can get back, then there's a hole you can climb up."

"No, no," she wailed. "I'm not going in the water. I'll drown. You should have got them to send a boat for me."

"Who? Get real, Georgina," said Tom. "There wasn't time for a boat. No one even knows you're here for starters."

The sand bar had halved in size since he had first spotted them and they were fast running out of time.

"Look, I'll swim to the cave and you hold onto my shoulders," Tom said, desperately trying to remember all he had learnt in his life-saving classes. Georgina seemed to calm down at this suggestion.

"OK, I'll hold onto you and you drag me," she said.

"Right," said Tom, getting more impatient by the minute. "Let's go."

"Chancey," he called. "Chancey, I'm coming back for you. Don't do anything silly." The horse was sidestepping around the sand bar, his eyes rolling uncontrollably.

Tom strode into the waves and plunged forward as Georgina held onto him. She was clinging on so tightly, that for a moment he panicked that she would drag him under. Once they had started, she calmed down though, and her grip slackened. Doggedly, Tom swam forward and forward until eventually they could stand.

"Stand Georgina, stand. Your feet can touch the bottom here. Walk forward." Quickly, he led her into the cave.

"Right, now this is the hole," he said pointing upwards. "Up you go."

"I'm not going up there."

"Yes you are," Tom said firmly. "Or you'll drown."

"I need you to show me how to do it," Georgina cried hysterically.

"I've got to go back for Chancey, Georgina."

"Never mind the horse," she screamed. "What about *me*?" Tom looked at her in disbelief.

"I'll drown," she said. "He's only a horse, he can be replaced."

Tom looked out to sea at the familiar figure still struggling on the sand bar, now a silhouette against the bleak horizon.

"No," he said firmly. "I'm going back. If I guide him, we can swim to the path. I've got you this far. Once you're on the top of the cliffs, you'll be safe. You know the way back."

"It's dangerous," Georgina yelled.

But Tom didn't listen as he turned and headed back into the sea. It wasn't long before he was up to his neck. He spluttered as he took in a gulp of water. Moving his arms was nearly impossible as the weight of his sweatshirt dragged him down. Out of breath, he scrambled onto the sand bar and quickly grabbed Chancey's bridle.

"Come on my boy. We're going to get off here. We're going to be all right. You've got to swim to the shore – straight ahead, towards the path. I know that it looks a long way, but you're strong. You can do it."

Tom had a job keeping Chancey still as he scrambled on top of him. Chancey circled the sand bar and pawed at the ground.

Tom patted his shoulder to settle him down. Then he urged him forward and they plunged into the waves. When Chancey realized that he could swim, he wasn't so frightened. But in spite of his words of encouragement, Tom really didn't know if they could make it. Chancey was a courageous horse, but two hundred yards was a long way to swim.

They seemed to make good progress at first, but after the first five minutes, Chancey was beginning to struggle. The current was stronger than Tom had anticipated and he felt exhausted as he clung on, gripping until his legs were numb. Were they nearly halfway now? Tom didn't know. Surely they must be. But the shore didn't seem to be any closer. Bravely, they battled forward. Chancey snorted and spluttered as the water swirled, until slowly, the shore grew larger. They were getting closer. Tom started to feel more positive. Surely they could make it now. He thought he heard voices carried to him on the sea air. They were almost there.

And suddenly they must have hit the sand. Chancey nostrils were a fiery red as he forced his way through the crashing waves. He seemed to be walking along the sea-bed. They were at the foot of the cliffs. Tom felt shivery as they reached the path. He slid to the ground, unable to hold on any longer and everything went black...

14

CHANCEY FOREVER!

Nick was startled when Feather clattered into the yard, her reins dangling broken by her sides, her coat dank with sea water. His heart sank. She had come from the beach. Someone was in danger. He looked at his watch. He looked at the tide sheet. Someone was in serious danger.

There wasn't a moment to lose. Nick hurried over to where Whispering Silver was basking lazily in the sun and climbed into the saddle. Turning out of the yard, he called to Sarah to bring the Land Rover round the old coastal track to the top of the cliffs. There wasn't time to answer any questions.

Slipping through the back gate, he headed for the cliffs, taking the same route Tom had taken no more than half an hour ago... through the fields, through the woods, to the open stretches beyond.

Nick reached the path at the top of the cliffs at a

quarter to five just as Georgina was scrambling her way up the blowhole.

Nick gazed anxiously out to sea, willing himself to see something... anything. But there wasn't anyone around. Or was there? And then he saw it – the outline of a horse on a sand bar. He looked harder. It looked like Chancey, but where was his rider? Now he could see a tiny speck moving halfway between the cliffs and the sand bar. Nick craned his neck further forward. It seemed to be getting closer to the sand. It was a person. And then he saw someone else on the far side of the cliffs. It looked like Georgina.

"What on earth is going on?" he bellowed. "Who's that on the sand bar?"

"Ch...Ch...Chancey," Georgina stuttered.

"I can see that," he said. "But who's that out there with him?"

"Tom."

"*Tom.*" Nick was flabbergasted. "What's he doing out there?"

"It's... it's my fault," Georgina spluttered, shivering now from both cold and fear. "I got caught and he wanted to go back for the horse. They will be able to make it won't they? They will be all right?"

"Well, we'll soon see," Nick said grimly, scrambling down the path to the beach where the waves were crashing fiercely against the rocks.

It was a long way to swim. Nick had never felt so completely powerless. All he could do was watch. The pair seemed to be progressing slowly. And then he heard the noise of a car engine and Sarah appeared at the top of the cliffs. As she hurried down the path to join Nick, she needed no explanation. Training her

105

eyes on the moving figures, she held her breath. The current was so strong but they were about halfway now. Could they make the shore?

"Clever lad," Sarah was saying. "He's following an angled route to take account of the currents."

Nick's mind was whirling. He couldn't watch. He couldn't stop watching. He couldn't think straight. He didn't know what to do. Turning from the sea, he listened to Sarah's running commentary. And he couldn't stop himself from looking back and remembering the day he had first met Tom. Had it come to this?

"They've only got fifty yards or so to go," said Sarah.

Nick snapped out of his trance as he realized that he hadn't been listening to a word Sarah had been saying. He rushed forward as Chancey clawed at the rocks and stumbled up the path. Tom collapsed at his feet.

* * * * * * * * * * * * * * * * *

When Tom awoke, he was back in his bedroom at home. The curtains were drawn, but as his eyes became accustomed to the dark, he could just make out the shape of the large china horse on his book shelf. Perhaps it had all been a dream. He reached up to his forehead. There was something on it, something cold and damp. It felt like a flannel.

Tom's head felt fuzzy. His heart started to beat faster

as slowly it all started to come back to him.

"Mum, Mum, where are you?" He was panicking now. Mrs. Buchanan rushed into the room.

"Why am I in bed?" he cried. "Where's Chancey? Did it all really happen?"

"Calm down Tom," his mother said sensibly. "One question at a time. Everything's OK. You're just exhausted. Yes, it did all happen and you hit your head when you fell."

"But Georgina," said Tom.

"She's fine," said his mother. "In disgrace, but fine. She managed to climb up the blowhole. And Chancey's all right too. Showing off, but still in one piece. You've slept through the night, so you haven't missed out on anything."

"Oh," said Tom, a wave of relief spreading right through him. "I shouldn't have saved Georgina, should I?" he joked. "Then I would have had Chancey all to myself."

"You were extremely brave," said his mother. "A lot has happened since then. You might find you have a few surprises," she said, drawing back the curtains. "Look outside."

Tom's head ached as he leaned out of his bed and looked out of the window. Then he laughed, for there was Chancey, walking on Mrs. Buchanan's garden. Alex was holding onto his head collar and waving up at Tom.

"What's going on Mum?" he said, stifling a giggle as Chancey pawed at Mrs. Buchanan's prizewinning dahlias. Mrs. Buchanan frowned.

"Well, I think your visitor will explain," she said mysteriously, as the door opened and a rather shamefaced-looking Georgina entered.

"I'll leave you both to it then," said Mrs. Buchanan. She smiled encouragingly at Georgina as she let herself out of the room. Nervously, Georgina approached the side of Tom's bed.

"What are you here for?" he asked, bemused.

"Just hear me out, Tom," said Georgina. "I know what I did was foolish," she stammered. "I thought I knew best."

Tom couldn't believe what he was hearing. His cousin Georgina was standing in front of him, admitting she had been in the wrong. Was he dreaming? He sat up and rubbed his eyes.

"I can't thank you enough," Georgina went on. "You saved my life... I'm sorry for being so awful. And I want you to have him."

Tom looked up and caught her gaze.

"Who?" said Tom.

"Chancey," she said.

"Chancey?" Tom spluttered. It was the last thing he had expected. "You mean you're giving him to me? Are you mad?"

"Maybe a little," Georgina smiled. "But I don't want to ride any more. I only took it up because I thought Daddy wanted me to. Now it turns out he would have been as happy for me to do ballet," she laughed. "So, if you want him." She hesitated, waiting for Tom to answer her. "We would like him to go to a good home."

"Want him... *Want him*?" said Tom, getting more excited by the minute. "I can't believe what I'm hearing. Things like this don't really happen. Tell me I'm not dreaming."

And, as if in response, there was a loud whinny

from the garden. It was as though Chancey was trying to tell Tom what he thought about it all. He was Tom's horse forever now, he seemed to be saying... not just for the summer.

THE
RUNAWAY
PONY

Susannah Leigh

CONTENTS

1

THE RUNAWAY PONY

Jess Adams free-wheeled her bicycle down the gentle hill. "No more school!" she cheered as she sped past the fields. "Hooray for the Easter holidays!"

She turned sharply into the drive of Sandy Lane Stables and skidded the bike to a halt. It was early morning, not quite seven o'clock, and no one else was around. Only the ponies were awake, shuffling in their stalls and whinnying softly for their breakfasts. Jess cast a glance at the little stone cottage tucked away behind the stables.

"I bet Nick and Sarah won't be up for hours," she said to herself.

Nick and Sarah Brooks were the owners of Sandy Lane. Last night had been a rare evening off. They had gone to a ball.

1

"It's in aid of the *Horse Rescue Society*," Sarah had said as she twirled excitedly around the stable yard, the emerald satin of her borrowed ball-gown matching her green eyes.

"You'll probably be dancing till midnight," Jess had sighed. "Sipping pink champagne and slurping caviar."

"Probably," Nick had said as he adjusted his black bow tie.

"And you're bound to be back very late and be terribly tired in the morning," Jess had continued, forking the last of the hay into Minstrel's hay net. "So perhaps I ought to come in early and start the ponies' breakfasts for you. And then maybe..."

"...Maybe you could have a free ride later on in the day?" Nick smiled and finished the sentence off for her. Money was tight in Jess's family since her dad had lost his job. There wasn't much spare cash for her riding lessons.

"You can have the eleven o'clock hack for free," Nick had said in an understanding voice. "I'll *even* try to be up and about early tomorrow morning to give you a hand..."

That was last night. And now it was morning and Nick wasn't up. But Jess had learnt a lot in the two years she had been coming to Sandy Lane. She certainly knew enough to start getting the ponies ready for the day.

"Perhaps Nick will even let me ride *you* this afternoon, you beautiful pony," she said as she drew nearer to Storm Cloud's stable.

Storm Cloud, a dappled-grey Arab, greeted Jess eagerly, poking her delicate, dished face over the stable door. Jess slipped her the sugar lump she had been saving especially. She had never seen a pony so breathtaking.

She thought back to the day Nick had first found Storm Cloud at the Ash Hill Horse Sale. Storm Cloud had been weak and neglected, but even then Nick had been able to see the pony's potential. And with love and patience, he had brought her back to her former glory. She was a natural jumper and it wouldn't be long before she was competing.

In Jess's mind, Storm Cloud was the best pony at the stables. She might look fragile, but she was really gutsy and strong-willed. Whenever Jess had been lucky enough to ride her, she had felt as though they had the potential to do anything; jump any fence, outrun any other pony. She loved to imagine jumping Storm Cloud in a show and riding off with the championship trophy, although she had never told anyone else this dream. It was her secret.

"What a team we'd make, eh Stormy?" Jess whispered into the pony's ear. Storm Cloud neighed gently in reply and at the same time, Jess heard a whinny from a nearby stable. She grinned as Minstrel, the little skewbald pony, showed his big yellow teeth and rolled the whites of his eyes at her.

"Don't worry Minstrel," Jess laughed. "I haven't forgotten about you."

Minstrel was Jess's regular pony at Sandy Lane –

the one she rode the most. He was a good, solid riding school pony and Jess was very fond of him.

"I expect I'll be riding you later on, Minstrel," Jess began as she made her way over to the pony's stall. "Bet you can't wait..."

"Come here!"

Angry shouting and the crunch of hooves on gravel stopped Jess in her tracks and made her spin around sharply. Careering towards her down the drive, wild-eyed with fear and long tail flying behind, was a palomino pony. It was completely out of control. Jess's heart began to pound and her breath came in sharp gasps, but almost without thinking she held out her arms.

"Whoa, little pony," she said, as calmly as she could. "Slow down."

Jess stood her ground and now the pony was only inches away from her. At the sound of Jess's voice it clattered to a halt. It dropped its head and nuzzled a velvety nose into Jess's shoulder. Jess sighed with relief. The next moment she had located a stray mint in the depths of her jodhpur pocket. Gingerly she fished it out and offered it to the palomino. The pony, a pretty little mare of about 14 hands, crunched contentedly. For a brief moment, girl and pony stood nose to nose talking softly to one another, the white gold of the pony's mane contrasting sharply with Jess's own dark curls.

"Come back you!" A stocky man ran into the yard. His face was red from shouting and he was panting hard. In his hand he waved a muddy head collar. The pony started, but Jess calmed it with a steadying hand.

When the man saw Jess he gasped. "Thanks! Thanks a lot. You've saved my bacon."

"That's all right," Jess said, trying to sound as if catching runaway ponies was something she did every day.

"Well you were very brave," the man acknowledged. "It can't have been easy standing your ground like that."

Jess shrugged her shoulders in what she hoped was a casual way. She couldn't help stealing a glance at the cottage in case Nick or Sarah happened to be looking out. She was sure they would have been impressed by her actions. But there was still no sign of them.

The pony butted her nose against Jess's shoulder. Jess laughed.

"She's lovely," she cried, gently pulling the pony's ears. "What's her name?"

"Um... Goldie." The man leaned forward and put his hands on his knees. He took deep breaths. "Because her coat shimmers like gold," he finished.

"She looks as precious as gold, too. Don't you, pretty girl?" Jess turned to the pony again.

"She may look like an angel," the man agreed crossly. "But she's a devil to catch. I was trying to load her into the horse box when she took flight. I'm parked miles back up the road..."

"She probably caught the scent of the horses here

and decided to investigate," said Jess.

"You could be right," the man replied. "It's a good job you were here to stop her. She's not my pony... she belongs to my daughter. I'm no good with the animal–" the man stopped abruptly. "Anyway, I can't stand around here chatting all day. I've got to get this pony back." He moved swiftly towards the palomino who started and shied.

"She won't be caught," he muttered.

"Here, let me try," said Jess, holding out her hand for the head collar. Talking gently to the pony and murmuring words of encouragement, she stroked the mare's nose firmly with her left hand while deftly slipping on the head collar with her right. Goldie didn't flinch. Taking the lead rein in her hand, Jess turned back to the man as he let out a low whistle.

"Well done. You've been a real help. A real help," he repeated softly. He tugged at the lead rein and this time the pony trotted obediently behind.

Jess stood watching as they disappeared out of sight. Now they had gone she felt strangely deflated. She thought of all the other questions she had wanted to ask the man. Where was Goldie kept? Why didn't his daughter catch the pony herself?

Minstrel whinnied loudly from his stall, cutting into her thoughts.

"All right boy." Jess dragged her mind away from the palomino. "It's breakfast time. Now, what shall it be this morning? Hay or bacon and eggs?"

2

NICK HAS SOME NEWS

"Finish up your cereal for goodness sake, Jess." Her mother looked on in exasperation as Jess pushed the soggy corn flakes around the bowl.

"Sorry Mum, I was miles away." Jess lifted her head from her hand and yawned loudly. Going to the stables so early and having to come home for breakfast had been more tiring than she'd imagined.

"What time did you leave the house this morning?" her mother asked, shaking her head.

"Six... six thirty," Jess answered nonchalantly.

"And on the first day of the holidays, as well." Her brother, Jack, looked up from his toast with a mixture of disgust and disbelief. "You're mad, Jess."

Jess's mother sighed loudly and continued her lecture. "You spend far too much time at that stables,

7

Jess. I hope you don't think you're going to be down there every day of the holidays. What about your homework?"

Jess sank down in her chair. She knew it was no good trying to explain how utterly and totally necessary ponies were to her life. Instead she gobbled down the rest of her cereal and bolted for the door.

"I've got a ride at eleven. It's free," she explained hastily, "in return for the work I did this morning."

Her mother accepted defeat. "Oh Jess... if only you spent as much time on your school work as you did at that stables," she sighed. "Don't be back late."

"I won't," Jess promised. "See you later. Bye!"

Jess grabbed her bicycle from the tiny front garden and tried to put her mother's remarks out of her mind. She didn't want to think about school work – not now... not when the sun was shining and there were ponies to ride. As she cycled away from her house in Colcott, she thought again about Goldie, the palomino pony that had run into Sandy Lane that morning. Soon she had drifted off into a daydream. In her mind she wasn't pedalling along the road to Sandy Lane, but cantering cross-country. As she swung into the stable yard the rusty red bicycle beneath her was a beautiful pony. Just the lightest touch on the reins was all that was needed...

"Look out!"

Jess snapped awake from her dream just in time to see her friend, Tom, wheeling a barrow full of hay directly across her path. She slammed on the brakes and her trusty steed, now a rusty red bicycle once more, swerved to the left and screeched to a halt.

"Phew. That was a close one," Jess gasped, just managing to stay upright on her bike. She blushed madly. "Sorry Tom, I was miles away."

"That's OK," Tom grinned and pushed away the strand of brown hair that had fallen across his face. He walked off, whistling softly to himself.

Jess shook her head. Of all the people to look clumsy in front of, why did it have to be Tom? He was easily the best rider at Sandy Lane. He even had his own horse, Chancey, who was kept at half-livery at Sandy Lane. Although Chancey was ridden by everyone, he really only had eyes for Tom. Jess sighed, turning her bicycle towards the tack room.

"Hey Jess, hang on a moment!" Her best friend, Rosie, came pedalling up the drive, her blonde ponytail flying in the breeze. "Have you been here all morning?"

"No, I went home for breakfast," Jess smiled.

"Did you earn yourself a free ride?" Rosie asked.

"Yes. I'm going on the eleven o'clock hack. And something else happened too," Jess said to Rosie. "I made friends with a new pony."

"A new pony?" Rosie was immediately interested. "Where? Whose?"

"It was a palomino mare," Jess began. "Her name's Goldie. She came running into the yard."

"A palomino," Rosie sighed. "How lovely."

"I had to hold out my arms and stop her, Rosie,"

Jess said proudly. "She was charging towards me, really really fast."

"Lucky she didn't trample you," Rosie shivered. "Why was she running into Sandy Lane anyway?"

Jess explained about the man chasing the palomino. "The pony belongs to his daughter. He didn't seem to know much about it at all..."

Now they had reached the fence beside the tack room. All the regular junior Sandy Lane riders chained their bicycles here. There was Tom's green racer, and Charlie's smart and shiny black mountain bike too. Rosie parked her bike neatly and Jess dumped hers down on the ground next to it.

"Come on you two, stack those bikes properly." Nick Brooks appeared on the steps of the tack room, blinking painfully in the bright April sunshine. "This is a stables, not a junk yard."

"Oops, my fault," said Jess, swiftly straightening the stack.

"Sorry I wasn't up to help you out this morning, Jess," Nick smiled ruefully. "I think I'm getting too old for this dancing-all-night lark. My legs are killing me," he groaned. "Anyway I've managed to put the list for the eleven o'clock ride up on the notice board. You're on Minstrel." Nick wandered off across the stable yard, limping slightly.

"I hope I'm on Pepper," Rosie said as she followed Jess into the tack room. "Brilliant," she continued as she ran her hand down the list of riders and ponies and saw her name next to Pepper's.

"I don't know what you see in that pony," Jess wrinkled up her nose. "He's so stubborn."

"Only with everyone else," Rosie reasoned. "He's always been a dream with me."

"It's because you're such a fantastic rider," Charlie teased as he entered the tack room, running a hand through his grubby blond hair. Rosie gave an embarrassed laugh, but Jess was quiet. Charlie was right about Rosie. She *was* a fantastic rider, even if she was too modest to admit it.

Jess didn't begrudge Rosie her riding ability. She was pleased for her best friend, but she couldn't help feeling envious of Rosie's skill, which lay in her calmness and poise. When Rosie sat on a horse she looked completely in control.

Not like me, Jess thought now. Hands flapping everywhere, feet slipping out of the stirrups.

"You're a good rider, Jess," Nick had often commented, "But it's your style that lets you down. Try and be slightly less *messy* when you ride."

Rosie was never messy, thought Jess. She was neat, and patient too. Perhaps that's why Pepper responded so well to her.

But *I* had patience this morning, Jess thought to herself. And I was calm, too. I couldn't have stopped that runaway pony if I hadn't been...

"Hey!" Jess's thoughts were interrupted as Rosie tapped her lightly with a crop.

"You're meant to be using that on the ponies, not me!" Jess said indignantly.

11

"You need a bit of waking up today, Jess," Rosie laughed. "I must have asked you five times to pass the hoof pick. Didn't you hear me? Come on, it's almost eleven. We'll be late for our hack."

"Sorry. I was dreaming of that beautiful palomino."

"I wonder why we've never seen her around here before," Rosie said as they left the tack room. "Is she stabled nearby?"

"I'm not sure," Jess admitted as they reached Minstrel's stable. She paused at the door and absent-mindedly patted the skewbald's neck. He bent his head and pushed his nose into her shoulder.

Rosie moved away towards Pepper's stall. "I'd better get a move on," she called. "See you when I've tacked up. What did you do with that hoof pick by the way?"

"What? Oh, it's still in my hand, sorry." Jess handed the pick to Rosie and unbolted Minstrel's door. She tacked him up quickly and went to join the rest of the ride in the stable yard. Tom was there on the back of Chancey and Charlie waved down at Jess from Napoleon, a huge horse of 16.2 hands.

"My dad took me out to dinner at that new restaurant near Ash Hill last night," Charlie called as he leaned forward in the saddle. "You know, the one where they play all those music videos in the background. It was amazing."

Jess flashed Charlie a smile. He was always trying to impress, but she didn't mind. She knew things hadn't been too easy for him since the divorce. He didn't see much of his dad these days.

"Sounds great," she said. "Lucky you."

"Come on you lot," a voice interrupted their conversation.

It was Sarah. She was taking the hack out and waited patiently by the gate. There were dark shadows under her eyes, but she was smiling happily. "Let's get going."

In no time at all, the ride was out of the stables and walking in single file down the lane. Sarah rode Storm Cloud as she led them up the bumpy old coastal track towards the lighthouse. Jess could already feel Minstrel leaning on the bit.

"OK, we'll have a gallop across the grass. It's nice and flat," Sarah called out as they neared the lighthouse. "We'll head towards Larkfield Copse. Stop on the edge of it and don't let the ponies run away with you. We don't want anyone scalped by the trees. Right then, at my signal."

Then they were off, galloping across the field. Jess gave Minstrel his head and they flew across the ground. Thundering to a stop where the grass met the trees, Jess gave a whoop of joy. There was nothing to match the feeling of being out on a pony on a crisp day.

"Pepper's going brilliantly," Rosie cried as she drew alongside Jess.

"So's Minstrel," Jess replied. "Isn't this fantastic?"

At the end of the hour, the ride wound its way back to the stables. As they clattered into the yard and dismounted, Alex and Kate Hardy, the last of the regular junior riders, came racing up to greet them.

"Where have you two been?" Jess called out as she ran Minstrel's stirrups up. "Weren't you booked on the eleven o'clock?"

"No, I've got a lunch time lesson," Kate replied, giving Minstrel a pat. "And Alex is riding later."

"Well you missed a brilliant ride," Rosie joined in as she led Pepper past.

"But it was a good job I was here," Kate replied mysteriously. "There's pony trouble afoot!"

Jess laughed. Kate could be rather dramatic sometimes. "What *are* you talking about, Kate? It sounds exciting."

"Not really," Kate admitted. "It's a bit of a sad story really. A girl came into the yard, about ten minutes ago. Her pony's missing and she wondered if anyone had seen it. Apparently she keeps it in a field a few miles up the road and this morning when this girl, Belinda..."

"Get on with it, Kate." Alex barged in on his sister's conversation. "What happened is – this girl, Belinda, went to get her pony from its field this morning and it wasn't there. Vanished. The gate was open so it must have escaped."

"What's it look like?" Charlie joined in the conversation.

"What's it called?" Tom asked.

"Um, it's a palomino mare apparently," Alex said. "Goes by the name of Golddust."

Jess was immediately alert. "It sounds like the pony

14

I saw this morning," she cried. "I wonder if it's the same one."

"But your one was called Goldie," said Rosie.

"Goldie, Golddust, same thing really, isn't it?" Alex interrupted. He had already become bored with the conversation.

"Well, she's left a phone number," Kate said, handing Jess a scrap of paper.

"Belinda Lang, Colcott 2562. Palomino pony. Golddust." Jess mumbled the words. "Maybe I'll phone her from the tack room once I've seen to Minstrel," she said aloud to no one in particular.

As Jess rubbed Minstrel down with absent-minded strokes she thought about Goldie and the man chasing her, and about Belinda too.

"I wonder if it could be the same pony," she reasoned aloud to Minstrel. "A man catching a pony, then this girl saying her pony's lost. I'm sure there must be an explanation for it all." She shrugged her shoulders and gave the pony a final pat. Fingering the scrap of paper in her jodhpur pocket she walked over to the tack room. But when she got there, Nick was standing at the door and the others were gathered around him.

"I've got some news," Nick said to them all. "Can you take a seat inside?"

Everyone piled in and Nick smiled at the expectant faces turned towards him. Leaning against the messy desk where the rides were booked, he folded his arms.

"As you are probably aware," he began. "The

Southdown Show is three weeks away."

How could they not be aware? Southdown! It was one of the most prestigious shows in the area – better even than the Benbridge show, where Sandy Lane had done so well in the past. Last year Nick and Sarah had taken the Sandy Lane regulars to Southdown to watch and Jess had loved every minute of it.

"This year at Southdown," Nick continued, ignoring the murmurs of anticipation, "there's to be a special show jumping event for juniors and I've been invited to enter three riders from Sandy Lane. It's a great honour, but obviously not all of you will be able to take part."

Nick's last words echoed in Jess's head. Nick must choose me to ride. He just *must*, she thought as everyone began talking at once.

"The Southdown Show – brilliant!"

"It's a *proper* horse show."

"Even my mum's heard of it!"

"Which horses will you take?"

"Who will you enter?"

At this last question, the room fell silent again. Who would Nick choose?

"Ah yes." Nick shuffled the papers on the desk in front of him. "The crucial question." He paused for a moment. "Well, there's valuable experience to be gained from taking part in such a prestigious event."

Jess held her breath as Nick continued.

"So I think that the riders who would most benefit from this sort of competition right now are Tom,

Charlie..."

Tom grinned madly. Charlie gave a whoop and shot his fist in the air.

"Thank you Charlie," Nick continued dryly, "and Rosie."

Suddenly Jess felt as though she was looking at everyone through the wrong end of a telescope. From far away Nick's voice carried on.

"Tom will ride Chancey, Charlie will be on Napoleon and Rosie will take Pepper," he continued. "Now as I said, the show's in three weeks. Everyone should work hard in lessons until then, whether you're competing or not. I'm sorry that not everyone can compete, but there will be other shows and other chances. You're all excellent riders and I have confidence in all of you." And then Nick was finished. He pushed his chair away from the table and stood up. "Now haven't you got jobs to do?" he said, smiling as he left the tack room. And that was that.

"Sandy Lane at the Southdown Show," Kate cried, breaking the silence that followed Nick's departure. "Well done you three."

"We haven't actually done anything yet," Tom said cheerfully.

"Ah, but you will," said Alex, nudging him in his seat. "You cleaned up at the Benbridge show last year. You can do the same at Southdown."

"You bet we can," Charlie grinned. "The question is, who'll come first?"

"I'll just be glad to get round the course," Rosie

said. "It's a scary thought."

"You'll be brilliant, Rosie," Jess managed at last. "Well done."

Rosie shot her friend an apologetic look. "I don't think I filled Pepper's hay net. Come with me while I do it, Jess?" she asked.

"OK." Jess shrugged, following Rosie out of the tack room. The little piebald looked up at their approach, surprised to see them again so soon.

"I've no idea why Nick picked me, Jess," Rosie said softly, drawing back the bolt. "It's a complete surprise."

"Don't be silly, Rosie. You're a really good rider," Jess sighed, picking splinters of wood from Pepper's stable door. "Nick can see that."

"But you wouldn't be scared to jump in a competition, Jess," Rosie wailed. "My legs feel like jelly at the thought of it."

Jess tried to grin. "You'll be fine, Rosie," she croaked at last. "Especially with me there to cheer you on. So – roll on Southdown!"

"But not too quickly," Rosie groaned.

* * * * * * * * * * * * * * *

A little while later, as Jess wheeled her bicycle across the yard, Nick stopped her with a wave.

"Thanks again for getting the ponies' breakfasts this morning, Jess," he said. "And don't be too disappointed about Southdown. It's quite a disciplined event. I'm not sure it's the right competition for you at the moment."

"I know," Jess sighed. "I'm a clumsy rider. I've got no poise."

"Nonsense," Nick laughed. "Although I'm glad to see you're being self-critical – that's an important quality for a show jumper. You're a dedicated and instinctive rider Jess. Your chance will come."

"Instinctive," Nick had said. *"Dedicated."* Suddenly everything was all right again. The grey cloud of gloom that had floated into Jess's view lifted and the sun poked through.

"Really?" Jess answered.

"Yes," Nick grinned. "Really."

When Jess returned home later that afternoon she was in a much better mood. She laid the table for tea *and* did all the washing up without even being asked.

"Are you sickening for something, Jess?" her mother asked.

It was only as she was undressing for bed and thinking back over the events of the day that a terrible thought struck Jess. In all the excitement she had completely forgotten to phone Belinda about the runaway palomino.

19

"It's too late now," Jess groaned aloud. "I'll have to do it first thing tomorrow. Oh why did I forget?"

Jess crawled underneath her duvet, but it was a long time before she slept. When at last she did, her dreams were disturbed by pictures of the runaway pony jumping a clear round at Southdown. But, try as she might, Jess couldn't see who was riding her...

3

JUMPING LESSON

"This is Colcott 2562," a mechanical female voice intoned at the end of the line. "I am sorry there is no one here to take your call at the moment, but if you'd like to leave a message we'll get right back to you."

Jess grimaced. She hated answering machines. She twisted the telephone cord between her fingers as she stood in the tack room, Belinda's number on the table in front of her. As the tone sounded she spoke quickly.

"Hello," she said. "I'm ringing for Belinda. I think I've seen your pony. My name is Jess Adams and I'll be at Sandy Lane Stables all day if you want to talk to me." She replaced the receiver and looked at her watch. Twenty minutes until the next lesson. They were practising jumping today and all the regulars were taking part.

Jess raced over to Minstrel's stable. Storm Cloud stood looking over her door and whinnied as Jess went by. Jess grinned and reached into her jodhpur pocket for the sugar lump she had saved especially.

"Here you go Stormy," she whispered in the pony's grey ear as she gave her the sugar lump. "Don't tell anyone else, or they'll all want one."

Storm Cloud tossed her mane in conspiratorial reply and crunched on the tasty treat.

"See you later," Jess called as she went to get Minstrel ready.

In the stable next door, Rosie was tacking up Pepper.

"I hope the jumps aren't too high today," Rosie said as they led the ponies out of their stables and took them down the drive to the outdoor school.

"Bring your horses into the middle here," Nick called as they approached. "And I'll hold them while you walk the course."

"This sounds serious," Rosie muttered as she followed Jess through the gate.

Charlie and Tom had just finished inspecting the jumps as Jess and Rosie followed Kate and Alex around. There were eight obstacles in all, starting with some cross poles and ending with a small wall. There was also a low, but nevertheless, tricky, double in the middle.

"They look quite difficult," Rosie said to Jess as they walked back to collect Minstrel and Pepper from Nick.

"It's only because Nick has tried to set up a proper

course, Rosie," Jess smiled. "We've jumped higher before."

"Right," said Nick. "So what do you think of my course?" He turned to them and smiled. "I was tempted to bring along a bell to ring and a loud speaker to announce each rider as they entered the ring – just like a real show jumping competition."

Everyone groaned.

"Don't worry," Nick continued. "These jumps are no harder than anything you've tried before. I'm confident they shouldn't present too many problems."

Jess turned to Rosie. "See, what did I tell you?" she smiled encouragingly.

"Piece of cake these jumps," Charlie said in Jess's ear as he rode by on Napoleon.

"OK you lot," Nick called from the ground. "We've got work to do here. Now, I know you're all at varying levels of riding ability, and some of you," he shot a quick glance at Charlie, "may think this course too easy. However, there's more to a successful round than just getting over the jumps. It requires planning and preparation if you want to do it swiftly and carefully. There are no short cuts. That's why it's essential to walk the course first. Got that?"

They all nodded vigorously.

"Good," Nick said. "Tom, would you like to test the course for us please?" He winked in Tom's direction.

Tom smiled ruefully and urged Chancey on. The pair jumped swiftly with fluid movement.

"Tom makes it look so easy," Rosie breathed as he jumped the wall and rode out clear.

"He's fantastic," Jess agreed.

"Well done, Tom," said Nick. "Now, who wants to go next?"

Before anyone had a chance to answer, Charlie stormed ahead on Napoleon and jumped clear. Jess was just thinking how like a proper show jumper he looked, when Nick's words cut across her.

"Not bad Charlie," he said. "Let's have a little more thought and a little less flourish next time please. You almost skidded poor Napoleon on some of those turns. It's important to jump swiftly, but it isn't worth risking your horse by cutting the corners too much."

Charlie reddened and Jess felt a pang of sympathy. She could tell he had been pleased with his round, but Nick's words had brought him down to earth with a bump. For the first time, Jess began to feel a little nervous. If Nick finds fault with Charlie, what's he going to think about my jumping? she wondered.

Rosie took the course next. She wasn't fast but she was steady, popping Pepper over the jumps in a self-contained way. Jess could see why Nick believed Rosie had a chance at Southdown.

"Come on Jess," Nick called now as Rosie rode out of the ring. "It's your turn. Take it slowly. Think of your centre line and keep the jumps directly in your sight as you approach."

Jess nodded and turned Minstrel towards the first. She knew that Nick's course wasn't actually too difficult. She tried to approach the first jump with confidence. Minstrel took it in his stride and Jess began to enjoy herself as she let Minstrel race on. Suddenly the double loomed sooner than she had anticipated.

"I haven't judged the pacing correctly," she muttered to herself as she felt Minstrel alter his stride. She tried to remember Nick's words of advice – "*Think of your centre line... keep the jumps in your sight...*"

Crack! Minstrel just clipped the top pole of the second part of the double. It rocked precariously and fell to the ground with a dull thud. Jess's heart plummeted.

"A bit impulsive, Jess," Nick said as she finished. "That's four faults. If it's any consolation, your time was fast."

Jess tried to smile, but she was annoyed with herself. If she had been more careful she would have jumped clear.

"Come on Hector," Alex urged, as he rode him forward. Hector, practically a carthorse at over 16 hands, took the jumps slowly and steadily with a lumbering stride, but they made it.

"Good work, Alex," Nick called. "You did well to push Hector around that course. OK, Kate. It's your turn to jump."

Jess's brain was whirring. I'm the only one to have misjudged the jumps so far, she thought.

She was so wrapped up in herself that she wasn't even watching Kate's round on the little bay pony, Jester. Then...

"Oh!" Rosie gasped and Jess looked up to see Jester running out at the brush.

"Do you know what you did wrong, Kate?" Nick called.

"Yes," Kate answered miserably. "I checked him too early. It was my fault."

"Well, learn from your mistakes," said Nick. "Have another go at that one."

Kate turned Jester and introduced him again to the jump. Face set in grim determination, she gave the signal just at the right moment, and Jester flew over the brush with inches to spare.

Outside in the lane, after the lesson, Jess swung herself down from Minstrel's saddle. Taking the pony by the reins she led her towards the loose boxes. Rosie came up behind them, leading Pepper and grinning madly.

"You jumped really well, Rosie," Jess said.

"You were faster than me, though," Rosie offered in reply. "Oh that was fantastic, Jess. I don't know why I always get so nervous before a lesson. I love it when I'm up there."

The two friends led the ponies into the yard and began rubbing them down after the sweaty ride.

Alex and Charlie were halfway through their chores as Jess and Rosie tied up Minstrel and Pepper and set to work. Tom had already taken Chancey to his stable and Kate was jumping Jester one last time.

"That was a good lesson," Charlie called. "I thought we all did rather well. Alex and I were just discussing who would have won the Southdown junior trophy based on today's performance."

Jess groaned. "Don't start getting all competitive, Charlie."

Alex laughed. "Uh oh, looks like you've touched a raw nerve there, Charlie," he grinned. "You should know better than to joke about the Southdown Show with Jess. She's a sensitive little soul you know."

This was almost more than Jess could bear. She *wasn't* upset about Southdown. Not really. But that still didn't give Alex the right to tease her about it. He would have to be taught a lesson. Dipping a dandy brush into the bucket of water, she flicked it towards Alex. Water sprayed over Charlie too. Rosie shrieked with laughter at the sight and Jess grinned triumphantly.

"Water fight!" the boys whooped excitedly.

Soon there was water everywhere and the four children were drenched. Water soaked into the hay on the ground and stuck in clumps to their feet. Alex leapt back to avoid another soaking and caught his elbow on a pile of yard brushes stacked in the corner, bringing them clattering down around him.

"Hey what's going on here?" Sarah said firmly as she rounded the corner of the stables. "I hate to interrupt your fun," she said, "but someone is asking for you at the tack room, Jess."

"It must be the Southdown talent scout!" Charlie couldn't help saying.

Before Jess could douse him again, Sarah spoke. "It's a girl actually, about your age Jess. Says her name's Belinda. Something about a missing palomino."

Jess's heart skipped a beat. "Did she have a pony with her?" she asked Sarah eagerly.

"No," Sarah replied. "She's on her own. Come on you lot." Sarah turned to the others. "Let's get this mess cleaned up now."

Jess cast a glance at Rosie. "I wonder if Belinda's found Goldie yet?" she said.

"Go and find out," Rosie urged. "I'll finish up here, don't worry."

Jess gave her friend a grateful wave and raced towards the tack room. There, waiting outside the door, was a tall, slim girl. She stood staring into the middle distance. She wore soft beige jodhpurs and a white shirt. Jess was suddenly horribly aware of her own rather dishevelled appearance. Her hair lay in wet rats' tails from the soaking she had been given, and hay stuck to her T-shirt in clumps. Slowly she approached the girl with none of the confidence she had mustered the morning she had caught the palomino.

"H-Hello," she stammered. "I'm Jess. Are you Belinda?"

The girl turned her gaze towards Jess and stared at her for a few moments. Jess shifted from one foot to the other.

"That's right," Belinda said at last. "You said on

the phone you'd seen Golddust."

On closer inspection, Jess saw that Belinda's face was pinched and white.

"Well, I think I must have done. A palomino mare came racing into the stable yard yesterday morning," Jess explained. "She was about 14 hands. She had the most beautiful white gold mane and a long, flowing tail."

"That sounds like Golddust," Belinda said quickly. "I went to her field at seven yesterday morning, like I always do, and she wasn't there. So is she here now?" Belinda asked. "Did you catch her?"

"Yes, I caught her," Jess began slowly. "But she isn't here. There was a man chasing her."

"A man? What man?" Belinda suddenly looked panic-stricken.

"Um," Jess stammered. "This man who was running after Golddust... only he called her Goldie. He said she was a devil to catch... he said Goldie was his daughter's pony..." Jess's words came out in staccato breaths.

Belinda's face looked blank with amazement at what Jess was saying and she started to stammer. "That's impossible," she said. "I don't have a father... he's dead."

Jess opened her mouth to say something, but before she could get the words out, Belinda had spoken first.

"It's obvious," she cried, and in that moment Jess realized the awful truth. "Golddust hasn't run away at all," Belinda wailed. "She's been stolen!"

4

JESS IS SORRY

Jess sat at the desk in the tack room, her head in her hands. "It all makes sense now. That man must have been actually stealing Golddust! And I helped him. What an idiot I am. Oh Belinda, I'm so sorry." Belinda stood, fiddling with Storm Cloud's bridle, which was hanging from a peg on the wall. Now she turned to Jess and shrugged sadly.

"Look, you weren't to know," she began. "You didn't do it on purpose."

Jess looked up and managed a smile. "You're being very nice about all this," she said. "It's making me feel even worse. I'd be furious, if I were you."

Belinda sighed. "What's the point?" she reasoned. "Golddust is gone, and there's nothing we can do about it."

At that moment Sarah appeared at the door of the

tack room, followed closely by Rosie. Sarah smiled encouragingly at Jess.

"Rosie's just been telling me about yesterday morning and the palomino pony," she said.

Jess's heart sank. Of course, Sarah didn't know yet that Golddust was stolen. And nor did Rosie. Quickly Jess explained what had happened. When she had finished, Rosie gasped in dismay. "Oh, Jess, that man must have been a thief! But how did he know the pony's name?"

"I suppose Goldie is just as obvious a name for a palomino as Golddust," said Belinda. "Not a very imaginative choice, I know, but it does describe her exactly."

"Look, I think it would be a good idea to go to the police about all this," said Sarah. Her voice was reassuring and capable. "You must give a statement Jess. And a description of the man you saw, if you can. It might help them find Belinda's pony sooner."

The police! Jess swallowed hard.

"Do you want me to come with you for moral support?" Sarah asked. "I could drive you in the Land Rover if you like. I've got some spare time now."

Jess nodded gratefully. If she had to go to the police, she would rather Sarah came with her.

"Yes please," she replied.

"What about you, Belinda?" Sarah said gently. "Would you like to come with us?"

Belinda shook her head. "They already know

Golddust is missing," she explained. "I went to the police station earlier today. My mum took me. They had no news of course. There's no point in me going back there again."

"Well, if you'd rather stay here and wait until we come back, I understand," said Sarah.

Jess didn't understand at all. If Golddust was *her* pony she imagined she'd be wanting to check the police station every five minutes for news.

"I'll stay with you if you like, Belinda," Rosie looked hesitantly at Belinda. "I think there's some lemonade in the fridge. Would you like some?"

Belinda shrugged her shoulders. "All right," she said.

Jess shot Rosie a look of thanks and followed Sarah to the Land Rover.

When they arrived, Jess found that giving a statement to the police wasn't actually too difficult. She had to go over the whole morning in tiny detail.

"You will find Golddust won't you?" Jess asked, concerned. "You will catch the thief."

"Well, we'll do our best," the friendly desk sergeant assured her. "But it's not always that easy."

"What do you think he might have done with Golddust?" Jess asked.

The sergeant shrugged. "Well, he could be planning to sell her at auction. He could have a private buyer..."

Jess sat hunched miserably in the Land Rover on the short drive back to Sandy Lane.

"These things happen, Jess," Sarah said to her. "It's why we have to be extra-cautious about security. I'm afraid ponies are easy targets."

The Land Rover crunched into the stable yard and Jess got out. While Sarah parked outside the cottage, Jess walked back to the tack room. Rosie was waiting eagerly for her, but there was no sign of Belinda.

"How did it go?" Rosie asked.

"Oh, all right I suppose," Jess replied, sinking down into the old basket chair in the corner of the room. "The police aren't exactly rushing around looking for clues with sniffer dogs and magnifying glasses though."

Rosie laughed. "Well I guess they know what they're doing," she said.

"Where's Belinda?" Jess asked abruptly.

"She's gone home," Rosie replied.

"Gone home?" Jess was incredulous. "Why? If *my* pony was missing I'd be out there looking for it, not sitting at home. Honestly, she hardly seemed angry or upset. *I* feel really worried and nervous for Golddust and she isn't even my pony!"

"I think Belinda *is* upset." Rosie paused as she tried to explain. "She's just not showing it the way you would. Listen to this – she told me her dad died six months ago and she's just moved to Colcott where she doesn't know anybody and now her pony's been stolen. If that had happened to me I'd probably lock myself in my bedroom and bawl my head off for months."

Jess thought about what Rosie had said and was silent for a moment. She hadn't thought of it like that.

"Maybe, Rosie," Jess sighed. Then she perked up. "So it's a good job she's met us!" she cried.

"Uh oh, why's that?" Rosie said slowly.

"Well, it's obvious really," Jess replied. "Golddust is out there somewhere, Rosie, and *we're* going to find her."

"We?" Rosie croaked.

"Yes! It's partly my fault Golddust is missing anyway. So it's the least I can do," Jess continued. "Just you wait, Rosie. Belinda won't be miserable for much longer. Not with Jess Adams and Rosie Edwards on Golddust's trail!"

5

NEAR DISASTER

The next day was Monday and Jess was at the stables again. She was keen to make a start on searching for Golddust right away. The local paper had been lying around in the tack room and Jess wanted to check it for details of horse sales. She passed Storm Cloud's stable on the way. The beautiful grey was looking out over the top of the half door. Jess gave her an affectionate pat.

"Hello Stormy," she said. "You're looking lovely today."

"Jess," Nick called, walking across the yard. "I've got a job for you. Sarah's at the saddler's and I have to go to the fodder merchant's. Someone's coming for a hack in twenty minutes. Could you tack up Minstrel?"

"Yes, of course," said Jess. "Who's riding?"

"A new girl, called Petronella Slater."

"Has she ridden before?" Jess asked.

"Yes, but not here," Nick replied. "She's trying out Sandy Lane for the first time, and if she likes it, I hope she'll come back. We need the business," he muttered, almost to himself. "Anyway, I spoke to her father on the phone. Actually I know him vaguely. He seems to think Petronella's quite a good rider. He's going to buy her a pony of her own quite soon."

"Lucky her," Jess sighed.

Nick laughed sympathetically. "Well, he wants Petronella to ride for a while at Sandy Lane before she takes on that responsibility anyway."

"Who'll be taking her out?" Jess asked.

"Tom," Nick answered. "He should be here any minute." Nick climbed into his Land Rover and drove away.

"See you later," Jess called as she headed for the tack room. No one else had arrived for the day. Jess reached up to get Minstrel's saddle from its hook. Glancing to the left, she realized that Chancey's tack was still in its place. Tom was running late. That wasn't like him. He was normally very reliable and always on time. For a fleeting moment Jess was concerned. But at that moment the tack room door swung open and Tom stumbled inside.

"There you are," Jess said. "I was beginning to worry. Did you know you've got a hack in about ten minutes' time? I was just about to tack up Minstrel. You're taking out someone called Petronella Slater.

What a name!"

Jess stopped abruptly as she caught sight of Tom's face. He was ghostly white and could hardly stand straight.

"Are you all right Tom?" she asked. "You look awful."

"I'm not sure." Tom collapsed heavily into the wicker chair. "I feel terrible. I was a bit sick when I woke up this morning. I've just cycled here and my stomach's killing me. I feel all hot and shaky."

"Oh poor you," Jess sympathised. "Perhaps you've got flu."

"Ow ow ow," Tom groaned. "No, it feels worse than that. I don't think I can take that hack, Jess. I can hardly stand straight. Where's Nick?"

"He's gone to get some feed. And Sarah's at the saddler's. What are we going to do Tom? It's too late to cancel this girl."

"Well, we'll just have to explain and ask her to come back another day," Tom said.

"Or I could take her out!" Jess cried impulsively. "I could ride another horse. Hector perhaps. He's really reliable. It'd be miles better than having to turn her away. It would be bad for business. That's what Nick would say."

Tom managed a half smile, despite his obvious pain. "Well," he began. "Nick has let you take a hack before, hasn't he?"

"Yes, I've done it twice," Jess replied proudly.

Tom seemed to make up his mind quickly. "Go on

then," he said. "You've got two ponies to tack up in under ten minutes!"

"OK," Jess smiled happily. She wanted a chance to prove she was capable. Everyone had heard the story of Golddust by now and how she had practically handed the pony over to a thief. She had been expecting some teasing about it, especially from Charlie. But no one had said anything. Still, she was determined to make everyone, especially Tom and Nick, see she wasn't a complete idiot. She would take the hack and show them how responsible and competent she really was.

"I'll come back for Hector's things in a moment," she called to Tom. But Tom was silent, his face pinched with pain.

Jess raced to the stable. She had just finished Minstrel and was on her way back for Hector's tack when a shiny white Range Rover pulled into the yard. A haughty looking girl in immaculate fawn jodhpurs stepped out. In her hand she held a black riding crop. She was about Jess's age. A tall man got out from the driver's side. The girl gave the stable yard an imperious once over as the man turned a questioning gaze towards Jess.

"I booked a ride for my daughter," he began.

"It's a hack Daddy," the girl hissed loudly. "You booked a hack."

"Ah yes, I did indeed," the man agreed.

What a fright this girl is, Jess thought. Aloud she said "Are you Petronella Slater?"

"Yes I am," the girl replied.

"Right. Well, hello," Jess continued. "I'm Jess Adams, and I'll be taking you out today. And this," she said turning to Minstrel, "is the pony you'll be riding, Minstrel."

Petronella looked scornfully at the pony.

"Bit of a nag, isn't she? She doesn't look very fast."

"She's a he, actually." Jess flushed angrily. Did this girl really know anything about riding? How dare she call Minstrel a nag? Jess bit her tongue. It wouldn't be a good idea to upset a new rider.

"He loves galloping," she said through gritted teeth. But Petronella wasn't impressed.

"No, he won't do at all," she said, waving her riding crop dismissively. "Far too ordinary. Ah, now that's the kind of thing I should be riding."

Jess turned to where Petronella was pointing – right at Storm Cloud, who was hanging her head over her stable door as usual.

"Oh I'm sorry," Jess said quickly, jumping to defend the grey pony. "That's Storm Cloud. No one's allowed to take her out unless they've been riding here a while. She's part-Arab and really precious. She's also quite flighty and a bit unpredictable."

"Exactly what I'm looking for," said Petronella. "I *am* an experienced rider you know. Obviously no one explained that to you." She turned to the man with her. "Daddy, tell the girl I can ride her."

"Well," Mr. Slater began, turning to Jess. "That horse..."

39

"Pony," Jess muttered.

"Ah, yes, pony. She does look rather nice. So what's the problem?" he asked. "Is Nick Brooks about? I spoke to him on the phone."

"No, he's not." Jess shifted uncomfortably. The situation was slipping away from her and she wasn't sure what to do.

"Daddy, if you're going to make me ride at this stables before I'm allowed my own pony I should jolly well be allowed to ride who I want," Petronella interrupted peevishly.

"All right my Pet," Mr. Slater soothed, and Jess began to feel sick.

"Now look here young lady," he said, addressing himself firmly to Jess. "Why don't you let Petronella ride that Storm Cloud creature? Don't worry, I'll square it with Nick when he comes back. We're old friends, you know, so it will be all right. And I *am* paying for this after all."

Jess was furious, but managed to bite her tongue. Well, if Petronella and her dad wouldn't listen to her advice, that was their problem. Handing Minstrel's reins to Petronella, she ran to the tack room to get Storm Cloud's things. For a fleeting moment Jess wondered if what she was doing was such a good idea. But Jess was determined to prove she could manage this hack and Mr. Slater had been so insistent, she couldn't back down now.

Hurrying back to Storm Cloud's stable, she tacked her up and led the little pony out. Storm Cloud was excited to be going out and Petronella had a job to mount the pony, who skipped and pirouetted around the yard.

"See you later, Daddy," Petronella called and then she was off down the lane at a brisk walk. Jess winced as Petronella sawed furiously on the reins and waved her crop dangerously high around the pony's eyes. Storm Cloud tossed her neck as she fought for control of her head. Jess urged Minstrel into a lively trot and followed them out of the yard.

"She's raring to go," Petronella called over her shoulder.

Jess nudged Minstrel on and overtook Petronella, leading them along the bumpy coastal track towards the lighthouse where Sarah had taken them only a few days before.

"There are some good places for a gallop around here," she called back to Petronella.

To the right of them the grass stretched away invitingly, and Jess could feel that Minstrel was eager for a race. Storm Cloud was positively foaming at the mouth and the more she pulled, the tighter Petronella tugged at the reins, until poor Stormy's ears were almost touching the girl's scornfully turned up nose. Jess winced.

"Perhaps you should give her a little more rein," she said. "And stop waving that crop. She'd probably calm down a bit then."

"Rubbish," Petronella sneered. "You have to show them who's boss. Besides, who wants to ride a calm pony? This is far more exciting. I'm off!"

And with that, she gave Storm Cloud a terrific whack with the crop. For a fraction of a second Storm Cloud seemed to hover in midair, almost stunned by the pain. And then she shot off and bolted across the field. Petronella pulled desperately on the reins, but it was too late. She had lost control.

"You stupid girl," Jess cried in dismay and disbelief.

For a moment Jess watched helplessly as the fragile grey careered across the fields at breakneck speed. Swerving round to the left, she pounded on towards Larkfield Copse. Jess gasped as the pony gathered pace. She was headed straight for the trees and Petronella couldn't turn her. Jess went cold as she thought of the low-hanging branches.

Now Jess urged Minstrel on into a gallop. The little pony didn't need much encouragement and he raced off, mane and tail flying in the breeze.

Ahead, Petronella screamed loudly and shut her eyes tight with terror. Minstrel's pounding hooves rang in Jess's ears and her eyes streamed with water as the wind bit into her face. Faster and faster Minstrel raced. Storm Cloud was well in front, but she was weaving from side to side. Jess concentrated on keeping Minstrel on a straight line, and soon they were gaining on them. All the time the low-hanging branches of Larkfield Copse loomed nearer.

The sweat rose on Minstrel's neck, and still Jess urged him on. Now at last they were galloping alongside Storm Cloud. They were only feet away from the trees. Petronella had dropped Storm Cloud's reins, and they were hanging loosely as she clung to his mane. Minstrel and Storm Cloud were neck and neck. With a supreme effort, Jess leaned over as far as she dared and grabbed Storm Cloud's reins. It seemed the only thing to do. She pulled hard and brought Storm Cloud's head round to the left, turning Minstrel at just the same time.

Storm Cloud seemed surprised that someone had taken charge and followed immediately. But Petronella stayed where she was and, as Storm Cloud and Minstrel changed direction, Petronella went flying forwards, sailing over Storm Cloud's neck. She landed with a thump in a patch of mud at the edge of the trees.

Jess brought Minstrel to a stop alongside the field and Storm Cloud followed obediently. As she gathered up Storm Cloud's reins, the little grey sprang back nervously. Her nostrils quivered and her heaving flanks were covered in foam and sweat.

"Whoa there, Stormy," Jess cooed softly as she jumped out of the saddle. "You're all right now."

Slowly, Storm Cloud calmed down. She listened intently to Jess and nuzzled her nose wearily into Jess's shoulder. Positioning herself between the two ponies, Jess looked over to Petronella.

"Are you all right?" she called.

"No, of course I'm not all right," Petronella howled, brushing the dirt from the seat of her pants. "That animal is dangerous. She shouldn't be allowed out."

Jess was furious. "You insisted on riding her," she couldn't help saying. "Couldn't you see that she was worked up already? The last thing she needed was a beating from a crop to get her going."

"How... how dare you," Petronella retorted. "*You're* the one to blame. You and this stupid horse. I wasn't properly supervised! I'm going to report you to... to Nick Brooks."

"What's going on here?" a familiar voice interrupted.

Jess spun around. Nick! The Land Rover was parked at an angle in the field and Nick was striding towards them. Jess's relief at his reassuring presence soon gave way to trepidation at the thought of what he might say.

"I was worried when I got back to the stables and found that Storm Cloud missing and Chancey was still in his stable. What's happened? Where's Tom?"

Quickly Jess explained everything – Tom's illness, Petronella's insistence on riding Storm Cloud and Jess's own part in it all too.

Nick looked sternly at her and took a deep breath. "Well, we'll talk about this later, Jess," he said. "Are you OK?" he asked, turning to face Petronella. "Can you stand up?"

Petronella got shakily to her feet. She swayed a little as she stood up and put a hand to her head. Nick held out a steadying hand. "Take it slowly now," he said.

"I'm all right," Petronella said fiercely. Her face was determined, but Jess saw tears in her eyes.

"I'll take you back in the Land Rover," Nick said gently. "Jess can lead Minstrel and Storm Cloud."

"No!" Petronella cried. Then, seeing Nick's startled face she tried to explain. "I mean... I can't let my father see me like this. You won't tell him?" She looked at Nick despairingly.

"Well, I don't know..." Nick began. Petronella pleaded again.

"If he hears about this he'll never let me have my own pony," she continued. "Not a really good one, anyway. He'll get me some safe, plodding old thing."

Jess looked on in amazement and Nick shook his head slowly. "You can't fool him that you're a better rider than you are, Petronella," he said. "Look, why don't you continue to have a few lessons at Sandy Lane before you get your pony? I think you'd find it a big help. Even the best riders still have lessons," he added hastily as Petronella tried to speak. "And the more experience you have, the more you'll enjoy having your own pony."

"Well..." Petronella hesitated. "If I come and ride at Sandy Lane, will you promise not to tell my father what's happened today?"

Jess let out a gasp of astonishment. What a cheek! Fancy talking to Nick like that! Even Nick seemed a little taken aback, for it was a while before he spoke. When he did, his voice was serious.

"I don't make bargains, Petronella," he said sternly.

"And I do think you need some more practice. Now, do you think you're up to riding Minstrel back, under Jess's supervision?" Petronella nodded quickly.

"OK. Good girl," said Nick. "Jess." He turned to her. "I think it's best if you ride Storm Cloud back to the yard, and I'd like a word with you once you've untacked the ponies."

He turned on his heel and walked back to the Land Rover. Jess looked on in astonishment and it was a moment before she came to her senses. Nick had told her to ride Storm Cloud. Not in the school, not around the yard, but out in the open – and after Storm Cloud had bolted too. For a moment, she wasn't even bothered about Nick's parting shot *I'd like a word with you*. Right now all that mattered was Storm Cloud.

She gathered up the reins and mounted. "Walk on," she said softly, and Storm Cloud moved forward.

Jess glanced back. Petronella followed on behind. She was calmer now, and Jess noted that she really wasn't such a bad rider when she wasn't showing off.

Jess turned to look ahead again. Storm Cloud's step was quick and eager as Jess kept a light but steadying control on the rein. She longed to have a gallop. She knew Storm Cloud would go like the wind, but she stopped herself.

"I'd better not try anything risky, or Nick will never trust me again. Come on Stormy," she murmured. "Let's go home."

6

A TURN OF EVENTS

"What exactly was wrong with Tom then?" Nick asked, in a stern voice. "You said he was ill."

"Yes, he felt sick," Jess answered quietly. "So I said I'd take Petronella out."

Jess stood in the kitchen of Nick and Sarah's cottage. She traced a small circle in the cracked red lino with the toe of her boot and stared at her feet. Nick stood with his back to the sink, leaning against it, his arms folded. He looked down at Jess and continued.

"I've given you permission to take hacks before Jess, but in this instance I knew Tom was the best person for the job. He's much more experienced than you are, I'm afraid."

Jess swallowed hard and tried to hold back the tears.

"And I think you know Storm Cloud wasn't a good choice for Petronella, too," Nick went on.

Jess nodded miserably. "I'm sorry Nick. I just thought I was doing the right thing. And I did try to warn Petronella, but Mr. Slater said he knew you and that it would be all right."

"I don't know him *that* well," Nick continued. "But I appreciate how difficult it must be to go against an adult's wishes."

"I'm sorry," Jess croaked again.

"Anyway, I was impressed with the way you handled Storm Cloud, Jess. You remained calm and collected in the face of a potentially dangerous situation. Well done." Jess blushed furiously.

"Right, that's the lecture over with. Back to the yard." Nick gestured with a nod towards the door. "It must be lunch time."

Jess gave a grateful wave and hurried to the tack room but there was no one there. She settled down by herself to eat her sandwiches. As she munched, Jess replayed the ride on Storm Cloud over and over in her mind.

Sandwich in one hand, she spread the local paper out on her lap and hunched over the crumpled page, scanning the list of open air markets.

"I'll show everybody I can do something right," she said aloud. "Now where are we? Benbridge Women's Institute Floral Display... April 14th-21st. St. Olaf's Parish Church." She ran her finger down the small black lettering, brushing aside crumbs.

"Livestock day at Bucknell Pig Farm."

And then she found what she was looking for – "The Ash Hill Horse Sale. 2nd Thursday of every month. Horses and ponies for sale at auction. 10 am at Ash Hill Showground."

Jess did some rapid calculating. It was Monday the 7th today – the second Monday of the month – so the sale was in three days' time.

"Caught you!" A voice shouted in her ear. Jess jumped up, startled and the paper slid to the floor.

"Looking for Golddust already I see," Rosie grinned.

"Yes, but something else has happened, Rosie. I've just had the most awful morning," Jess began, thinking back over the hack with Petronella.

"Another one?" Rosie grinned. "What was it this time? More runaway ponies? International horse thieves?"

Jess laughed and began to tell Rosie about the hack.

"Petronella Slater?" Rosie wrinkled up her nose as Jess finished her explanation. "I've never heard of her... she's not at our school, that's for sure."

"Thank goodness," Jess said heartily. She picked up the paper and stabbed at it with her forefinger. "Anyway, we've got more important things to think about, Rosie. There's a sale at Ash Hill in three days. It only happens once a month so the man who stole Golddust can't have been there yet."

"That's where Nick bought Storm Cloud," said Rosie.

"Exactly," Jess replied. "So that's a good omen." She smiled cheerfully and if she had been about to say more, her words were halted by the arrival of Alex and Kate. They came bounding into the tack room arguing with each other as usual. Charlie followed close behind and greeted everyone with a casual wave. Now all the regulars were here.

"Has anyone seen Tom?" she asked.

They all shook their heads.

"Not yet," Alex said. "We've got a jumping lesson though, so he should be here soon."

"I'm sorry, but I'm afraid he won't be." Sarah appeared on the step of the tack room, a hand held up for silence. Her face was solemn. "I've got some bad news. Tom's mother rang a little while ago. He's been taken into hospital," she went on.

"Hospital?" Alex gasped. "What's wrong?"

"They're not sure at the moment, which is why he's been taken in," Sarah replied. "His mother said he had stomach pains this morning, but he seemed well enough to cycle into Sandy Lane, though. You saw him, didn't you Jess?"

Jess nodded quickly. "He looked awful."

"Well he managed to cycle home again, but he was in a lot of pain," Sarah explained. "He insisted his mother phone us. He was afraid Chancey might be neglected if he didn't show up for his lesson."

"Typical Tom." Alex tried to laugh, but Jess could see he was worried.

"Now, look, he wouldn't want you to worry," said Sarah. "And he's in the best place. As soon as I have any more news I'll let you know. Anyway, I'm going to exercise Chancey now. And you've all got a jumping lesson, haven't you?"

Everyone stood around dumbstruck, until Sarah snapped them out of their trances.

"Get a move on then," she called. "Nick's waiting."

"Yes, come on everyone," said Charlie. "Buck up. Worrying isn't going to win us any Southdown trophies," he said gruffly. "I'm off to tack up Napoleon."

* * * * * * * * * * * * * * * *

"I wish we knew what was wrong with Tom," Alex groaned as the lesson came to an end. It had been a subdued hour. They had all jumped well, but without enthusiasm. Jess had cleared the course, but unspectacularly and with all her thoughts on Tom.

"Perhaps we should all go to the hospital, now," Kate said. "And not leave until we find out if Tom's going to be OK."

"Don't be silly, Kate," said Charlie. "Tom's mother is bound to ring again when there's any more news."

"Let's hang around the stables for a while then," Rosie said when they had finished the ponies. "We should wait for news."

"OK," Jess agreed as they flopped down on some

hay bales behind the big barn. "And to take our minds off things, we can make plans for finding Golddust. Apart from going to Ash Hill, I thought we should put posters up. We could try farriers and vets, local gymkhanas, that kind of thing. I know Belinda's already made a start on asking at riding stables – not that there are many around here. But there's much more we can do..."

Rosie stopped Jess with a laugh. "Whoa, slow down Jess," she cried. "Aren't you forgetting something?"

"What?" Jess asked eagerly. "Horse sales, posters... what should I have remembered?"

"Belinda!" Rosie reminded her. "Shouldn't she be involved as well? After all, Golddust is her pony. Maybe she's had the same ideas as you."

"Oh yes," Jess paused. "Maybe Belinda would start to feel happier if she really started to search for Golddust too."

"And if she knew we wanted to help she might feel a bit better," Rosie pointed out.

"You're right, Rosie," Jess said. "I'll ring her now and tell her we'll help."

"Take it slowly, Jess," said Rosie. "You don't want to frighten her off. You can be a bit overwhelming sometimes."

"I know," Jess smiled as Kate raced towards them.

"Come quickly!" Kate cried. "Sarah's got news about Tom. She's going to tell us all in the tack room."

Jess and Rosie raced with Kate to the tack room. Charlie and Alex were already there and Sarah began to speak.

"It's appendicitis," she announced. "Tom's going to have an operation this afternoon. He'll be in hospital for several days," she went on. "But it will take quite a lot longer than that before he is completely better."

"When will he be able to ride again?" Alex asked.

"Not for a while I guess," said Sarah. "A month or so, maybe more."

"So he'll miss Southdown?" Charlie said.

"It looks like it," Sarah replied.

"Poor Tom," said Rosie.

"Poor Chancey," said Jess.

* * * * * * * * * * * * * * * *

Jess was still thinking about Tom later that evening as she cycled through Colcott and on to the new houses at the edge of town. She was going to see Belinda.

Jess had rung her earlier and arranged to come over. Belinda had been hesitant on the phone, but Jess sensed a hint of curiosity in her voice. Jess was quite excited.

In her mind, she had already found Golddust and was receiving Belinda's heart-felt thanks. This thought pleased Jess so much that it carried her swiftly along the road and right past Belinda's house. Turning her bike sharply she pedalled back and checked the house number. 34 Archway Avenue. This was it. The grassy front garden was encircled by a low privet hedge, and a small stone statue of a dancing horse stood guard on the front step.

"You must be Jess," Belinda's mother said as she opened the door. "Come in." She called up the stairs. "Belinda... you have a visitor!"

Belinda appeared on the top step. She was wearing jeans and a dark blue guernsey and her hair was pulled back in a ponytail. She gave Jess a half smile. "I suppose the police didn't have any news about Golddust?" she said.

"No, sorry," Jess shook her head.

Belinda shrugged. "Oh well, you can come up to my room, if you like." She disappeared through a door at the top of the stairs.

"See you later, Jess," Belinda's mother smiled as Jess followed Belinda to her bedroom a little doubtfully.

When Jess stepped into the room, she relaxed immediately. Belinda's bedroom walls were plastered with posters and pictures. Horses and ponies of all shapes and sizes stared down at Jess. There were rosettes of all colours, but mainly red, Jess noticed enviously.

"I won those with Golddust," Belinda said, following Jess's eye to the rosettes. "She's quite a good showjumper."

"Lucky you," Jess said.

"Do you ride at Sandy Lane regularly then?" Belinda said.

"Yes," Jess replied eagerly. "I don't have my own pony or anything, but the Sandy Lane ponies are lovely. Especially Storm Cloud. She's my favourite."

"Is that the little grey one?" Belinda asked, Jess's enthusiasm igniting a flicker of curiosity.

"Yes," Jess said in surprise. "How did you know?"

Belinda smiled again. "Just a guess. I noticed her when I came to the stables yesterday..." She stopped suddenly and looked sad again.

"Belinda," Jess said quickly. "I've got something to tell you. Rosie and I want to help you look for Golddust. We thought we could put up stolen notices and look around horse sales. There's one on Thursday..." She stopped and thought for a moment. "If you want our help, that is," she finished.

Belinda was quiet but her eyes were shining.

"Would you really help me?" she cried at last. "Oh thank you!" And then she was off. She started telling Jess what had happened and didn't stop for ages. Jess sat and listened and didn't interrupt. She heard how Belinda's mother had had to look for a job after Belinda's father died. She had finally found one in Colcott and they'd had to move. And how Belinda was going to be starting at a new school after Easter.

Belinda told Jess how she had been keeping Golddust in a field on the edge of town for the time being until her mother earned enough to pay for stabling. She told her how she had made a start on looking for Golddust. And finally Belinda told Jess how upset she had felt when she had gone to Sandy Lane Stables and seen how friendly everyone was, and how she had felt very alone.

"But you're not alone now," Jess cried. "You've got Rosie and me! And we've got this horse sale to go to on Thursday."

"You're right, Jess," Belinda agreed happily. "Oh wouldn't it be brilliant if we found Golddust there?"

"Yes, it would," Jess smiled and looked around at Belinda's lovely horsy room. "Hey!" she exclaimed, pointing to a colour snapshot of a girl and a pony perched on Belinda's book shelf. "Is that you? Can I have a look at it?"

"Of course." Belinda took the photo down and gave it a quick dust with her elbow. "It's me and Golddust at the novice jumping at Benbridge last summer."

"The Benbridge show?" Jess exclaimed. "How fantastic... Tom jumped there last year too. He won the open jumping," she said. She looked down at the photo in her hands. She looked and then she looked again.

"Hey, hang on a minute," Jess said, her voice tightening.

"What's the matter?" said Belinda.

But Jess hardly heard it. All of her earlier optimism vanished in an instant, like a light being switched off. When she spoke her voice didn't sound like her own.

"But Belinda... this isn't Golddust!" she mumbled.

"Of course it's Golddust," Belinda laughed. "I should know. She is my pony. "

"No, I don't mean that, I mean..." Jess swallowed hard and then the words came spilling out. "I mean.. this isn't the same pony I saw at Sandy Lane the other morning. This isn't the pony I helped to catch!"

7

ASH HILL HORSE SALE

"It was awful, Rosie." Jess walked along beside her friend, telling her about the visit to Belinda's house. It was Thursday morning, the day of the Ash Hill sale, and the pair were on their way to the bus stop to meet Belinda. It was the first time they had been properly together since Monday. On Tuesday and Wednesday, Jess's mother had put her foot down and reminded Jess of her other responsibilities. And when her mother was in one of her organising moods it was, Jess knew, best to obey her. Especially since she wanted to visit Tom in hospital that afternoon too.

Nick had caught Jess yesterday morning as she was leaving Sandy Lane and told her that Tom wanted her to go and see him in hospital. Nick was rather mysterious about it, but was gone before Jess could ask any more.

Now Jess filled Rosie in about what had happened at Belinda's house.

"There I was looking at this photo of Golddust and I could see it wasn't the same pony I helped to catch the other morning," she explained. "The palomino *I* saw was pure gold, but I could see from the photo that Golddust has a circle of white hair on her forehead."

"So what did Belinda say?" Rosie was curious.

"She asked me if I was sure and then she just sat there very quietly and didn't really say much. Which made me feel pretty miserable. I thought I could help Belinda find Golddust. Now Belinda has no idea if Golddust has been stolen, has run away, or is lying dead in a ditch somewhere."

"Well at least you know it's not your fault Golddust has disappeared, but what a mystery," Rosie said. "I wonder what happened to the palomino pony *you* saw then. I wonder where it came from."

"I wish I knew," Jess replied. "I went to the police station again this morning... on my own this time. I cycled all the way there. And I told them that I made a mistake... that I hadn't seen Belinda's pony after all."

"What did they say?"

"I saw a different policeman this time. He didn't say much, but he raised his eyebrows a lot and shook his head and wrote everything down in a big book and asked me to sign my name. Oh Rosie, is all this pointless? Going to Ash Hill, I mean... trying to help Belinda find Golddust."

"We said we'd help her look, so we must," Rosie reasoned. "Watch out, here's Belinda now," she said, seeing the tall girl waiting at the bus stop.

"Hello," Belinda said quietly.

"Hi," Rosie said. "Jess has just been telling me about Golddust not being Golddust. It's very odd."

"Isn't it?" Belinda said as the bus appeared and they clambered aboard. "Strange that two palominos should be running loose on the same day."

Rosie didn't know what to say. They rode in silence for the rest of the way. Jess reached up to ring the bell and the bus shuddered and stopped. The doors swished open and the three girls jumped off. They followed a steady stream of cars and trailers along the road until they came to a turning and a sign in a field that said *Ash Hill Horse Sale*.

They weaved their way through the crowd until they came to the group of horses and ponies up for auction.

"Right, let's be logical about this," said Rosie as she bought a sale catalogue. "Are there any ponies that match Golddust's description?"

Jess thumbed through the auction catalogue. "If Golddust is here, she'll be a late entrant," she reasoned. "After all, there hasn't been much time between her being stolen and this sale."

"That's true," Rosie agreed. "The late additions are on this slip of paper at the back. Look."

There weren't many, but there was still plenty to read.

"Here we go," said Jess, reading aloud.

"Lot forty-two. Palomino pony. 13.2 hands without shoes. Fully warranted."

"Hmm. A bit small, but worth a look."

Belinda peered over her shoulder. "Here's another one. Lot fifty-five. Palomino show pony. 14.2 hands. Rising five. Some blemishes, but sound."

"They don't make that one sound very attractive. Still, we can't afford to miss it. It's about the right height." She turned the page. "Lot sixty-six. Registered palomino. Show jumper. 14 hands without shoes. Ideal jumper."

"Hmm, that sounds promising," Rosie chipped in. "Any more?"

Jess thumbed through the rest of the catalogue and shook her head. "No, that's it. Not many to choose from."

"Good," said Rosie. "That means we can check them out quickly."

"How shall we do it? Should we wait for their numbers to be called?" Belinda asked.

"Maybe we should go and have a look at them now," Rosie suggested. "Pretend we're interested buyers."

"What, three girls with no more than a bus fare back between us?" Jess was suddenly hesitant. For a fleeting moment she wondered if this was such a good idea after all. Then she saw Belinda's face, and she knew they had to carry on.

"It's the only choice we have," Rosie said firmly. "Shall we go together or split up?"

"Together, definitely," Belinda said.

As they were faced with row upon row of sad and neglected horses, Jess felt less and less cheerful. There were good ponies of course – the ones destined for riding stables and some for a lucky handful of children who would leave with their very own pony. Jess looked longingly at these fit and healthy animals. At the same time, there was another pony who kept calling for her attention. The runaway palomino she had seen the other morning at Sandy Lane. 'Goldie,' that man had called her. Where was that pony now?

"Lot forty-two," said Rosie. "Here it is." They drew to a halt beside a pony tethered to a pole. Belinda gave one look at the little pony and shook her head.

"Nope. This isn't her."

"That's not even a palomino," said Jess when they came to lot fifty-five. "It's a dun. Definitely a dun."

"That must have been the one with blemishes?" Rosie said. "Maybe they were trying to compensate by choosing a pretty colour for her."

Lot sixty-six was beautiful. A really gentle palomino with kind eyes. "But it's not Golddust," Belinda sighed. She began to look defeated and Jess felt despondent.

"Come on," Rosie said. "I've got a packed lunch. Let's share it."

Slowly they walked away from the ponies and flopped down as they reached a small group of trees.

"Cheese and tomato or ham?" Rosie said, offering the sandwiches around.

"Cheese," said Jess. "Actually, I'd better eat this pretty quickly," she cried, glancing at her watch. "I've got to go and see Tom this afternoon. I must get a move on."

* * * * * * * * * * * * * * * *

"You look a bit green, Tom."

"Thanks a lot, Jess. You'd look a bit green if someone had sliced you open, rummaged about with your insides and then stitched you back up again with a needle."

"Yuk." Jess screwed up her nose. She fished about in her plastic bag and pulled out a pile of dog-eared magazines. "I know people are meant to give you grapes in hospital but I couldn't find any, so I brought you some pony magazines. I've read them already. There's a really good story in one of them about a ghost rider and a lost foal..." Jess hovered by Tom's hospital bed. She could hear herself blabbering on and on.

There were eight beds in Tom's ward, and four of them were occupied. Tom's bed was by the window. Opposite, a girl of about Jess's age slept soundly. There were dark circles under her eyes, but her hair was bright gold.

"That's Mary," Tom said, following Jess's eye.

"She's got a pony."

"Lucky her," Jess said as she sat down on the bed. "Nick said you wanted me to come and see you," she blurted out, curiosity getting the better of her.

Tom smiled. "So you're not here to wish me a speedy recovery then?" he teased.

Jess looked downcast. "No. I mean..." she stopped and laughed. "Sorry, Tom. Of course I'm here to see how you are. But..."

"You're right," Tom interrupted her. "We've got a proposition to make to you. Me and Nick, that is. Nick said I should be the one to tell you, but he's backing this all the way. It's about Southdown," Tom explained. "I won't be able to ride, so would you like to take my place?"

There was silence. Jess knew it was her turn to speak, but she didn't know what to say. She was going to ride at Southdown!

"I'm no replacement for you Tom," she managed at last. "You're a much better rider than me."

"Well obviously no one expects you to do as brilliantly as *I* would have done," Tom grinned. "Oh dear, I sounded just like Charlie then, didn't I?"

"Horribly," Jess agreed happily.

"But I reckon you'll be in with a chance," Tom continued seriously. "I'll be out of here by then and I'll be able to come and cheer you on."

"Oh, that would be brilliant!" Jess cried.

"So how's Chancey, Jess? Is he pining away for me?" Tom asked.

"He's fine. But he does look a bit sad," Jess said, trying to drag her mind back to normal conversation as little bubbles of excitement burst in her stomach. "Don't worry," she continued. "We've all explained where you are and that you'll be back soon. He understands."

"Of course he does," Tom agreed. "He's a very intelligent horse. Oh look, here's my mum."

Jess turned around to see Tom's mother walking towards them, tall and elegant. Jess stood up to greet her. She had only met Mrs. Buchanan a few times and she didn't want to make a bad impression.

But as Mrs. Buchanan came nearer, the smile froze on Jess's face. Walking a few paces behind her, jacket bundled under his arm, was a stocky man. A man whose face Jess remembered well.

"You!" Jess croaked, as the man drew up alongside her. Ignoring Mrs. Buchanan's surprised expression, Jess spoke again. "You're the man with the runaway pony!"

8

EXPLANATIONS

Jess stood and stared. She knew she was being rude but she just couldn't help it. The last time she had seen this man he had been chasing a palomino pony into the yard at Sandy Lane Stables. Jess stared some more.

"What's the matter, Jess?" Tom began.

Mrs. Buchanan looked shocked at her behaviour, but Jess couldn't move. She was face to face with this man – this thief! She didn't know what to do. He peered at her now and a smile spread slowly across his face.

"I recognize you!" he exclaimed at last. "You're the young lady who helped me catch Goldie the other morning!" He turned to the girl in the bed opposite Tom, who was just waking up. "Mary... this is the girl I told you about... the one who helped me with Goldie."

66

Mary turned and rubbed her eyes. She propped herself up on her pillows and smiled at Jess.

"So is Goldie your pony?" Jess stammered slowly.

"Not mine," the man explained. "She's Mary's actually. You were marvellous. I was rather upset that morning. You see Mary had been rushed into hospital the night before and I was taking Goldie to be looked after by some friends. I was trying to load her into the horsebox, but I wasn't making a very good job of it. That's why she took fright and bolted. If you hadn't caught her, I don't know what would have happened."

"She's a beautiful pony." Jess wanted to say more, but she was still in shock.

"She's lovely, isn't she?" Mary said eagerly, her eyes shining. "I miss her so much. What's your name?" she asked.

"Jess. Jess Adams."

"I'm Bob Hughes," said the man. "And this, as you know by now, is my daughter, Mary."

Mary smiled at Jess who still looked dazed.

"Would you like some of Tom's orange juice Jess? You're looking a little unwell." Tom's mother was full of concern.

"No, I..." Jess started.

Then Tom began to laugh. "Ouch my stitches!" he yelped. "I'm sure I heard that pony was stolen," he continued when the pain had subsided.

"Stolen?" Mary's father looked astonished.

Of course, Tom didn't know that Goldie wasn't the

same pony as Golddust. Jess shook her head and began to explain until at last it all came out. About mistaking Goldie for Golddust and about Belinda and – even worse – about reporting it all to the police.

Mary's dad laughed at this. "So I'm a wanted man now am I?"

But Mary was quiet. "Poor Belinda," she said. "Her pony's still missing."

Jess nodded in silent agreement. One mystery had been solved. The palomino pony Jess had caught running into the stable yard hadn't been stolen at all. She was safe and well... unlike Golddust.

* * * * * * * * * * * * * * * *

"Concentrate!" Nick called. "Come on Jess, you're letting Minstrel get away with murder. He'll run out if you don't check him."

"Sorry Nick," Jess mumbled. She shortened Minstrel's reins and turned again towards the first jump. Urging him on, she balanced the little pony so that he met the fence at exactly the right spot and they flew over the cross poles with inches to spare.

"Better," said Nick. "Much better."

It was Easter Saturday and the Southdown entrants were having a special lesson. The show was less than two weeks away now.

"We've got the early evenings," Nick had reassured them. "It's still light enough to see what's going on. Don't worry, you're all doing very well."

"Tom gets out of hospital today," Rosie said as they rode back to the stables at the end of the lesson. "I heard Nick talking to his mum."

"I wonder how Mary is," Jess said. She had told Rosie – and Belinda – all about Mary and Goldie.

"She must miss Goldie terribly," Rosie said.

"Not as much as Belinda misses Golddust I bet," said Jess.

Both girls were quiet for a moment. They hadn't found Golddust at Ash Hill on Thursday and there weren't any more horse sales for a while. Belinda had put posters up all around the area, asking for information, but so far there had been no response. It seemed like the end of the trail for the moment. For now, the Southdown Show loomed and for Jess at least, there was no more time to search.

Feeling guilty that she couldn't help Belinda any more, Jess had asked her to come to Southdown. But Belinda had been hesitant.

"I'm not sure, Jess," she had said. "I had been hoping to ride Golddust at Southdown. I don't know if I'd feel right going there without her."

Jess replayed this conversation in her head now as she led Minstrel into the yard.

"Don't untack Minstrel, Jess," Nick said, interrupting her thoughts. "He's got a lesson in a minute."

Jess was surprised. "OK," she said. "But I thought I was booked on him for a hack."

"Sorry about that," Nick said. "You'll have to ride someone else. Let's see. Which horse can you ride instead?" He paused for a moment, mentally checking off the list of Sandy Lane ponies in his mind. "It'll have to be Storm Cloud," he said finally. He shook his head, but there was a grin in his voice.

"Storm Cloud?" Jess breathed. "Really?"

"Lucky you," Rosie whispered.

"She's the only one available," Nick smiled. "Anyway, it's the least I can do, seeing as I'm commandeering Minstrel for a lesson with our old friend, Petronella Slater. Well don't stand there. You better get Stormy tacked up."

"I'm going," Jess said quickly, before Nick had a chance to change his mind.

Fifteen minutes later the eleven o'clock hack was ready to leave Sandy Lane. Jess kept an eye out for Petronella, but there was no sign of her. As Sarah led the ride on Feather, Jess looked back at the stable yard to see Nick checking his watch and muttering angrily. It looked as if Petronella was late.

"Walk on everybody," Sarah called and Jess drew her attention back to the hack. Sarah turned Feather to the gate and the ride clattered out of the yard and down the lane.

For the next hour, Jess planned to forget about Petronella; forget about mistaking Bob Hughes for a thief; forget about Golddust even. Something told her that the chances of finding the pony were getting slimmer and slimmer every day. She tried to ignore the guilty feeling that she was letting Belinda down, but she had important things of her own to think about. Anyway, right now, she wanted to concentrate utterly and completely on Storm Cloud. It was such a treat to be riding her.

The little grey's step was light and easy. Her ears pricked forward, alert and attentive. They had reached the open fields at the back of the stables and Sarah gathered the ride around her.

"Those who want to can gallop to the end of the field. There are three cross-country fences to jump. Can you see them?"

Jess looked ahead and saw three low tree trunks lying in a row.

At Sarah's signal the ride began to gallop. Storm Cloud was first and she didn't need any further encouragement. Jess gathered up her reins and nudged her forward, moving smoothly from a trot to a canter and then into a gallop. Three long strides and a signal from Jess and Storm Cloud had cleared the first tree trunk, then the second and the third.

On Stormy's back, Jess felt the smoothness of movement and hardly even noticed as they sailed through the air. She brought Storm Cloud to a neat and collected stop at the end of the field. Rosie drew Pepper to a halt beside her, her cheeks were flushed and eyes were glowing. Pepper snorted heartily.

"You looked fantastic!" Rosie cried. "Storm Cloud jumps like a stag."

"She's just brilliant, isn't she?" Jess sighed happily.

9

SOUTHDOWN AT LAST!

The next few days flew by... before Jess knew it, there was only a week to go, and then four days. Then it was the day after tomorrow and now – now it was Friday evening and tomorrow was the Southdown Show!

Jess wandered restlessly around the house, unable to concentrate on anything or settle anywhere. She picked up the TV remote control and flicked from channel to channel but there was nothing she wanted to watch that evening.

Jess padded into the kitchen and opened the fridge door, contemplating the choice inside.

"Close the door, Jess," said her dad. "You're letting all the cold air out."

"What you need is a warm bath and an early night,"

her mother sympathized. "Stop worrying, Jess."

"I'm not worried," Jess said crossly. "Just excited."

Her mother smiled at her. Jess had been afraid her parents wouldn't approve of her riding in a horse show as it meant more time spent with ponies and not on her school work. But they had been surprisingly encouraging.

"We'll all be there to watch. We wouldn't miss it for the world," they had said.

Jess went to bed early that night. She didn't think she'd sleep at all. She put her head on the pillow and tried to fill her mind with pleasant thoughts of jumping ponies. The next thing she knew, daylight was streaming in through the curtains and it was seven in the morning. Saturday and Southdown!

"We'll be by the ringside if we don't see you first," her mother said at breakfast. "Now, are you *sure* you don't want a lift to Sandy Lane?"

But Jess wanted to cycle as she always did.

"It's probably some sort of mad good luck routine, Mum. I'd leave her to it," her brother, Jack, muttered as they waved her off.

Sandy Lane was a buzz of activity as Jess cycled into the yard with the plastic bag containing her show kit hooked over the handlebars.

The horse boxes stood ready for loading with their precious cargo. Riders were scurrying about grooming, plaiting manes, picking out hooves. Jess went to fling her bicycle down. Then she had second thoughts and leaned it carefully against the wall of the tack room.

Alex and Kate called out to her. "We're your cheerleading team today – good luck Jess!"

Charlie was in Napoleon's stable, madly brushing the horse's brown coat. "A perfect job," he said, standing back to admire his work.

"You've missed a bit," Jess grinned, leaving Charlie inspecting every inch of Napoleon's coat for imaginary specks of dirt.

She walked over to Minstrel, who stood waiting patiently, peering over the stable door. The pony snickered gently when he saw Jess, and his nostrils quivered with quiet excitement.

"You know you're going to a show, boy, don't you?" Jess whispered in his ear. "Well, it's not just any show you see. It's the Southdown show, and I know you're going to be brilliant."

"CLANG!"

Pepper's stable door swung open and Jess's peaceful moment was interrupted by a clatter of hooves and a flurry of flying feet as the little pony jogged out of his box, into the yard and off down the lane. Rosie followed close behind.

"He's spooking like mad," Rosie called breathlessly over her shoulder.

She bolted after the little pony, but Pepper saw her coming and, with one effortless leap, he had cleared the pond and landed in the grass on the other side. Unconcerned, he trotted lightly toward the overhanging trees and, straining his neck, he began to munch at the leaves. Twigs caught in his mane, making a complete mess of the tidy plaits Rosie had spent ages over.

"Bad luck Rosie," Charlie called as Rosie hurried off to catch him.

When each of the ponies were almost ready, Nick called the team together.

"Horsebox loading," he said. "You must all be responsible for getting your pony into the horse box as calmly and as swiftly as possible. So here's the order. Minstrel first, then Pepper in this box. Sarah will drive it. I'll be driving the other one with Napoleon, Feather and Storm Cloud in it."

"Storm Cloud?" Jess was immediately alert. "But, I didn't know she was coming. And Feather as well? Who'll be riding them, Nick?"

"Not so fast, Jess," Nick smiled. "Storm Cloud and Feather won't be entering any competitions today. But they will be competing soon and they need to get used to a show atmosphere."

Jess squirmed with embarrassment at her eager outburst.

"Everything ready?" Nick was saying now. "Let's go!"

"Wait for me!" A breathless voice made them all look around. Belinda, dressed in pale beige jodhpurs and a dark jacket, climbed out of her mother's car and ran towards them.

"You came after all!" Jess cried. Belinda stood in the stable yard and smiled at Jess.

"Well, there didn't seem much point moping around at home," Belinda explained. "The least I can do is come and help cheer you lot on."

"Let's hope you've brought a few miracles with you then," Jess grinned ruefully. "I'll need them if I'm going to jump anything today."

And then they were off at last – to Southdown and the show.

As the Sandy Lane boxes pulled into the Southdown showground, Jess felt a swirling mix of excitement and fear race through her. Everywhere was bustling with activity. Official stewards with tannoys and clipboards ran around, barking out instructions and organizing everyone. Horse boxes of all shapes and sizes were everywhere they looked. Tied to each box were horses and ponies in various states of grooming. A perfectly poised little girl on a tiny roan mare popped backwards and forwards over a practice jump with effortless ease. Riders in smart black jackets and cream jodhpurs strode past confidently, greeting each other.

Over in the main field there were stalls and marquees selling everything from saddle soap to riding hats, hot dogs to smoked salmon. Was it really only last year that she and Rosie had been enthralled spectators here, the chances of them taking part only a dream? And now they were official competitors! They tethered the ponies and gave them a final groom while Nick went off to check everyone in.

"I'll meet you by the ring," he called as he left,

"and we'll walk around the course together."

Jess struggled into her show jacket. She turned to Rosie excitedly.

"Can you believe we're really here, Rosie?" she breathed.

"I would be excited if I wasn't feeling so nervous," Rosie groaned in reply.

Jess looked around for Tom. He had promised he would be here. She hadn't seen him since the day at the hospital. She hoped he would be well enough to come.

They met up with Nick again at the show ring. He handed out their numbers and then led them around the course. Belinda came too, for moral support, and Alex and Kate followed on behind. The course was quite tricky and the fences looked big. Jess didn't like the look of the combination, but Nick had some words of advice.

"Keep the impulsion as you come around the corner and don't over ride it, Jess," he warned her before he left for the competitors' tent.

"Have you jumped a course as hard as this, Belinda?" Jess asked.

"Um, no, actually," Belinda grinned ruefully. "It looks pretty challenging. You'll just have to take it steady and, well, enjoy it."

"Easier said than done," Jess groaned, but her insides had calmed down a little. She was even almost looking forward to jumping. It was time to go and warm Minstrel up.

"I'll meet you back at the horse boxes," Belinda said. "I'm going to have a look at the dressage."

"And I promised to meet my mum by the stewards' tent," Rosie called as Belinda went. "I won't be long."

Jess waved goodbye and followed Alex and Kate back to the boxes.

"Is Nick with you?" Sarah asked as they approached.

"No, he had to check something out at the competitors' tent," Alex answered.

"I'd better go and find him," said Sarah. "There's some man... says he knows Nick, who's keen to buy Storm Cloud. I said she wasn't for sale but he's very insistent. He's just gone off to find his wife. I need Nick to sort this one out. Will you keep an eye on the horses? Watch out for Pepper. He's been spooking a bit."

Buy Storm Cloud? Jess shook her head. Surely they would never sell her, but if this man was a friend of Nick's...

She went over to the grey mare who stood grazing in the shade, ears alert to the sounds around her, her tail twitching nervously. As Jess approached, Storm Cloud lifted her head and snickered. She nuzzled her soft nose into Jess's shoulder and her tail relaxed.

"Don't worry, Stormy," Jess whispered. "Nick and Sarah would never sell you. You're far too precious to them. And to me," she added silently.

Suddenly, a small brown dog tore around the corner of the box yapping and snapping. Storm Cloud started but Jess laid a steadying hand on her neck and she was still again.

"Rags! Come back here," a child cried.

But Rags took no notice as he darted and weaved between the ponies' hooves.

Pepper shifted nervously and, at the small dog's shrill barking, he kicked out in a blind panic, hitting Minstrel squarely and sharply on the fetlock. Minstrel whinnied in pain and reared up. When he landed again, he was limping ominously.

Jess held onto Storm Cloud while Alex and Kate did their best to calm Minstrel and Pepper. Rags scampered off and his small owner finally caught up with him. But the damage had been done. Minstrel was limping badly. Nick and Sarah came running up but Jess knew from their faces that they had seen everything. It didn't look good.

"Oh no," Nick groaned as he ran a reassuring and calming hand down Minstrel's foreleg. "I think we'd better get the vet to come and look at this. It doesn't look like you'll be riding Minstrel today, I'm afraid."

As Nick made his way to the secretary's tent, Jess stared in disbelief. This couldn't be happening. Poor Minstrel. Poor her! Was this the end of her Southdown dream?

Jess didn't have time to dwell on it though, for in an instant, her thoughts were disturbed as Belinda came charging up the field.

"Listen, oh listen everyone."

"Slow down," Sarah said as Belinda gulped for

breath. "Now, what's the matter?"

"I've seen her. She's here," Belinda gasped.

"Who's here?" Sarah asked.

"Golddust," Belinda cried. "She's here at Southdown!"

10

STRIKING GOLD

Golddust! In all the excitement preparing for Southdown, Jess had quite forgotten about her. Belinda's words were greeted with stunned silence. It was all too much to take in. Finally, it was Sarah who spoke.

"Are you sure, Belinda?" she asked.

"Of course I am," Belinda cried. "I'd recognize Golddust anywhere." She stopped short as she sensed the subdued atmosphere, the glum faces. "What's happened here?" she finished.

Jess found her voice and quickly explained about the runaway dog and Minstrel's accident, but before she had a chance to say more, Sarah had taken charge of the situation.

"I need to stay and wait for Nick, Jess," she said.

"Can you go with Belinda and find out what's going on? But be very careful what you do and what you say. Come and get us if there are any problems." And when she saw Jess hesitating, she said urgently, "Go on now – and hurry!"

Jess nodded and the two girls darted off through the crowds. The hustle and bustle around them only added to the confusion in Jess's head.

"She was over here," said Belinda as she led the way through the throng to a small copse of trees. At first Jess couldn't make out where Belinda was pointing. She screwed up her eyes to get a better glimpse of the ponies. Blacks, bays, a roan and a grey. And suddenly she saw her. Standing slightly apart from the others, kicking her heels and dancing on the spot was a beautiful palomino pony with mane and tail the colour of white gold. On her forehead was a small circle of white hair.

"Golddust!" Belinda breathed.

"Wait a minute, Belinda," Jess said, grabbing her arm. "There's someone with her. Look!"

A small girl with long plaited hair was hanging desperately onto the end of Golddust's lead rope with both hands, trying in vain to calm the jumpy pony. But with every tug of the rope and with every yank of her hands, Golddust became even more frantic. Belinda winced.

"I can't stand it, Jess," she cried. "That girl is scaring Golddust half to death. I have to go." She raced towards them.

"Wait for me!" Jess called, and ran after her.

Belinda slowed down as she neared Golddust, and began to talk in low soothing tones. "It's all right girl, here I am," she said.

At the sound of her voice, Golddust's ears twitched forward.

As Belinda drew up alongside her and laid a soothing hand across her pony's neck, Golddust whinnied again, and this time the sound wasn't of fear, but one of sheer pleasure. Belinda buried her head in Golddust's mane.

"It's all right my beauty," Jess could hear her saying, "I'm here. I've found you at last!"

The girl hanging onto Golddust looked relieved.

"Thank you, oh thank you for calming her down!" she cried. "I don't know what I would have done if you hadn't come along."

Jess looked at the small upturned face streaked with sweat and tears and felt sorry for her. She looked very young and bewildered.

"Are your parents here?" she asked.

"They were, but they've gone to look at a pony they want to buy for my sister."

"Is this your pony, then?" Jess asked, pointing to Golddust.

"No, she's my sister's. I'm not into riding. We haven't had her long and she's a bit of a handful. Daddy's gone to look at another pony that might be more manageable. Oh–" she stopped abruptly. "I'm not supposed to talk to strangers. Who are you?"

Jess smiled. "I'm Jess," she said. "And this is Belinda."

"My name's Sally," the girl replied. "My sister's meant to be riding in the junior jumping today. Rather her than me – this pony's practically wild."

"She isn't wild, she's just frightened," Belinda said lifting her head and tuning into Sally's stream of chatter. "Wait a minute – where did you get this pony?"

"Daddy bought her," Sally replied. "Why?"

"Sally," Jess said as softly as she could. "This pony is called Golddust. She belongs to Belinda. She was stolen from her a few weeks ago."

"Stolen! But that's impossible." Sally's eyes widened in disbelief. "Daddy paid for her... he did."

"I'm sure he did," Belinda said quickly. "But she had already been stolen from me."

"Oh." Sally fell into a stunned silence.

Jess shifted uncomfortably. This was the last thing she had expected... to find Golddust in the hands of someone else.

"I think we ought to find your parents," Jess said quickly. However nice Sally was, the fact remained that her dad had bought a stolen pony, and would have to give it back.

"Oh good." A look of relief spread across Sally's face. "Here they are now. And my sister's with them too."

Jess turned to follow Sally's eager gaze. Sure enough, a girl was striding purposefully towards them, closely followed by two grown-ups. The girl was dressed in an immaculate black riding jacket, cream jodphurs and shiny black boots. She was horribly familiar.

"Petronella Slater!" Jess cried.

"You!" Petronella sneered.

Behind her, talking in loud voices, strode Mr. Slater and a woman with the same disdainful expression as Petronella, so that Jess could only imagine she was her mother.

"What a shame Nick Brooks wouldn't sell that lovely grey pony. And after you rode her so well at Sandy Lane, Pet," the woman trilled.

"I didn't *want* that pony anyway," Petronella hissed.

Jess couldn't believe her ears. They must be talking about Storm Cloud. But Petronella *hadn't* ridden her well. She had been arrogant and reckless and had frightened poor Stormy half to death. What a cheek – if only Petronella's mother knew the truth. Jess's thoughts were interrupted by Sally's anxious voice.

"Dad, come quick. Petronella's pony's been stolen!" she cried.

"What are you talking about, Sal?" Petronella said quickly. "She's right here. Look."

"No," Sally cried. "I mean she's a stolen pony!"

"What rubbish," Mr. Slater boomed. "Of course she's not stolen. I bought her fair and square."

"Look, I'm sure you did," Belinda burst out. "But she is my pony and I can prove it. She's freezemarked right here." She pointed to a number on the little palomino's neck. "And I have all the documents at home."

Mrs. Slater looked furious. "I knew there was something fishy about that man who sold her to you," she barked. "I told you so at the time, Colin. But you didn't listen to me. You never do."

Mr. Slater looked harassed. "Oh dear," he groaned. "But Pet wanted that pony so badly. How was I to know..." He paused anxiously. "Look," he said at last. "I think we should call the police, resolve this straight away."

Jess couldn't agree more. Right now, her head was beginning to ache with trying to think sensibly.

"Why don't we go and get Nick," she said to Belinda.

"No!" Petronella spat.

Mr. Slater looked straight at Jess for the first time. "Don't I know you?" he asked.

"Yes," Jess had to admit. "I took Petronella out for a hack at Sandy Lane. She rode Storm Cloud," she said. *Or tried to*, she couldn't help adding in her head.

"Ah yes," Mr. Slater smiled affably. "It was after that we got Petronella her own pony. She had such a good time that day. And she told me how well she had ridden."

Jess shot Petronella a quick glance. Petronella shifted uncomfortably. She cast her eyes downwards and kicked at the grass with her heel. For a brief moment Jess considered telling Mr. Slater the truth about that day, but what was the point? Petronella obviously had him wrapped around her little finger. Besides, the fact remained, there were more important things to sort out. Mr. Slater seemed to have read her mind.

"Look, I'm going to get the police," he said. "I want to sort this out once and for all."

"Yes, I think you'd better, Colin," Mrs. Slater barked, "What would people say if they found out we'd been handling stolen goods?"

Jess was relieved that things were starting to get moving. Which was just as well, because a terrible thought had just struck her. Minstrel! Jess looked at her watch. Time was running out. The junior jumping would be starting soon. Was Minstrel fit enough to enter? Jess had to find out what was going on.

"I must get back," she cried to the startled Slaters. "It's Minstrel," she explained to Belinda.

"Of course." Belinda understood immediately. "Off you go, Jess. Everything is under control here."

And so Jess raced back to her Sandy Lane team mates. When she arrived at the horse boxes, she was greeted by a sea of glum faces. Rosie was the first to speak. Jess could tell that she was dying to know about Golddust, but news of Minstrel came first.

"It doesn't look good, Jess," Rosie said. "The vet left a while ago, and Nick and Sarah have been in a conspiratorial huddle for absolutely ages. We're just waiting to find out what's going on."

Jess groaned. Time was running out. They would be starting the junior jumping any minute. Charlie was mounted and raring to go and Rosie was circling Pepper, warming the piebald up. They were low numbers, twelve and fourteen respectively, so they had to get a move on. Jess was number thirty-eight – second last. She sighed. There didn't seem much point in wearing it any more. Minstrel stood patiently under a tree, ominously favouring his right foreleg. Jess walked over and began to stroke him gently.

At long last, Nick and Sarah stopped talking and came over.

"It's bad news, I'm afraid, Jess," Nick said. "Minstrel's got a badly bruised left foreleg. He'll be all right, but there's no way he can jump today."

Jess lowered her head and tried to fight back the tears that welled in her eyes. She had expected this but it was still a bitter disappointment. To be given the chance to ride at Southdown and then to have it so cruelly snatched away from her at the last moment was almost more than she could bear.

But now Sarah was speaking and although Jess tried to focus on the words, it was a while before she understood. At last Sarah got through to her.

"Did you hear that Jess?" she said. "You can ride after all."

"Ride after all, but how?" Jess was confused.

"It's Sarah's idea," Nick explained. "But I agree with her. We're going to let you ride Storm Cloud, Jess – if you want to, that is. She's an excellent jumper and you've ridden her well before. I'm not saying it will be easy, but if you take it steady I'm sure you'll be all right. So what do you say?"

What could she say? Jess could only beam. She saw Rosie beaming back at her.

To ride Storm Cloud would be a dream come true. She felt proud that Nick and Sarah had so much faith in her. Minstrel was injured and that was terrible, but she had been given another chance. She had to make the most of it.

"Oh thank you so much. Thanks Nick, thank you Sarah," Jess gasped. "I will ride Storm Cloud. We'll do our best to make Sandy Lane proud of us!"

11

SHOWJUMPING

Storm Cloud stood steady and alert as Jess sprang lightly onto her back. She followed Rosie and Charlie to the collecting ring to warm up. As they drew near, Alex and Kate spotted them and came over. Wide-eyed, they immediately wanted to know what had happened to Minstrel, and why Jess was riding Storm Cloud. Jess hurriedly explained.

"Poor Minstrel. But how exciting for you," Kate exclaimed. "We've been watching the jumping so far. Some of the fences are really difficult."

"They're not too bad," Alex said calmly. "Jump five, the square parallel, seems to be causing problems. And judging the combination at the sixth looks tricky too."

"Jess, Jess!" an eager voice at stirrup level called and Jess looked down to see her little sister Em gazing up at her.

"What a beautiful pony," said Em.

Her mum and dad joined her. "You look very professional Jess. Good luck," they smiled.

Jess smiled happily when suddenly an announcement over the tannoy caught her ear.

"Competitor number ten, Belinda Lang on Golddust. This is a rider change."

What? Jess could hardly believe it. Belinda must have sorted everything out with the Slaters. Jess jumped down from Storm Cloud and tethered him at the box. Then she made her way to watch as Belinda and Golddust entered the ring. She felt as nervous as if it were already her turn.

Golddust tossed her head playfully, her flaxen mane blowing freely in the breeze. She held her magnificent tail up high and the sun glinted and danced on her golden coat. Belinda sat poised and calm, controlling Golddust with no perceptible movement, seemingly unaware of all around her. But then she caught Jess's eye and grinned madly. Jess saw her confidence and began to relax. She would enjoy watching Belinda. She knew they were in for a treat.

With the ring of the bell, Golddust cantered off and took the first fence with easy strides. She hardly seemed to notice there were jumps beneath her feet as she all but flew over the bars and onto the brush, then the gate. Then she was over the difficult square parallel and onto the combination. One and two and it was cleared before Jess had time to blink. Now they were at the triple bar, almost as tall as Golddust herself, but Belinda urged the pony on and they landed lightly, and onto the final wall. Jumping clear, they were finished and out of the ring. A roar from the crowd signalled their appreciation and Jess exhaled slowly as Rosie gasped in delight beside her.

"Clear round," boomed the tannoy.

"Wow, they were brilliant!" said Rosie.

"She's good!" Alex said. "Really, really good."

"That'll take some beating," said Kate, shaking her head.

"Well, I'm going to give it a try," Charlie grinned, bringing them all back down to earth with a bump. Wish me luck!"

"Good luck, Charlie!" everyone called as the tannoy announced that competitor number eleven had clocked up four faults.

But Jess said nothing. She was thinking about the way Belinda and Golddust had looked together; about the practised ease with which Belinda handled Golddust; the way in which the pony seemed to have complete trust and faith in Belinda, and responded eagerly to her every command. As Belinda came up to them, leading Golddust, Jess joined in with the congratulations of the others. She wanted to ask about Petronella, but now wasn't the time. Belinda was flushed with pleasure.

"It's all thanks to Sandy Lane," she said. "I would never have come to Southdown today if it hadn't been for you. And now I've found Golddust and I don't care if I win or lose. I think right at this moment I'm the happiest person alive."

"Competitor number twelve. Charlie Marshall on Napoleon," came the announcement.

"Quick, we mustn't miss this," Kate said eagerly.

Charlie certainly cut an imposing figure as he rode Napoleon confidently into the ring.

"He's gorgeous," whispered a girl in front.

"Yeah, and the rider's not bad either," her friend replied.

Kate and Jess nudged each other in fits of giggles. But they were soon lost in the swiftness and capability of Charlie's ride. Before they knew it, he had ridden triumphantly out of the ring.

"Clear round!" the tannoy called.

"Oh no, it's me now," Rosie cried as competitor number thirteen sent the square parallel crashing to the ground. "Wish me luck," she called, riding away.

"Go on Rosie," Jess whispered fiercely.

Slowly and steadily and with great determination, Rosie and Pepper cleared the ascending oxer and the bars. They clipped the top of the brush but the jump remained intact. Next it was the parallel, the combination, and finally the wall. They were over and clear. It wasn't fast, but it was effective. Pepper stalked out of the ring, tail held high.

"Oh well done, that was brilliant Rosie," Jess cried as the pair came towards her.

"I was a bit slow." Rosie wrinkled her nose.

"But you jumped steadily and clear," Jess reassured

her.

Nick joined their little group. "Well, I must say things are looking very good so far. Two clear rounds for Sandy Lane. And a clear for Belinda, our honorary member."

Belinda's eyes shone with delight at Nick's words. Jess smiled wanly. Would their good luck last? It was all up to her. Quietly she took herself away from the crowd and began to warm Storm Cloud up. Round and round they walked in the practice field, every lap bringing them closer to their turn. In the show ring, the competition carried on until at last competitor thirty -seven left the ring, a trail of spectacular destruction in her wake.

"Sixteen faults for Amanda Matthews on Cinnamon," the tannoy confirmed.

"It's going to be a tough one, Storm Cloud," Jess murmured into the pony's alert ears.

"You'll be fine, Jess." A voice at her side startled her. She looked down to see...

"Tom! Oh you made it. Brilliant! How are you feeling?"

"Delicate," Tom smiled. "But excited too. I'm looking forward to seeing you jump. There have been eight clear rounds so far – yours will be the ninth." Jess's heart soared and suddenly she didn't feel so bad. If Tom thought she could do it, well... she'd try her very best.

"Thanks Tom," she grinned. Then she leaned over

to whisper in Storm Cloud's ear. "It's our turn now, girl. Let's show them what we can do."

Circling Storm Cloud as she waited for their number to be called, Jess tried to shut everything else out – the hum of the crowd, the activity around her. Suddenly a voice echoed across the field.

"Competitor number thirty-eight, Jess Adams on Storm Cloud."

They trotted into the ring. Suddenly Jess was nervous again. This was it. She was here. She was really going to jump at Southdown! She felt Storm Cloud quiver with anticipation and bent down to pat her dappled neck.

"We can do it together, Storm Cloud. I know we can!" she whispered.

She trotted Storm Cloud around the edge of the ring, battling hard to stop her nerves interfering with her concentration. Suddenly the bell sounded.

"Let's take our time, Stormy," Jess murmured. "The clock isn't ticking yet."

And before she knew it, the first fence was behind them. Jess felt a surge of confidence. The competition had begun! Now they were clear on course for the bars.

"Jump," she breathed as she urged Storm Cloud forward. Don't look down, she reminded herself, and kept her gaze firmly fixed between Storm Cloud's alert ears. The spirited pony knew exactly what was expected of her and gathering her strength she soared through the air, leaving inches of space between her and the jump.

Onwards they rode, up and over the brush and towards the gate. Storm Cloud reached high for the obstacle and cleared it, but she overbalanced on landing and Jess was flung forward. Swiftly she tried to right herself as she turned Storm Cloud in the approach to the parallel. But Jess felt she was still leaning too far forward. She was losing contact. Storm Cloud sensed Jess's dilemma and knew what was expected of her. Valiantly she attempted the jump. As the pony's head came up, Jess was struck on the chin. She bit her lip heavily and tasted blood. Her pain increased as she heard Storm Cloud's hind legs rap the top pole. Jess's heart stopped and time stood still. Then she regained her balance and cantered on, all the time straining to hear the thud of pole hitting grass. She couldn't look back, but the gasp of relief from the crowd told her it was all right. The pole had stayed in place and Jess had been offered a stay of execution.

"Well done, Storm Cloud," she breathed. "I won't make that mistake again. We can do it!"

With renewed confidence, she rode Storm Cloud straight and square towards the combination. Storm Cloud flicked her tail and thundered on. But Jess was prepared.

"Steady, steady," Jess chanted under her breath.

One, two, three, jump! And they were over the first combination. Storm Cloud flew through the air. Touchdown! Take off! And they were soaring again. Clear and away. They flew over the cross poles as the final fence loomed. They jumped the wall with ease and then they were finished and out of the ring. Jess barely had time to catch her breath before she realized what had happened.

"Oh well done, Storm Cloud," she cried, flinging her arms forward around the pony's neck. "We did it!"

As if to confirm this fact, the tannoy boomed out the result.

"Clear round for competitor number thirty-eight, Jess Adams on Storm Cloud."

Everyone gathered round to congratulate her.

"Amazing, Jess," Nick approached her and gave Storm Cloud a pat. "You rode very well."

Jess glowed with happiness and pride. But it wasn't over yet. She was through to the jump-off – against the clock this time – and she needed to gather her thoughts and regain her composure.

She led Storm Cloud off to cool down beneath the trees before their big moment arrived. She knew her friends would be jumping too, but all she could think about now was how to get the best performance out of Storm Cloud – how to ride like the wind.

There were ten riders in all for the final competition. Jess was jumping fifth, Belinda was ninth. Charlie was seventh. Poor Rosie was to jump first. As much as Jess wanted to cheer Rosie on, this time the suspense was too much for her, and she knew she couldn't watch.

When her number was finally called, she had no idea what time she had to beat. She would just have to jump the round of her life. Storm Cloud seemed to have picked up on the urgency of it all and skipped and danced beneath her.

"This is it, girl," Jess whispered.

"Good luck, Jess," Tom called from the side of the field.

Storm Cloud tossed her smoke-grey mane in nonchalant reply and trotted once again into the ring. Jess held her in check with just the lightest touch of the reins.

"Relax, relax," she whispered softly as she circled Storm Cloud. And then there was the ring of the bell and they were off! Swift and steady to the first jump. A light tap of her heels and Storm Cloud was over and riding squarely for the bars. Up and away and they were down again and Jess felt as light as a feather. Turning nimbly, she headed Storm Cloud for the brush, counting the strides with every thunder of Storm Cloud's hooves. One and two and three and they were over and then they had cleared the gate before Jess had time to catch her breath.

Now they were entering the turn for the parallel. But this time, Jess was ready for it. She was in control. She checked Storm Cloud and set her square and then they were racing toward the jump. Jess felt Storm Cloud's front legs tuck well underneath her as she sprung high into the air and over the pole. Clear!

Now was the combination and it was one, two and over. Storm Cloud turned on a sixpence as she rounded the corner. They flew over the triple bar and now there was just the wall to go. Storm Cloud took that in her stride and they were clear! Jess's heart pounded and reverberated loudly in her ears as she clasped her arms around Storm Cloud's neck.

"Fantastic!" she cried.

"Jess Adams, clear in fifty-three seconds," the tannoy boomed.

Jess was exhilarated. It sounded fast, but was it fast enough?

"Well done Jess!" Nick called. "You really got the best out of Storm Cloud!"

"Oh Jess, that was amazing!" Rosie cried as she rushed up. "You did miles better than me. Pepper clipped the wall with his heels. That's four faults automatically."

Alex grinned madly at her. "That was some performance Jess. I think you're in with a chance of a rosette. Well done."

Jess shook her head. "It was all Storm Cloud," she protested.

They all turned in time to see the next competitor crash into the brush and net herself four faults.

And then it was Charlie's turn. As he rode into the ring once more, Jess had to admit they looked magnificent. Napoleon's healthy, brown coat shone in the bright sunlight and Charlie pressed him on over the jumps. He seemed to have remembered all Nick's words of advice, for this time he didn't rush the course but took it steadily and swiftly too. And then he had finished and was clear.

"Charlie Marshall on Napoleon, jumping clear in forty-nine seconds!" echoed the tannoy.

"He was fantastic!" Jess cried.

"He's in the lead!" Rosie shouted at Jess's side.

The next rider, a tiny girl on top of a sprightly little roan pony jumped clear also, and the tannoy confirmed this. "Melissa James, jumping clear in fifty-one seconds."

"Not as fast as Charlie," Alex muttered.

"But faster than me," Jess couldn't help thinking. Yet somehow she didn't care. She had jumped and she had jumped well. She had done her best and she was happy. Now it was time to watch Belinda.

Jess stood close to Storm Cloud as she watched Belinda enter the ring with Golddust. She gazed in silent admiration as Belinda cantered the golden pony easily around the ring.

"Wow, what a fantastic pony," a girl whispered next to Jess.

Jess stood enthralled at Belinda's performance. Swiftly and efficiently Golddust cleared the jumps in quick succession, and at what a pace!

"Clear in forty six seconds!" the announcement came. "Belinda Lang takes the lead on Golddust!"

Tears shone in Belinda's eyes as she left the ring. After all this time without her beloved pony, Belinda and Golddust had been reunited and had returned in triumph. Jess knew she and Storm Cloud had jumped superbly but it was Belinda who had been the best and really deserved to win. She was so wrapped up in her thoughts that it took Jess a few moments to take in what Rosie was saying to her.

"Come on, it's all over!" Rosie cried as the final competitor left the ring. "Belinda's won!"

"I know she has," Jess said.

"And we've got to follow her into the ring to collect our prizes," Rosie urged.

"Prizes? What for?" Jess was confused.

"You came fourth, silly," Rosie laughed. "And I was sixth. Guess what Jess? We're winners at Southdown!"

Jess was astounded. She could hardly believe it. She climbed into Storm Cloud's saddle once more and rode into the ring.

"Get behind me Jess," Charlie grinned as he rode past. "I came second you know!"

At the side of the ring Jess saw her family, grinning with pride. Tom was there too, and Alex and Kate jumped up and down, cheering and clapping. Jess's heart jumped as she caught a glimpse of Petronella and Sally watching them closely. In the background, Nick and Sarah were talking urgently to Mr. Slater and a policeman. But nothing else mattered to Jess now. As she followed Charlie into the ring for the celebratory lap of honour she could only beam and beam.

12

RUNAWAY RETURNS

"I can't believe Mr. Slater gave Golddust back so easily in the end," said Rosie.

Jess and Rosie were sitting in the tack room at Sandy Lane on the Saturday after the Southdown Show. A tin of saddle soap stood open on the table in front of them and, as they talked, they polished their way methodically through a jumbled pile of stirrup leathers.

"Well, there wasn't a lot he could do about it," said Jess. "The police told him because Golddust was stolen, she still belonged to the original owner. Petronella was furious about Belinda riding her, but her mother said she wasn't allowed to have anything more to do with a stolen pony. And it seems that what Petronella's mother says goes..."

So far the police hadn't managed to track down the

man who sold Golddust to the Slaters, although they hadn't given up hope of catching him. Golddust was back with Belinda again, and Nick and Sarah had offered Belinda the use of the spare loose box at Sandy Lane on a temporary basis. With a thief still around, Belinda couldn't be careful enough.

"Who am I booked on for the 11 o'clock hack?" Alex strode in to join Rosie and Jess in the tack room.

"Hello Alex. You're on Hector I think," Jess said.

"What, that lumbering old thing?" Alex groaned, but he was only joking. Alex loved Hector and Jess and Rosie knew it.

"Who's a lumbering old thing?" a familiar voice enquired.

"Tom!" Jess and Rosie exclaimed together. "You're back! Are you riding today? Are you feeling better? Have you missed Chancey?"

Tom stumbled back in mock horror, fending off the barrage of questions with fake blows. "Good grief, what an onslaught," he grinned. "Well, to answer your questions. No, I'm not riding today – I'm not quite up to that yet, although I am feeling better. And – yes – yes, I have missed Chancey."

"Hey, everyone," Charlie mooched in. "Who am I riding then?"

But no one had time to answer him as an angry Kate appeared at the doorway, hands on hips.

"Right, Alex, that's it!" she said, her eyes glinting furiously. "Just because your bike's got a puncture, it doesn't give you the right to take mine!"

"Sorry, Kate." Alex shrank guiltily into a corner. "But you were so long getting ready this morning, and your bike was just sitting there looking all shiny and tempting and..."

"Hello everybody," Belinda appeared. "I've come to take Golddust out. How's Minstrel today, Jess?"

"He's much better," Jess replied. "I'm riding him later."

Amidst the chatting and laughing Nick popped his head around the tack room door. "There's someone asking for you outside, Jess," he said.

"It's Petronella Slater. She wants a private lesson!" said Charlie. By now everyone at Sandy Lane knew Petronella's story. Jess glared at him and walked out. It was bright outside after the dimness of the tack room but when Jess could see clearly, she found herself face to face with a stocky man. It was Bob Hughes.

"I brought Goldie and Mary to see you," he smiled.

Jess blinked. Sure enough, in front of her sat Mary on top of a beautiful palomino pony.

"Goldie!" Jess breathed. "Hello Mary. Can I stroke her?"

"Of course," Mary smiled down at Jess. "It's my first ride on Goldie since I came out of hospital," she explained. "We only live up the Ash Hill road so we thought we'd pop in and say hello."

"I'm glad you've come," Jess said. "That's Belinda's pony, Golddust, over there," she said, pointing to where Golddust stood in her loose box. "She's the one I confused Goldie with. They don't actually look the same at all, do they?"

"No," Mary smiled. "They're completely different. Both lovely, but different."

At that moment, Belinda came out of the tack room. "Is that the runaway palomino pony?" she asked.

"Yes," said Jess. "Funny to see both Goldie and Golddust together."

"Mary!" Tom's voice called from the tack room and they all looked round. "How are you feeling?"

"Hello Tom," Mary replied as she slipped down from the saddle. "Ok-ish. You look much better."

"Thanks, I feel it."

"What a lovely pony!" Rosie, Charlie, Alex and Kate crowded eagerly around Mary. Goldie jumped back in startled surprise at all this attention and moved nearer to Golddust. The two ponies neighed gently at each other and stood nose to nose, breathing softly.

Jess stood back a little way from her friends and watched them all, eagerly chatting and laughing. She wanted to stand on the edge for a while and see what Sandy Lane looked like to an outside eye.

"It looks just brilliant," she said to herself.

From the stable behind her came a soft whinny. Storm Cloud was hanging her head over her door as usual, her delicate grey face turned towards Jess. Jess walked slowly towards her and breathed softly into the little pony's nose.

"I haven't forgotten you, Stormy," she whispered into the pony's ear. "We'll ride again together soon. Nick's promised me that."

"Come on Jess," a voice at her elbow interrupted. Rosie stood there smiling. "It's nearly 11 o'clock. Minstrel and Pepper are waiting. Let's go and tack up."

STRANGERS AT THE STABLES

Michelle Bates

CONTENTS

1

SOME BAD NEWS

"If we have to close down the stables, we'll close down the stables..."

Rosie Edwards just caught the end of the telephone conversation going on in the tack room and looked up, startled. Nick Brooks – the owner of Sandy Lane Stables – sounded unusually tense. As she watched him run towards the cottage, her stomach turned itself in knots.

What was going on? Surely Nick and his wife Sarah weren't thinking of packing it all in, not when things were just starting to take off? Why would they close down Sandy Lane? Questions rang in Rosie's head like alarm bells.

She felt uneasy. She hadn't been riding at Sandy Lane long, but already it was her life. It had been hard for all of her family, uprooting themselves with her father's job, but hardest of all for Rosie – new home, new school, new friends. It wasn't until she'd discovered Sandy Lane that she really started to feel settled. Here at the stables, she had made all of her friends, even her best friend Jess Adams. Rosie felt hot tears pricking her eyes as she remembered how awful it had been before she had known any of them.

Rosie walked over to the cottage and glanced in through the kitchen window. Nick and Sarah were talking inside and she could just catch the tail end of what they were saying. She wouldn't normally be seen dead eavesdropping, but this sounded serious.

"We'll have to discuss it with Beth immediately," Sarah was saying, as Nick paced up and down the floor. He had his back to the window, so Rosie couldn't catch his reply. Before Rosie even had time to step out of the way, the cottage door had been flung open and Nick hurried out. Rosie jumped back, embarrassed.

"I didn't see you there. Are you OK, Rosie?" he said, breathlessly.

"Yes, fine Nick." Rosie swallowed hard. "What time do you want us in the outdoor school?" she asked, quickly changing the subject.

"Sorry. What was that?" Nick looked up distracted.

"I was just asking what time..." Rosie started.

But her words were cut short as the ring of the telephone sounded around the yard and Nick rushed off to answer it.

Rosie sighed. Deep in thought as she crossed the yard, she saw Kate and Alex Hardy, two more of the Sandy Lane regulars, sprinting up the drive... late as usual.

"Morning, Rosie," they called.

"Morning," she answered.

2

On the other side of the yard, Tom Buchanan, Sandy Lane's star rider, sprang neatly into the saddle of his horse, Chancey. It was the start of the Easter holidays and everyone was in high spirits, but Rosie didn't feel like joining in. Putting on a brave face, she waved as she saw Jess cycle into the yard.

"All ready for Tentenden training this morning?" Jess called.

"Sort of," Rosie answered flatly.

It was their first training session in preparation for the Tentenden Team Chase, and normally any mention of the cross-country race made Rosie feel better instantly. But this morning there were more important things to think about – would there even be a team, for instance, if Sandy Lane was to close down?

The day Nick had announced that she, Tom, Charlie and Jess would make up the team, had been one of the most important days of Rosie's life. She would be devastated if they couldn't enter now. Pulling back the bolt to Pepper's stable, she determined to put it out of her mind and stepped inside. Absent-mindedly, she ran the body brush over the pony's shoulder. Before she knew it, someone had crept up behind her and...

"BOO!"

Jess pounced on her.

Rosie nearly jumped out of her skin as Jess collapsed into fits of laughter.

"Jess, you frightened the life out of me," Rosie said crossly. "Can't you take anything seriously?"

"Like what?" Jess asked, munching on a mouthful of apple.

"Well, if I tell you something... something awful," Rosie continued. Immediately, Jess looked concerned.

"Go on then. Spill the beans. Don't keep me in suspense."

And in a moment Rosie had blurted everything out... about the telephone call, Nick and Sarah's worried faces, her fears of the stables being closed down...

"What do you think it can mean, Jess?" Rosie asked at the end of it. "It sounds as though they're going to pack it all in."

"They wouldn't do that," Jess said quickly. "Nick and Sarah would never leave Sandy Lane. Besides, they'd tell us about it first, wouldn't they? Are you sure you heard things right?"

"Of course I did." Rosie shrugged her shoulders.

"Well, maybe Charlie knows something about it," Jess said, and quickly she called their friend over. "Charlie, Charlie."

Charlie Marshall looked up from where he was sweeping the yard and ambled over. He listened carefully to what Rosie had to say, but he didn't seem to think it could be serious either.

"Tell her it's nonsense then," Jess begged, "or we'll never hear the end of it."

"It's nonsense," Charlie began. "But that doesn't mean..."

"Doesn't mean it's not true?" Rosie said frostily. "Why doesn't anyone ever believe me? It was like that time at Christmas when I tried to tell Charlie there wasn't any school the next day and he went in anyway," Rosie finished.

"Well, I admitted I was wrong then, didn't I?" Charlie said humbly. "I thought you were joking. Nobody told me the boiler had broken down and I was the one who looked stupid turning up at an empty

4

school. It's not that we don't believe you, Rosie. It's just that it seems so unlikely. I know Sandy Lane's had its rough patches, but it's come through all that. Nick and Sarah have been doing so well lately, and they'd hardly have taken on a new stable girl if they were about to close down the stables, would they?"

Rosie looked unconvinced. "But don't you see, Charlie," she said in frustration, "I don't think this is something they've been planning. I think it's something awful that's just happened!"

"I give up with you two," Charlie groaned. "Stop panicking. Nick will tell us everything in good time. There's work to do. I'm going to tack up Napoleon."

"Yes, come on Rosie," said Jess. "We'd better get a move on if we're going to get our horses ready."

"Look, here's Nick right now," said Charlie, seeing Nick stride across the yard. "Let's ask him what's going on."

"No... no don't do that," Rosie said urgently. "It'll look as though I was listening in on them."

"Well, you were weren't you?" Charlie said grinning.

Rosie shot him a filthy look. "I don't want Nick to know that," she whispered, in an annoyed voice.

"Fair enough," Charlie said. And before he had a chance to say anything anyway, Nick began talking.

"I'll be taking the training session at eleven," he called, "and I need to see everybody in the tack room at twelve. Can you spread the word? I've got some important news... news that's going to affect all of you, I'm afraid. And if you see Beth, can you tell her to come and find me at the cottage?"

"See," said Rosie as Nick hurried off. "I told you.

Sandy Lane's going to be shut down."

"Oh, come on Rosie," groaned Charlie. "Stop being so dramatic."

"Well, I think we ought to tell the others what Rosie's heard anyway," said Jess. Charlie shrugged his shoulders. "It's only fair that everyone knows," she continued.

Charlie nodded. "OK then. I suppose you're right."

Rosie grimaced as Charlie and Jess disappeared. It wouldn't take long for the news to go round.

"Whatever are we to do Pepper?" she asked the little black and white pony as she gave his coat a quick going over with the body brush.

"Talking to yourself Rosie?" Beth's smiling face appeared over the door of Pepper's stable.

"There you are, Beth. Nick's been looking for you," Rosie said. "He wants you to meet him at the cottage with Sarah."

"Sounds serious. Hope I'm not about to get the sack!" Beth smiled.

Rosie felt quite uncomfortable. Beth was the new stable girl. She hadn't been at Sandy Lane long, but she had fitted in straight away. Rosie had been worried when Nick had told them he was employing someone to help out... worried that she would try to take over. But as soon as Rosie had met Beth, she knew she needn't have worried, Beth wasn't like that. She was more like a friend really. She was kind, not bossy at all, and absolutely brilliant with the horses. Rosie couldn't help liking her.

Making her way across the yard, Rosie collected Pepper's saddle from the tack room. Word of her news must have got round already, for her friends were looking very gloomy. Anxious to escape another postmortem of Nick's words, Rosie hurried back to Pepper's stable. She patted Pepper's shoulder and tacked him up, leading him over to join the others. Tom, Charlie and Jess were already making their way down to the outdoor school.

"All here?" Nick called distractedly as he opened the gate and let everyone in.

"I want everyone to start by mounting and dismounting properly on both sides," he called. "Then start walking around. I'll let you know when I want you to trot on. I'd like to see some turns on the forehand from a halt, rising trot on each diagonal and cantering on a named leg. Are you all ready for that?"

"OK," he went on when no one answered. "Tom, you take the lead."

Tom led the way around the perimeter of the school and Rosie brought up the rear. She was trying desperately to keep her mind on her riding. But Pepper was fidgeting and she knew she wasn't really concentrating. She looked across at the others. Charlie was frowning and didn't seem able to get Napoleon to respond and Storm Cloud was napping with Jess.

"Come on everyone," Nick called. "Pay attention."

"One two, one two, one two," Rosie chanted, trying to stop Pepper from trotting into the back of Chancey.

After twenty minutes of loosening up their horses, Nick didn't look terribly impressed.

"I think everyone's blundered through those exercises enough for now. Let's try some jumping."

Rosie looked anxiously at the course laid out in front of them. The jumps weren't that high, but she felt all jittery.

"All ready?" Nick called out. "Charlie, do you want to start and show us how it's done?"

"Sure," said Charlie, and with a flourish of his whip, he turned Napoleon to the first. Rosie held her breath. They were going very fast as they flew over the brush and cantered on to the stile. They soared over the next two fences in swift succession, but Charlie wasn't going to jump clear. As he turned Napoleon to the gate, the little bay firmly refused, and although Charlie turned him three times, he still couldn't get him to jump it.

"Try him over the parallel bars to relax him," Nick called, and quickly Napoleon went on to clear them.

Rosie watched grimly as Tom took a turn at the course and knocked down two jumps. And Jess did no better, knocking down three.

"My turn," she muttered to herself, trying to focus her attention on the course ahead of her, as Nick called her forward. She gritted her teeth and kicked Pepper on for the brush. But her mind was elsewhere, and although she jumped clear, she knew it had been a plodding round.

"That's enough for one day," Nick said at the end of the session. "I don't know what's wrong with you lot. I haven't seen such laborious riding in a long time. You'll have to work harder if you're going to be ready for Tentenden – it's only four weeks away. And don't forget – everyone's to meet me in the tack room in five minutes time." He turned on his heel as he spoke and strode out of the school.

Gloomily, Rosie led the way back to the yard, taking Pepper to his stable. She was furious with herself. She hated riding badly in front of Nick.

Impatiently, she fumbled with Pepper's girth as she tried to undo the buckle. "More haste, less speed," she muttered under her breath. "And you can take that look off your face too, Pepper," she snapped, closing the stable door behind her. "I'll be back later to sponge you down."

She knew she should really do it straight away but the news in the tack room simply couldn't wait. Slinging the saddle across her arm, she hurried inside and hung the saddle up on its peg before she sat down. Nick looked serious as he sat leaning against the desk, his arms folded in front of him.

"Are we all here now?" he asked.

Rosie looked round at the expectant faces. Tom was there and Charlie too. Even Alex and Kate had managed to turn up on time. This was important news after all. Jess gave Rosie a 'don't worry' kind of look as she shifted uneasily in her seat.

"I'll come straight to the point," said Nick. "Sarah and I have had some rather bad news."

Rosie's heart skipped a beat. She sat rooted to the spot. This was it, he was going to tell them it was all over for Sandy Lane.

Nick glanced across at his wife and took a deep breath before he went on. "I'm afraid Sarah's dad in America has been taken ill. He's had a heart attack and been rushed into hospital."

The news was greeted by low mutterings, followed by an embarrassed silence.

"He's all right," Nick went on. "But he needs time to recover. He's going to be in hospital for a while and, in the meantime, we've agreed to go and run his stud farm for him in Kentucky."

Rosie felt a wave of relief flood through her. So Sandy Lane wasn't closing down forever. Then, almost immediately, she felt terrible. How could she have been so selfish? Sarah's father was ill, and all she could think about was the future of her beloved stables.

"We've asked Beth to take charge of Sandy Lane while we're away," Nick went on. "At the moment we'll be gone for three weeks, but obviously we'll get back sooner if we can. Beth's going to come and live at the cottage until we get back. And I was rather hoping that you lot might offer to help out. It is the start of the Easter holidays after all. And I'd feel a lot happier knowing you were giving Beth a hand down here. What do you say?"

"Of course we'll help out, Nick," said Tom, taking charge of the situation. "There's no question of that, is there?" He turned to look at the others. His friends all nodded in swift agreement.

"When are you going?" Tom asked, turning back to face Nick.

"Well," Nick sighed heavily. "We've managed to get flights for Monday morning which doesn't give us long to get everything organized – just two days." His voice tailed off as Sarah started to speak.

"You'll have to bear with us. There's going to be a lot to sort out before we go. It's going to be a tough few days for everyone." She smiled weakly.

"We should be back in time for the Tentenden Team Chase, but Beth has agreed to continue with the training," Nick continued. "I'll set up a programme with her before I go. I'm sure everything will be fine, but I'll leave you our number in America, as well as a contact number of a friend of mine in case of emergency." Nick smiled anxiously. "I'm sure you won't need them. You should be fine with Beth in charge."

Not knowing what else to say, Rosie and her friends trooped out of the tack room and tried to busy themselves around the yard.

2

THEY'RE OFF

Sarah wasn't wrong in saying it would be a tough few days for them all. There was so much to organize. Rotas had to be drawn up for mucking-out, feeding and grooming. Lessons and hacks had to be decided upon. Routines had to be established. In the end it was decided that it would be easier if the regulars were responsible for two horses each and, while Beth would take all private lessons, the regulars could lead hacks.

Eventually, Monday morning arrived. By nine, the last of the bags were squashed into a taxi and Nick and Sarah climbed in. They were off.

"I've pinned the phone numbers on the tack room notice board," Nick called out of the window. "We'll ring when we get there, but don't panic if you don't hear much from us, we're going to be very busy. Anyway, you'll be fine with Beth in charge."

"Sure, we'll be fine," Beth smiled. "What can

possibly go wrong in three weeks?"

"Practise hard," Sarah called as the taxi rolled out of the yard. "And don't forget to send off the Tentenden entry form!"

"Bye-eee..." the voices died away as the car disappeared down the drive and out of sight.

Rosie made her way to the water trough. Hunching her shoulders in the wind, she crossed the yard, struggling under the weight of the water buckets. It was a grey, blustery April day. Rosie's teeth chattered as she gave the horses their buckets and pulled down the sleeves of her jumper. She stopped for a moment, scraping her blonde hair into a tight ponytail before strolling off to take another look at the cross-country course.

Rosie knew it like the back of her hand. She'd spent long enough helping Nick set it up over the winter months. They all had.

"Without our own cross-country course to practise over, we won't stand a chance at Tentenden." Nick's words echoed in Rosie's ears as she thought back to the day he had started to plan it all. Although the jumps weren't all that high, the course he had laid out was a challenging one and each fence would have to be jumped clear, or the horse would take a heavy rap. Standing on top of the little tussock by the gate, Rosie's eyes narrowed as she took it all in and a rush of adrenaline ran through her. Absent-mindedly, she gazed into the distance when a voice from behind her disturbed her thoughts.

"I've been looking for you everywhere. Have you forgotten we've got a Tentenden training session?"

Rosie spun round to see Jess, walking towards her.

"How could I?" Rosie said, looking at her watch. "I was just checking out the course. Come on, let's go," she said, smiling.

The two friends chattered excitedly as they hurried back to the yard. Rosie collected her riding hat and made her way to Pepper's stable. The little piebald sniffed the air feverishly as Rosie folded back his rug and started to tack him up. Attaching the breast plate to the saddle, she led Pepper out of his stable to join the others.

Rosie sprung nimbly into the saddle and nudged the little pony on through the gate at the back of the yard, into the fields behind. A gusty wind was blowing and it was drizzling with rain. Rosie's cheeks felt flushed as she drew Pepper to a halt under the trees.

"Here we all are then. Excited?" Beth asked, reaching for her field binoculars. "As this is the first time I've taken you over the course, I'm not going to time you. It's quite slippery, so just concentrate on getting round safely. OK?"

"Yes Beth," came a volley of voices.

"Let's get going before it pours down. Try and take extra care through the woods. There are a lot of branches lying around from last week's storm. I don't want your horses to spook. The most important thing is to take things slowly. The jumps aren't that difficult. Now, you all know where you're going, don't you?" she said.

"Yes Beth," they chorused.

"Right then. Charlie, you go first followed by Jess, Tom and then Rosie," said Beth.

Rosie didn't know whether to feel pleased or disappointed. She didn't want to go first, but at the same time, she thought she would die waiting for her turn. Rosie watched closely as Charlie rode across the field and approached the first. He was so quick, she envied him his speed. She would see him up to the trees, then she would go and warm up.

She turned Pepper to a quiet corner of the field and started to trot the pony round. Then she pushed him on into a gentle canter. Pepper had such a smooth, rhythmical stride, he was a pleasure to ride. Soon Rosie began to relax. She didn't realize how quickly the time had gone. When she returned to the group, Jess was already back and Tom was halfway round the course.

"How was it, Jess?" Rosie asked.

"Brilliant," her friend answered, her eyes glinting brightly. "Storm Cloud was amazing. Weren't you?" She leant forward, shivering as the coastal rain swept in across the fields.

And then Rosie heard Beth call her name. Gritting her teeth determinedly, she turned Pepper to the start. Her skin felt taut as the wind whistled past and Pepper lengthened his stride. Rosie drove him forward with her heels and the pony jumped over the tiger trap as if it was alight. As Rosie steadied him before the brush, she felt a tremor run through his body. They took the fence in their stride and raced on towards the hayrack.

"Steady now Pepper. Easy does it," she crooned. "It's not as hard as it looks, it's only a hayrack."

Rosie sat deeper in the saddle and collected Pepper for the spread. Pepper snatched at the reins, impatiently waiting for Rosie to release him for the jump. Quickly, she urged him on, letting the reins ease through her fingers as the pony jumped clear and went on to soar over the hedge. Leaning forward as they entered the trees, Rosie swung Pepper towards the tree trunk. Determinedly, she drove him on. Without hesitating, Pepper rose to the challenge, up and over and on to the log pile.

Rosie knew they were going well. Bravely, Pepper gathered his legs up under him and they flew over the tyres. Galloping forward, clear of the water jump, they approached the zigzag rails. Rosie held her breath. But they jumped it squarely and the gutsy little pony landed lightly and went on to race over the gate. Rosie felt herself slipping and gripped harder with her knees as they thundered across the fields. The rain was teeming down now as they took the stone wall. Touchdown! They had done it. They had finished.

Pepper snorted, his breath spiralling from his nostrils like clouds of smoke, as Rosie slowed his pace to a trot.

Everyone was making so much noise when Rosie eventually returned to the group, that she couldn't get a word in edgeways.

"Quick everyone," Beth said, "we'll have to hurry back to the yard if we don't want to get drenched."

As the horses wound their way back into the yard, Rosie felt content. She was soaked through to the skin, but somehow it didn't matter. Leading Pepper into his stable, she removed his tack and started to rub him down. Then she hurried to the tack room to collect some grooming kit. She could hear trouble brewing between Tom and Charlie over who was riding Hector and Napoleon in the afternoon hacks. Putting her head over Blackjack's stable door, she glanced inside. Susannah – one of the younger pupils – was there with him.

"Did you enjoy your ride?" Rosie asked her.

"Yes," she replied. "Alex told me I was really improving," she added proudly.

"I'm sure you are," Rosie said kindly. "If you nip to the barn and get Blackjack's food, I'll take over grooming him if you like."

"Thanks. I think my mum's waiting for me," Susannah answered gratefully, scuttling off. Rosie picked up the body brush and made a start on Blackjack's mottled coat.

"Keep still Blackjack," she muttered.

"Here's his food, Rosie." Susannah's head appeared over the door.

"Great," Rosie said. "See you the same time next week then."

"Thanks," Susannah shouted over her shoulder as she ran off.

Impatiently, Blackjack shifted his weight as he eyed the food sitting outside the stable. Gently, he nosed Rosie's back as a little reminder that he was waiting.

"Don't you fret," said Rosie. "I haven't forgotten you, but you can't have your lunch till I've got you clean. There, that should do the trick." She bent down to pick out Blackjack's last hoof. Patting his hindquarters, she closed the door behind her. That was her two horses sorted. She hoped Jess had got Storm Cloud and Minstrel settled as quickly. After all, they did have plans for that afternoon.

"All set Jess?" Rosie cried as she saw her friend scurry past.

"Nearly," said Jess. "I'll check on Storm Cloud and then I'll be with you."

Five minutes later they were ready. Looking at her

reflection in the glass of the tack room window, Rosie wiped the smudges from her face.

"Come on," Jess urged, "or we'll be late."

Jogging down the lane, the girls headed for the bus stop at the corner of Sandy Lane. Out of puff and red in the face, they stumbled to the stop and clambered aboard the bus."

"Phew. We nearly missed it, slowcoach!" Jess teased. "Two halves to Colcott, please," she said, scrabbling about for some change.

The two girls chattered excitedly as the bus climbed the hill away from the coast. Fields of greenery sped past and buildings sprang up as the bus wound its way along the winding back roads.

As they neared the town of Colcott, the girls rang the bell. The doors swished open and Rosie and Jess jumped to the ground. The bus drove off, leaving them outside the old saddlery.

"Afternoon Jess... Rosie."

Mr. Armstrong's jovial face peered out at them from behind the counter. The Sandy Lane regulars spent so much time in his shop, he had come to know all of their names. His watery blue eyes twinkled at his two favourite customers.

"They're ready, girls. I hope these are what you wanted."

The girls grinned at each other as Mr. Armstrong placed four brand new skull cap covers, in Sandy Lane red and black quarters, on the shop counter.

"Yes, Mr. Armstrong," Jess breathed. "Those are just what we wanted. What do you think Rosie?"

"They're brilliant Jess. We'll look like a real team now. I can't wait to see the others' faces."

"Don't they know you've ordered them then?" Mr. Armstrong asked.

"No," Jess said mischievously. "Rosie and I have been saving up for them for ages. We wanted it to be a surprise."

"And how are Nick and Sarah?" Mr. Armstrong asked, as he totalled up what they owed.

"Haven't you heard?" Rosie said, glancing anxiously at Jess. "They're away at the moment. Sarah's father's been taken ill." She paused to draw breath. "So they've had to go to America to run his stud farm for him. We're helping Beth look after Sandy Lane while they're away."

Mr. Armstrong looked concerned. "How long are they planning to be away for then? Is it serious?"

"I'm afraid it is," said Rosie. "He's had a heart attack. They're going to be away for three weeks."

"Well, if you speak to them, do send them my best wishes," Mr. Armstrong said, looking worried.

Rosie nodded. "Come on, Jess. We'd better get going," she called over to where Jess was browsing through the bridles. "We'll miss the next bus back if we don't hurry, and we need to get the horses groomed and tacked up for the afternoon rides."

"Coming," said Jess. "Bye Mr. Armstrong," they called as they let themselves out of the shop. The low rumble of the bus sounded in the distance as Rosie and Jess waited patiently by the stop.

"Don't worry. We'll be at the stables soon enough," Rosie said as the bus pulled over and the two girls climbed on.

Twenty minutes later, the bus drew to a halt in Sandy Lane and Rosie and Jess jumped off. Rounding the corner by the sycamore tree, they walked on up the drive to the stables. Quickly, Rosie made her way to Pepper's stable, only to find it was empty.

"Uh oh," she said to herself. "Too late."

Jess looked equally sheepish as she met Rosie in the middle of the yard.

"Someone seems to have beaten us to it, Jess," Rosie said. "We're not going to be in anyone's good books at this rate."

"It can't be helped," Jess said briskly. "We're not that late. Wait till the others see what we've got for them. They won't be angry then."

"I hope so," said Rosie, unconvinced. "Let's go and find them."

Eagerly they hurried to the tack room.

"Hi everyone," Jess called to a wall of stony faces.

"Nice of you to drop by." Charlie was the first to break the awkward silence.

"Sorry," Rosie mumbled. "We didn't realize we'd been so long."

"Obviously," Charlie said sarcastically.

"It's not very responsible to go disappearing on the first day Nick and Sarah are away," Tom said in a more appeasing voice. "We've all had to help get your horses tacked up."

"Oh... um... sorry," said Rosie, shamefaced.

"We've got to pull together while Nick and Sarah are away," Kate added, crossly.

"We know all that," Jess answered. "We're not trying to get out of our jobs. It's just that we had to collect some things," she said.

"What things?" Charlie asked, frowning.

"These," said Jess, pulling the bag out from behind

20

her back. "Hopefully they'll make you less annoyed with us. We bought them for Tentenden."

The colourful caps spilled out onto the tack room desk. Everyone stood back, looking embarrassed.

"Well, it's a good idea," Alex said kindly.

"Oh Jess, Rosie. They're perfect. You'll all look really professional," Kate exclaimed.

"Yes, thanks you two," said Tom, running the silk caps through his fingers. Charlie grunted noncommittally.

"You might be a bit more excited," Jess said. "We went to a lot of trouble to get them."

"And they are very nice," said Tom. "It's just that there were only four of us to get the horses ready and Beth's lesson was late. We thought you'd just gone off and left everyone to do your jobs."

"Well thanks. Thanks a lot everyone," Rosie said huffily. "We didn't think you'd miss us for an hour and we wanted it to be a surprise."

"It was a surprise," Tom said appreciatively. "Come on you two," he said, linking arms with the two girls as he led them out of the tack room. "Don't look so upset. It's just that for a while, we've got to put the running of Sandy Lane above everything else – even Tentenden."

3

DISASTER STRIKES

"Don't let him puff out his belly when you're trying to tighten up the girth, Jess," Charlie called from the other side of the yard.

"I know that," Jess snapped. "But it's easier said than done. You're not the boss around here anyway. You know how Minstrel hates being tacked up. Why don't *you* put on his saddle if you think you can do any better!"

Rosie groaned. Not another quarrel. It had only been four days ago that they had waved goodbye to Nick and Sarah and already the arguments were in full swing – who was riding who, who was taking the lead, who was in charge of what. On and on it went. And it was getting worse. Yesterday they had all been bickering so much that one mother had lifted her child off Horace before the lesson had even begun.

Somehow, without Nick and Sarah around to

oversee the yard, things weren't quite so straightforward. Rosie liked Beth, but she just couldn't keep control like Nick did. Jess, for instance, was supposed to be in charge of Minstrel, but when Alex had brought him in from the hack yesterday afternoon absolutely plastered in mud, she had gone mad and refused to groom him. And nothing Beth had said would make Jess change her mind.

"If you were the one who had to clean him, you wouldn't have let him get that dirty," Jess had screamed at Alex. Rosie cringed as she remembered the scene.

They weren't getting anything done on time either. Rosie looked at her watch. It was five past eleven. Beth was supposed to have started the lesson in road-work at eleven o'clock and Pepper was the only one of the horses ready.

"Come on everyone," Rosie moaned. "I must have circled Pepper at least a dozen times. He'll have made his own track if I'm not careful."

Jess scowled as she tried to help a rider with a leg-up onto Napoleon. "Coming," she grumbled.

By quarter past eleven, Jester, Napoleon, Minstrel, Storm Cloud and Whispering Silver stood groomed, tacked up and ready to go.

"At last," Rosie mumbled under her breath.

"Who's going on this ride, Rosie?" Beth called.

"The lot training for their road-work test – George, Melissa, Anna, Mark and me," Rosie answered cheerfully.

"Excellent," Beth smiled. "All good riders. That should be fun. Let's go then," she said happily. "Follow on after me."

Rosie nudged Pepper forward, relieved to be leaving

the others behind her to argue things out. As the horses meandered down the tiny winding lane, Rosie thought what a fine spectacle they made. Their buffed coats gleamed as the April sun peered weakly through the clouds. Beth and Whispering Silver led the string of horses and Rosie took up the rear. Slowly, they picked their way along the grassy verge of the roadside, past gates and hedges heading for the open fields ahead of them. Rosie pushed Pepper on into a brisk trot to catch up with Napoleon.

The further they rode from the stables, the better Rosie started to feel. Of course it wasn't the same at Sandy Lane without Nick and Sarah around. She shouldn't have expected it to be really. But once things had settled down, they would be all right, she was sure of it. Rosie sighed contentedly as the wind rustled through the trees, stirring the leaves. The smell of the countryside enveloped her. It was so peaceful and the rest of the Easter holidays lay ahead of her to be spent at Sandy Lane.

Rosie didn't know when it was that she first heard the sound of the approaching car. Certainly it wasn't until it was right upon her as there were no warning calls from the front. It all happened so quickly. One moment, she was quietly ambling along the side of the road, the next, the low-slung red sports car had sped out of the Colcott junction and was heading straight for them at full throttle. Swiftly, she collected her reins and checked Pepper, but the riders ahead of her seemed to be having trouble as their horses danced skittishly from side to side.

Any minute now the car will slow down, Rosie thought to herself. But if anything, it seemed to accelerate. Rosie looked on in horror as the car swerved out of control across the road. At the last moment it careered left, not a hair's breadth away from the horses, and sped on. Rosie gasped as everything was thrown into total chaos. And later, when she was to look back on things, she couldn't remember anything very clearly. Horses and riders spun in a whirlwind of colours, shrieking voices and clattering hooves merged as one.

Rosie sat shell-shocked. She felt as though she was looking at a video that had been freeze-framed. Storm Cloud pirouetted in staccato movements, cannoning into the stampeding horses and then Whispering Silver reared, her eyes rolling in sheer terror, her legs flailing in the air as Beth clung on for dear life. Crash! In one split-second, Whispering Silver's shoes struck tarmac and Beth was flung sideways from the saddle. There was a sickening crunch as Beth hit the ground. Whispering Silver thundered off down the road, taking horses and riders with her. Suddenly, Rosie snapped to her senses.

"Pull on the reins! Try to turn them back!" She shouted instructions until she was blue in the face, but it was too late. Napoleon was the only horse left behind, and George was struggling to keep him under control. Jumping to the ground, Rosie rushed over to where Beth had fallen. She felt the panic rising in her throat as she looked at the pale face of the girl stretched out on the ground, her leg twisted awkwardly underneath her.

"She's dead!" George screamed.

"No she's not," Rosie said as she felt for Beth's pulse. "She's unconscious, but there's a very definite beat. We need help. Can you ride and phone for an ambulance? I'll stay here with her. Tie Pepper to that tree over there."

"Beth, Beth. Can you hear me?" She turned back to the girl, not waiting for an answer from George.

"Go on," Rosie said. "There's a house some way up on the left. I can't remember what it's called, but it's got a white gate. Call Tom at Sandy Lane too. Tell him what's happened. Get him to come out and look for the others. And hurry," she said urgently.

Rosie watched as George turned Napoleon up the road towards Ash Hill, and galloped away into the distance. Quietly, she bent over Beth, stroking her hair, talking to her all the time, not knowing what to say.

"You're going to be all right," she whispered. "It was only a little fall. It looks worse than it is. Please, please be all right," she said. But there was no reply from the white, immobile figure laid out beside her. It had started to rain now. Big drips of water ran in rivulets down Rosie's back as she took off her coat and laid it over Beth to keep her warm. She didn't know what else she could do. She felt so helpless kneeling there, waiting and waiting. Beth groaned as Rosie leant over.

"Beth... Beth can you hear me?" Beth opened one eye and groaned faintly.

"It's... it's my leg," she murmured.

"It's OK. It's OK," Rosie said, patting her hand. "They'll soon be here."

She looked at her watch. It could only have been five minutes ago that George had left for help, but it felt like ages. She thought she could hear something. Was it the sound of an engine in the distance? Her heart leapt as she jumped to her feet and then it sank again. Her mind was playing tricks on her. She grimaced as the sound faded away. Then she heard another noise and, as she stared into the distance, she could see a horse and rider cantering towards her. Rosie waited patiently as the figures got nearer and nearer. She breathed a sigh of relief. It was George.

"The ambulance is on its way." The words tumbled from the boy's mouth. "They should be here any minute. And I phoned Tom... he's coming out with Alex... how is she?"

"She's come round," Rosie said. "Her leg's hurting her, but I..." And then Rosie jumped up. There was a siren in the distance, getting louder and louder.

"The ambulance!" George cried, jumping off Napoleon.

Before Rosie knew it, an ambulance had appeared around the corner and everyone sprang into action. Neon lights flashed as three men jumped out and rushed over.

"What's her name?" one called.

"Beth. She's called Beth." Rosie answered weakly, watching them as they unloaded a trolley from the ambulance.

"Pulse is OK," she heard one of them mutter to the others, laying his hand against her brow.

"Temperature OK."

Rosie felt a wave of relief flood through her. Beth was groaning.

"Do you hurt anywhere?" one of them was asking her.

"She said something about her leg," Rosie intervened.

"OK, OK," the ambulance man said kindly, motioning to the others to fetch something. Rosie looked on as they attached a support bandage to Beth's leg. Gently, the three men rolled her onto a board and carried her over to the trolley.

"What happens now?" Rosie asked.

"We're taking her to casualty... to Barkston hospital," one of them said. "Can you phone her family?"

"Yes, I'll phone her mother," Rosie said.

"I'll radio the hospital and get them to call out the police," said the ambulance man. "Wait till they get here – they'll tell you what to do," he said, heading for the driver's seat.

"OK," Rosie said miserably, shivering as she shifted her weight from one foot to the other.

Beth smiled weakly as the men strapped her to the trolley and loaded her into the back, and then the ambulance drove off leaving Rosie and George standing on the roadside waiting. It had all happened so quickly.

"Tom and the others should be here any moment," George said. "In fact, there they are now."

Rosie turned around and looked back in the direction of Sandy Lane to see Tom and Alex running over.

"Rosie... George. Is Beth OK?" Tom asked, striding towards them.

"She's been rushed off to Barkston casualty, but she was at least conscious when they took her off. Her leg is hurting her," Rosie answered, clutching the reins of a rather impatient Pepper who was pawing frantically at the ground.

"We must phone Beth's mother as soon as we get back and tell her she's been taken to Barkston," Alex said sensibly. "Are you all right, Rosie?"

"Yes, I'm fine," Rosie said, looking down at her dishevelled appearance. "Just a bit shocked. The police are on their way. I can't get over it... the car didn't stop. It must have seen the trouble it caused. Beth could have been killed and yet it didn't stop."

"Did you get its number plate?" Tom asked.

"No," Rosie cried. "It all happened so quickly. It was a red sports car... a man driving it, but everything else is a bit hazy."

"What about you, George?" Tom asked.

"I'm afraid it's a complete blur," he answered, shaking his head.

"We've got to find the others," Tom said, suddenly taking charge of the situation. "You wait here for the police. Which way did they go?"

Rosie pointed vaguely in the direction of Ash Hill.

"Don't worry. We'll go and look for them. I'm sure we'll find them," said Tom, confidently. "We'll take Pepper and Napoleon off your hands. Just tell the police what you can remember."

Rosie watched as the two boys mounted the horses and disappeared into the distance. The police didn't take long to get there and soon Rosie found herself going over the events once more.

"I'm PC Dale," the first policeman said as he strode over. "Can you tell me what's happened here?" he asked kindly. "The hospital radioed that there had been an accident."

"Yes, yes there was," said Rosie hurriedly. "The ambulance has taken Beth off – the girl who was thrown from her horse," she explained.

"Where are the other riders then?" he asked. "I was told there were a lot of you down here."

"There were." Rosie paused for breath. "The horses bolted with their riders. Our friends have already gone to look for them... I told them which way to go... they've taken care of our horses..." The words tumbled out one after the other. "We were just waiting for you before we went back to the yard."

"We won't keep you long... just a few details, then we'll run you back to the stables," the policeman said, opening a notepad. Rosie watched as he drew a map of the surrounding roads.

"So where did this car come from then?"

"The Colcott junction over there," said Rosie. "And very fast."

"But it didn't actually hit anyone?"

"No," Rosie said hesitantly. "But it drove very close to us."

"And it seemed as though it speeded up," George added.

"What sort of speed would you estimate it was going at then?" PC Dale turned to George

George looked doubtful. "It's hard to say. It just looked very fast," he said.

"And where were the horses on the road?" he asked, turning back to Rosie.

"In single file." Rosie paused to draw breath. "We were practising for our road safety exams, so we wouldn't have ridden any other way."

"That's good," said PC Dale. "And how many people were there in the vehicle?" he went on.

"Just one – a man I think," Rosie answered. "But I

didn't get a clear view of him. It all happened so quickly."

"What about you?" PC Dale asked George.

"Well, no," said George. "I was too busy trying to hold my horse."

"And did either of you get the registration number by any chance?" he asked.

"No, I'm afraid not," Rosie said.

Rosie watched as PC Dale scribbled one last thing down and snapped his notepad shut.

"Is that all you need to know?" Rosie asked quietly.

"For now," the policeman said in a kind voice. "If you want to get into the car, we'll give you a lift back to the stables."

Rosie and George climbed into the back. Rosie stared out of the window. She couldn't believe all this had happened – only an hour ago she had ridden so confidently out of Sandy Lane.

"Do you think you might find the driver?" she heard George asking the police, as they drove back along the winding roads.

"Hmm." PC Dale was hesitant. "To be honest with you, we're in a very difficult position – as the car didn't actually hit anything..."

"But it was obvious the man drove too close to us," George interrupted.

"Maybe," PC Dale went on. "But it'll be very difficult to prove, and without a vehicle registration number it's unlikely we'll be able to find him anyway."

Rosie wasn't listening to the continuing conversation. As she stared dejectedly out of the window, her mind drifted off. That car had definitely speeded up, it had been no accident. Poor Beth. As the police car turned into the drive off Sandy Lane, visions of the girl lying crumpled on the ground flooded Rosie's mind. She took a deep breath. What on earth were they going to tell Nick and Sarah?

4

HOLDING THE FORT

"Well, it could have been worse," said Charlie. "At least all the other riders are back in one piece. And none of the horses are injured."

It was late in the day, and the Sandy Lane regulars were huddled in the tack room. It seemed as though they'd been there for hours, just trying to decide what to do. And it had been a long day. A day that had started off so promisingly and ended in disaster.

"It's as Rosie suspected," Tom said, putting down the phone from Beth's mother. "Beth's broken her leg." He took a deep breath. "They reckon it's going to take at least six weeks to heal, so she's not going to be around at Sandy Lane for some time. She's going to have to stay at home till she's fully recovered." Tom looked around the tack room at the gloomy faces staring back at him.

"What did her mother say we should do?" Rosie

asked. "Who's going to run Sandy Lane?"

"Don't worry, Rosie," Tom replied. "It's all in hand. I said we'd phone Nick's friend. Beth's mother was going to do it, but she seemed quite relieved when I offered instead. I suppose I'd better ring him now." Tom reached for the number on the notice board.

"What's his name?" Rosie asked.

"Dick Bryant," Tom answered. "Shhh." Tom motioned to his lips as he dialled the number and waited patiently.

"No answer," he said finally.

"We'll have to phone Nick and Sarah," Rosie said.

"No," said Tom. "I don't want to worry Nick and Sarah if we don't have to. They've got enough to think about at the moment. We'll pack things up here, then if we can't get hold of Dick Bryant tonight, we'll try him again tomorrow."

"But what about tomorrow's lessons?" Rosie said. "Shouldn't we cancel them?"

"No... not yet," said Tom. "We'll manage. It's only for a day. I can always take over Beth's lessons and then we'll divide the hacks between us."

Rosie wasn't convinced.

"Look," said Tom. "By tomorrow, we'll have got hold of Dick Bryant and things will be back to normal."

"Unless we don't phone Dick Bryant at all..." Charlie started.

"Oh Charlie!" Rosie exclaimed. "Not another of your mad schemes."

"Not that mad," he went on. "We could run Sandy Lane ourselves. It is the Easter holidays after all. I'm sure we could manage until Nick and Sarah get back. They'd be so pleased..."

"Don't even think about it," Tom said. "We can't possibly do that. Nick would go mad."

"I suppose you're right," Charlie said, shrugging his shoulders. "It was just an idea. You must admit, it would be fun."

"Fun, but totally mad." Tom was cross now. "But we can hold the fort till tomorrow evening can't we?"

There were faint murmurings and then everyone nodded in agreement.

"OK. If that's all agreed, I can think of twelve hungry horses waiting to be fed. Let's get going."

"I'll nip across to the cottage and lock up," said Alex. "Turn some lights on, make it look lived in... that sort of thing."

"Good idea," said Tom. "There's a spare set of keys in the drawer. Make sure you do it properly. Oh and don't let's say anything about what's happened yet," Tom went on. "Not until we've got everything sorted. You know what parents are like. They'll only worry and one of them is bound to try and get hold of Nick."

There was a quick pause as everyone exchanged nervous glances. Rosie felt uneasy. She didn't like keeping things from her parents. Still, it was only for a day and no one else seemed worried by it. She didn't want to be the odd one out.

Quickly, she followed the others into the yard as they set about packing up the stables for the night.

* * * * * * * * * * * * * * * *

The next morning passed uneventfully at Sandy Lane. Tom still hadn't managed to get hold of Dick Bryant. Every time he rang there was no reply. At two o'clock, the regulars met in the tack room and delegated tasks for the afternoon.

"I'll take that private lesson and Rosie and Jess – do you think you could take the 2 o'clock hack out?" Tom asked.

"Of course!" said Rosie, her eyes lighting up. It was the hack that went to the lighthouse – her favourite ride. Hurriedly, she skipped to Pepper's stable.

"Did you hear that, Pepper?" she called. "We're taking a hack out this afternoon."

Pepper turned round to look at her and snorted lethargically.

"Come on, where's your energy?' she asked the little black and white pony.

"All right Rosie?" Jess's head appeared over the door.

"Fine." Rosie smiled at her friend.

"Can you tack up Blackjack?" Jess asked. "David Taylor's here and his mother wants to see him mounted for his private lesson."

"OK, I'll be there in a moment," Rosie said quickly. "Hello Mrs. Taylor," she called, hurrying over to Blackjack's stable. "I'll just get Blackjack's saddle. Tom's taking David's lesson this afternoon."

"Tom?" Mrs. Taylor looked surprised. "But where's Beth?" she asked, concerned.

"She's had an accident," said Rosie. "She was knocked off her horse by a car."

"Is she all right?" Mrs. Taylor asked.

"I'm afraid she's broken her leg," Rosie said. "And

it's going to take six weeks to mend."

"Oh dear." Mrs. Taylor was hesitant. "But is Tom capable of taking lessons?"

"Yes. He's an excellent rider, and it's only for today – some of Nick's friends are coming in to help tomorrow," Rosie said, silently praying that she wouldn't be struck down for lying. Well, it was only a little white lie. She was sure that when Tom got hold of Dick Bryant, he'd come round straight away.

Rosie gritted her teeth as she tightened Blackjack's girth. "Come on, breathe in," she said to the little black pony. "We'll be back to normal tomorrow," Rosie went on, leading the pony out of the stable.

"Hmm," Mrs. Taylor answered. "I suppose that's all right then – if it's only for today. And you did say that Tom is a good rider..."

"The best," Rosie interrupted.

"If Nick trusts him, I'm sure it will be all right. Come on, David," she called to her son.

Rosie helped the little boy into the saddle and circled the pony around the yard as Tom hurried over.

"Hi David," Tom called. "Are you ready?"

"Yes," the little boy answered, his eyes shining.

Rosie smiled as she watched them set off to the outdoor school for the lesson.

"I'll be back at three to pick David up," Mrs. Taylor called, getting back into her car.

"All right Mrs. Taylor," Rosie answered. Hurriedly she made her way back to Pepper's stable and, after tacking him up, led him out to join the rest of the riders who had gathered in the yard for the hack.

There was a girl from the year below her at school on Minstrel, a boy with dark hair riding Hector, a blonde girl she didn't recognize with Jester and Jess was on Storm Cloud.

"All ready?" Rosie asked the riders.

"Yes," said the blonde girl, lifting up the saddle flap to tighten the girth.

Excitedly the riders wound their way out of the yard. Jess headed the line and Rosie brought up the rear. The horses trotted down the drive and into the lane. Rosie felt the spring in Pepper's heels as they turned into the fields.

"OK. Let's have a canter," Jess called from the front. "All meet up by those trees," she pointed. Rosie waited for the other horses to set off and then, with a little nudge from her heels, she pushed Pepper on. She sat tight to the saddle. Racing forward as they headed for the trees, Rosie felt a rush of excitement run through her. There was nothing like riding to exhilarate her.

It was a wonderful hack. At the end of the hour, the ride wound its way along Sandy Lane. As they rode back into the yard, Rosie breathed a sigh of relief – so far so good.

"How was David's lesson, Tom?" Rosie called, as she led Pepper back into his stable.

"Brilliant," he answered, his eyes gleaming. "I really enjoyed teaching him. I never thought I'd have the patience."

Rosie couldn't help smiling. Anyone who had the patience to spend a whole summer training a horse the way Tom had Chancey, was bound to be a good teacher. Rosie looked fondly at her friend. As he turned away, Rosie crossed the yard to check the appointments book. Pepper wasn't needed again that afternoon so she determined to make an extra good job of grooming him.

"Meeting in the tack room at five," Jess called into Pepper's stable.

"OK." Rosie smiled contentedly. Everything seemed to be going so smoothly. She wondered if Tom had got hold of Dick Bryant yet. Hurrying to the tack room, Pepper's saddle slung over her arm, she joined the others.

"OK everyone," said Tom. "As you know, I've been trying to get hold of Dick Bryant all day and there's still no reply, so we'll have to make a group decision here. I personally think we should wait one more day. We can cope can't we?"

There were low murmurings and everyone exchanged uncertain glances.

"I know we agreed that if we still hadn't got hold of Dick Bryant this evening, we'd phone Nick and Sarah, but things have run smoothly enough haven't they?"

"Definitely," said Charlie. Slowly, the others all nodded in agreement.

"Good," said Tom. "Let's wait until tomorrow and if we haven't got hold of him then, we really will have to phone Nick and Sarah."

It had all been decided so quickly that Rosie hadn't even had time to feel worried about it. In fact, the thought of spending another day running Sandy Lane filled her with nervous excitement. Today had gone so well. Tomorrow could be even better. Whistling to herself, she hurried out of the tack room.

5

THE NEWCOMERS

Rosie got to the yard early the next day. It was a cold, crisp spring morning and the sun peered weakly through the clouds. All was peaceful at Sandy Lane.

"Morning, Storm Cloud," she called as the dappled grey pony looked inquisitively from her box.

Rosie smiled to herself as she propped up her bike and hurried over to the tack room. She groped around under the mat to find the key and unlocked the door. Taking the appointments book out of the drawer, she glanced at the rides. Three hacks and two lessons. She could get used to running Sandy Lane. She would be quite disappointed when they finally got hold of Dick Bryant. And then a wave of guilt ran through her as she thought of the lie she had told Mrs. Taylor yesterday – that they were expecting Dick Bryant the next day.

Thrusting these thoughts to the back of her mind,

she rummaged around in the desk drawer for the key to the cottage and crossed the yard. Nick and Sarah's black labrador, Ebony, almost knocked her over with excitement as she opened the back door.

"All right, all right," Rosie laughed. "You'll have your breakfast in a moment," she said. As she turned around, she looked out of the window and saw a tall, wiry man walking up the drive. She glanced at her watch. Seven thirty.

"Strange time to be booking a lesson, isn't it Ebony?" she said. "Well, he'll just have to wait."

Paws perched on the kitchen table, Ebony looked anxiously at his food. Rosie pulled the tin opener out of the drawer and quickly spooned the dog food into his bowl.

"Rather you than me," she said, wrinkling up her nose as Ebony bounded over to his bowl.

She looked out of the window again, and this time the man was stubbing a cigarette out in the yard, grinding his foot into the ground. She felt irritated. You should never smoke in a stables, not with all the hay and straw around. Everything could so easily go up in flames.

Silently, she observed the visitor. She didn't like the look of him. The muscles in his cheeks twitched and his eyes narrowed as he turned and surveyed the yard.

"Now what's he up to, Ebony?" She smiled down at the black labrador.

He seemed to be counting the loose boxes. What was he doing? thought Rosie. And where had he come from? He hadn't arrived by car and the first bus to Sandy Lane didn't arrive till eight.

Hurrying out of the cottage, she approached the stranger.

"Can I help you?" she asked politely. The man spun around, startled.

"Phew, you made me jump," he said, looking her up and down. "I'm here to help *you* actually," he continued, smiling slowly. "I'm a friend of Nick and Sarah's."

Rosie looked puzzled.

"Nick and Sarah Brooks? You do know them don't you?" the man went on, waiting for a response.

"Of course," said Rosie. "It's just that we weren't expecting anyone..."

"Well, Nick gave me a ring yesterday," the man said, not giving Rosie a chance to finish her sentence. "He told me about Beth's accident and asked me to come along and help out. I got here as quickly as I could."

"Oh," said Rosie, looking the man up and down.

Rosie realized she had been staring and was quick to collect her manners. "So, you must be Dick Bryant then," she said.

"Dick Bryant?" Now it was the man's turn to look puzzled.

"Yes, Nick left us your number. We've been trying to get hold of you for the last two days, but there's been no answer," Rosie said.

"Oh... Dick Bryant." The man let out a low, throaty laugh. "No, I'm Sam Durant. Sorry, we haven't been formally introduced." He held out his hand. "Pleased to meet you. No, Dick's away at the moment. That's why Nick asked me to come and help out."

Rosie scratched her head, trying to make sense of

it all. "So Nick knows about the accident then, does he?" she asked.

"Yes, apparently your stable girl phoned him," the man went on.

"Oh," said Rosie, anxiously. "Well, what did Nick say? Was he worried? Are they coming back?"

"Whoa, hang on a minute," Sam said, holding his hand in the air. "One question at a time. Of course Nick was worried, that's why he called Vanessa and me in to help."

"Vanessa?" Rosie questioned.

"Didn't I mention my wife, Vanessa?" he answered. "She'll be coming too. Nick said we could use the cottage until he and Sarah get back," he said.

"Oh." Rosie's brain was working overtime. "I see," she said. "So you're coming to *live* at Sandy Lane is that right?"

"That's about the sum of it," he went on.

"Well, I think you'd better wait and talk to Tom and the others then," she said quickly.

"Tom?" The man looked cross. Rosie didn't really know why she was being so stubborn. There was just something about him she didn't really like; something about his silky smooth way of talking.

"I'm sure there won't be a problem, but you'd better speak to them," Rosie went on.

"Of course there won't be a problem, my dear," the man went on. "It's all been sorted out, so there's nothing to talk about *is there*?"

He was still smiling as he held Rosie's gaze, but his words had a sinister ring to them. Rosie felt uneasy as he turned away again.

"Vanessa and I will be back at two o'clock to move

in and meet the others," he called over his shoulder.

And that seemed to be the end of it. Before Rosie could say another word, the man had turned on his heels and headed off down the drive.

"But wait!" she called desperately.

Rosie's words rang out hollowly and the man's departing frame didn't turn back to answer her call. She felt worried. It had all happened so quickly. She should have asked some more questions. She felt cross at herself, and at the awful man. Who did he think he was? Just wait till she told the others.

Rosie picked up a broom and started to sweep. The more she thought about it, the less she was able to find a real reason for disliking the man. She hated to admit it to herself, but perhaps she would have felt the same about anyone stepping in to take over the stables when they had been managing so well on their own. If Sam and his wife really were going to be running Sandy Lane, it wasn't a good idea to be on the wrong side of them. Rosie felt a little nervous at the thought of having to tell her friends what had been said. Still, she hadn't liked the man. There was just something about him...

Rosie was lost in thought when she was suddenly brought back to earth with a bump by the sound of excited voices in the yard. She peered over the stable door. Everyone had arrived. Stepping out of the box, she tried to attract their attention.

"Listen everyone. I've got something to tell you all," Rosie started nervously. She cleared her throat as her friends gathered round and she began to recount the story of the early morning events.

As Rosie finished, there was a disappointed silence

and then she was hit by a barrage of questions.

"What about Dick Bryant?"

"When are Sam and Vanessa arriving?"

"What did Nick say?"

"Were they worried?"

"When are they coming back?"

"I don't know," Rosie wailed foolishly. "I didn't manage to find all that out. All I know is that Sam's coming back at two."

"But what was he like?" Jess asked.

"Awful," Rosie said despondently.

"Why?" Tom asked. "Why was he so awful?"

"Well." Rosie was hesitant. "He just didn't look right somehow, that's all," she said, waving her hands in a flustered fashion. "I don't know. I just don't like the idea of strangers coming in and running Sandy Lane."

"Tell us the whole story again," said Tom.

So Rosie ran through the early morning events again... with a few embellishments. Then she looked round at her friends, expecting to see agreement in their faces.

"I really haven't explained things at all well, have I?" she said.

"Perhaps we should phone Nick and Sarah in America," Jess started.

"Look, I think it's only fair to give Sam and Vanessa a few days to settle in first," Tom interrupted. "I know I sound boring and grown-up, but it's a big thing running a stables. We don't want to do anything to muck it up for Nick and Sarah, do we? And if Nick has sent Sam in to help, well we can't just send him away saying Rosie doesn't like him."

"Tom's right, Rosie," said Jess. "Let's wait a while.

"Yes... maybe they are awful, but we ought to put up with them," Charlie said grudgingly.

"And let's try and get everything looking spick and span around the yard," Kate added, "after all, if they're going to be reporting back to Nick and Sarah, we want them to say we've done a good job."

"OK," Rosie said uncertainly. "You don't think I was over the top do you?" she asked Jess as they headed to the loose boxes. "A bit rude?"

"Of course not," said Jess, tying to reassure her friend. "We don't want Sam coming in here and thinking he can totally rearrange things, do we? Not now that things are going so well."

"No, we don't," said Rosie, encouraged by her friend's faith in her. "You're right," she went on. "Come on, let's get mucking out."

Jess and Rosie hurried off in different directions. By eight thirty, twelve horses had been mucked out, groomed and fed.

"When's the first lesson of the day?" Jess called, as she entered the tack room.

"Nine o'clock," Rosie answered. "Tom's taking a private lesson and you and I are taking out the hack."

"Good," said Jess. "I want to get out. I feel as though I've been mucking out all morning."

* * * * * * * * * * * * * * * *

Two o'clock came and went. By three, there was still no sign of Sam and Vanessa.

"Come on," said Tom. "It's no good sitting around tapping our fingers. The 3 o'clock hack's waiting to go out."

"OK," said Rosie.

It wasn't until a quarter past five that a white Range Rover pulled up in the yard. A motley assortment of Sandy Lane heads – horses and all – popped over the stable doors to see the new arrivals to the yard.

Sam Durant jumped out of the car, followed by a stylish woman in her early thirties. Clad in a beautiful pair of designer black jodhpurs, a glossy silk scarf wrapped around her neck, she peered out from behind a pair of dark sunglasses. Her long blonde hair was tied back in a sleek French plait.

"They're not how I imagined them, Rosie," Tom whispered, obviously impressed.

"Why? What did you expect?" Rosie muttered back.

"Something less smart I suppose."

Rosie felt embarrassed. "They hardly look very horsy though, do they?" she grumbled.

"I don't know," Jess interrupted. "Horsy people don't have to be scruffs. They look important."

Now the man was striding over to Tom and holding out his hand.

"I take it you must be Tom," he said grandly. "I've heard all about you from Nick... said you were quite the little rider. I'm Sam Durant. You may have heard of me from my days as an eventer," he said.

"Yes, yes," said Tom, blushing with pride at the words of praise from an obvious expert.

Rosie shrugged her shoulders. She had never heard the name Sam Durant before and felt quite ill at ease with what she was hearing. Tom actually seemed to have warmed to Sam, and now all of her friends had gathered round.

"And this is my wife, Vanessa," Sam continued, introducing the woman beside him.

Rosie looked on, silently watching, as her friends avidly introduced themselves. Rosie stood back from the group and frowned. She couldn't go back on what she had said about Sam now. She had to stick to her guns.

"OK," said Sam turning to the group. "You seem to have been managing things just fine here. How have you been going about it all?"

"We've each been responsible for looking after two horses and then we take turns in leading hacks," Tom explained. "And I've been taking over Beth's lessons for the last couple of days," he went on hesitantly. "I know I shouldn't have really but..."

"Perfect," Sam said. "We could continue in the same way then. We'll share taking lessons. You can do the ones in the morning and I'll do the ones in the afternoon."

Tom beamed. Rosie couldn't believe what she was hearing.

"But Tom, you're not really qualified to take lessons are you?" she whispered.

"Rosie," Tom hissed. "If Sam thinks I'm up to it then I'm up to it." He turned round to smile at Sam.

"Right... all settled?" Sam went on. "I'm happy with that."

"I bet you are," Rosie said under her breath. "All

the less work for you."

"Vanessa can book in the rides, that sort of thing,"
Sam said now. "I don't want it to look as though we're
completely taking over." He flashed them a smile.

"And what about our Tentenden training sessions?"
Jess asked anxiously.

"Are you entered for the Tentenden Team Chase?"
Sam asked.

"Yes," Jess said. "Nick has already picked us four
to represent Sandy Lane." She indicated herself, Tom,
Charlie and Rosie. "And we've set up a programme
of training sessions."

"Good. I'll take over those sessions then, if you
want me to," said Sam.

"That sounds great," Tom enthused.

"OK," Sam said, taking the keys to the cottage that
Tom was holding out. "That's all agreed then. We'll
be settling in if anyone wants us," he added. Vanessa
gave them a regal wave. She hadn't said a thing.

"Well, at least that's the back of them for today,"
Rosie muttered under her breath, as the couple slid
off to the cottage.

"Don't be like that Rosie," said Kate crossly. "Why
are you being so funny about them? They're nice."

"Hmm. A bit too nice," Rosie said gruffly.

"Look, I don't know why you've taken this instant
dislike to them," said Tom. "It sounds like they're not
going to bother us too much. They'll leave us to do
pretty much as we like and help with Tentenden too.
It's perfect."

"But there's something not quite right about them,"
Rosie mused.

"You've been reading too many detective stories,

Rosie," Tom teased. "We're going to have to start calling you the Sandy Lane Super Sleuth if you're not careful." Rosie looked hurt.

"I'm only joking," he said, giving her arm a little squeeze.

"I know," said Rosie, following the others into the tack room. "And I suppose I did make a mistake over Nick and Sarah closing down Sandy Lane too."

That was it. She was being silly. Things would be all right in the morning, she was sure of it. She mustn't be so quick to judge people. Everyone else had liked Sam and Vanessa.

Settling down on the floor, she picked up a piece of saddle soap, and set about cleaning the tack. An uncomfortable silence pervaded the room. She looked at her watch. Half past six, and she'd said she would be home at seven for supper. She'd have to leave in ten minutes. Rosie's thoughts were interrupted as the phone in the tack room started ringing and Tom got up to answer it. It was Beth's mother.

"Yes Mrs. Wilson," Tom was saying. "We're fine... no, we didn't get hold of Dick Bryant, but it's all right. Nick and Sarah have sent some friends in to run the stables – Sam and Vanessa Durant... yes they're great. Tell Beth to hurry up and get better. We'll be round to visit her soon... yes that's fine."

Rosie looked at her watch. She'd have to hurry. Getting up from the floor, she crossed the room to the door. Everyone was tuned into the telephone conversation, carefully listening to what Tom was saying.

"Bye everyone," she called forlornly. "I'm off home now." But no one answered her. Rosie shrugged her shoulders and slipped out of the doorway, heading over to her bicycle. For the first time ever, Rosie felt like an outsider at Sandy Lane. Sadly, she turned her bicycle out of the yard, taking one quick glance behind her at the tack room, now lit up by a yellow glow, the laughter spilling out into the night.

6

STANDARDS SLIP

In the excitement following the arrival of the newcomers to Sandy Lane, the forthcoming Tentenden Team Chase seemed to have been quite forgotten. The Sandy Lane regulars found themselves extremely busy. There was so much to do – so many hacks to organize, so many lessons to take, that they hardly had time to fit in any training. Four days had passed and Sam had only taken them out over the cross-country course once.

"Where's Sam?" Rosie called, hurrying over to Alex and Tom. "I've been banging on the door of the cottage all morning. I'm sure he's inside, but there's no answer."

"But that was part of the deal, wasn't it?" Tom returned quickly. "I take lessons in the morning, he takes lessons in the afternoon and we all help around the yard. He doesn't need to be around all the time."

Rosie raised her eyebrows.

"They don't seem to be helping much around the yard though, do they?" she said gruffly.

"Oh Rosie. You're not still going on about that are you?" Tom said crossly. "Come on. Give them a chance. And Sam's excellent over cross-country."

"He may be very experienced," Rosie said hesitantly. "But personally I don't think I'm learning a great deal. He's too busy congratulating himself most of the time. Anyway, it's the yard I'm worried about, not his riding skills," she continued. "The takings have been down for the last three days in a row and Vanessa's completely useless. It was better when we did the appointments book ourselves. Yesterday, there were *two* double bookings. Nick and Sarah never turn pupils away, especially not regulars like Melissa White. And Melissa said that she might even try out the Clarendon Equestrian Centre. It's the last thing Nick and Sarah need – having another stables' takings boosted because of us."

"It was a mistake, Rosie," Tom said tersely. "Accidents do happen. Melissa wouldn't really go to the Clarendon Equestrian Centre. It's only been open six months and it's already got a bad reputation. The horses look all right, but they're really badly schooled. And as for the owner, Ralph Winterson, he's never there anyway. He just leaves the stable girls to do everything."

"He's been had up for cruelty to horses before too, Rosie," Alex added. "And I heard a rumour going round that he had to close down his last stables for rapping. He only got away with it because it was his word against a little girl's. But no one doubted for a moment that he'd been lifting the poles to get her horse to jump higher."

"Whatever you say," Rosie said crossly. "But I do still need to see Sam... and now rather than next year. He needs to sign the Tentenden entry form," she went on. "If it doesn't go today it'll miss the closing date. I'm almost tempted to forge his signature."

Rosie wandered away, trying to look as if she didn't care. But deep down she did care. She minded very much what her friends thought of her. She would have to keep quiet from now on, even Jess had started telling her to give it a rest.

Rosie hurried into the tack room to finish off the entry form. Methodically, she filled in the gaps in her neat, sloping handwriting, chewing the end of her pen as she carefully read the form. It was only when Jess put her head around the door that she realized how long she had spent poring over it.

"Look Rosie," Jess cried excitedly. "A postcard from Nick and Sarah."

"Read it out then," said Rosie, taking the pen out of her mouth.

"Dear all," Jess started. "Arrived safely. Sarah's dad is on the road to recovery, so all is well. Hope Beth is working you hard for Tentenden. Very busy out here, but should still be back on the 20th as planned. Tell you more about it when we see you. Love Nick and Sarah."

"It looks like they must have sent it before Beth's accident," said Rosie, thinking aloud.

"I suppose so," Jess said, "I can't quite make out the postmark. I'll pin it to the notice board where the others can see it. Come on, Rosie," she added.

"Pepper's waiting for you. And Sam has said he'll take us all over the cross-country course."

"Cross-country?" Rosie said puzzled. "I didn't know we had training this morning. Is Sam up and about then?"

"Yes and waiting," Jess grinned. "And he says he'll take Kate and Alex too, not just the team for Tentenden."

"Oh," said Rosie, shrugging her shoulders. Jumping to her feet, she left the application form spread out on the desk in front of her. It could wait another hour. She followed Jess out of the tack room, just as Tom led Whispering Silver out of her stable.

"Where are you going with Whisp, Tom?" Rosie called out.

"Sam wants to try her over the cross-country," Tom answered quickly.

"What? But Nick doesn't let *anyone* ride Whisp over the course," said Rosie. "Not even him. Her legs aren't up to it, not if she takes a heavy rap. She's getting older now. Nick wants to be careful with her."

"Sam thinks it'll strengthen her legs if he gives her a good bit of exercise and he's going to jump her carefully, Rosie," Tom said shortly. "Why are you always questioning his judgement? He is here with Nick's approval you know. And I'm sure he knows better than any of us what her legs can and can't take. He's been riding for years."

Rosie shrugged her shoulders and turned away. Tom had well and truly put her in her place. She wanted to say something to Sam, to question his decision to ride Whispering Silver, but somehow she didn't feel she dare. Leading Pepper out to join the others, she shivered as a gust of wind blew across the yard.

"Is everyone here?" Sam asked, opening the gate to the fields at the back. Rosie followed on after the others in a daze.

"Everyone gather over by the big beech tree," Sam continued.

The horses trotted over to the tree and stopped in a group. Sam cantered over to join them.

"OK. Let's get going. And remember, speed is the key."

Rosie felt a nervous tremor run through her. She knew that speed was vital but it wasn't her greatest skill. Surely care and safety were as important too? She had never been intimidated by the cross-country course before, never doubted her own ability. But suddenly she felt unsure. Was it just a week and a half ago that she had stood so confidently in front of the jumps? Suddenly the tiger trap seemed to tower above her and the other fences loomed dangerously in the distance.

"I'll go round once to show you how it's done," Sam said brusquely, snapping Rosie out of her trance. "And then, when I'm back, I'll watch you one by one. OK? And by the way everyone, I'm not sure about the choice for the Tentenden team," he laughed, looking at Rosie. "So convince me with your riding."

Rosie gulped. Sam couldn't alter the team now, could he? She looked around at the animated faces of her friends. None of them seemed worried by Sam's remarks. She opened her mouth to protest, and closed it again. Digging her nails into her hands to stop the tears, she turned to Jess.

"Did you hear what Sam said? He wants me out of

the team."

"Don't be silly, Rosie," said Jess laughing. "It wasn't aimed at you. I'm sure Sam wouldn't alter the team now... not after all the training we've put in. It's just his way of keeping us on our toes."

"I hope you're right," Rosie said despondently. She didn't know what to think. Maybe she was overreacting but it certainly hadn't seemed that way to her. She felt faint as she turned to look at the course.

Staring into the distance, Rosie watched Sam turn Whispering Silver towards the first fence with a crack from his whip. The horse stumbled and hurtled towards the tiger trap at breakneck speed as Sam crouched low onto her neck, his legs tucked neatly beneath him. They careered over the jump and, as they landed, Sam pushed her on. Faster and faster Whisp raced. Rosie hardly dared watch as the horse was spurred forward. Whisp responded bravely and battled her way over the next jump and then they went out of sight and into the woods.

"Wow. They're going fast," Jess cried, her eyes glinting brightly. "Are you all right there, Rosie?" she asked turning in the saddle and seeing her friend's white face.

"Yes," Rosie breathed.

But Rosie felt sick. She wasn't impressed. She knew Sam was asking too much of Whisp. Nervously she bit her lip, training her eyes on the outline of horse and rider. Nick would die if anything happened to that horse. Rosie dreaded to think what was going on.

"Here they are now," Tom cried, as the pair of them emerged from the trees and headed for the next jump. Horse and rider skimmed over the fence and plunged into the water. But Whisp was sinking, her legs thrashing about under her as she tried to gather momentum. Tired, she staggered up the bank.

Rosie held her breath as they rode over the zigzag rails and then the gate, onto the stone wall. The ground fell away as horse and rider galloped up the hill and neared the group. Rosie grimaced. Whispering Silver was in a lather, her body was bathed in sweat as she quivered in the wind. Sam's jodhpurs, clean on that morning, were splattered with mud.

"That was fast, Sam. It looked amazing," Tom gasped.

"It was," Sam said nonchalantly. "Now you try. I must say, I did have a bit of trouble in the woods. I think the old horse was tiring, took a bit of a rap."

Rosie trembled. Her heart felt heavy as she looked down at Whispering Silver's delicate legs. Sam's words echoed in her head as Tom galloped Chancey to the first fence and Sam clicked his stopwatch.

Rosie had never seen them go so fast. They were out of control. And she knew Chancey wasn't fit enough for it. It could strain his heart. But Tom must know what he was doing – Chancey was his horse after all. Thundering over the tiger trap, they raced to the brush hurdle. Rosie could hear the sound of hooves pulsating in her ears, the sound of metal shoes striking timber as the jumps were cleared in easy succession. Chancey hardly seemed to touch the ground as he came out of the woods and approached the water jump. But no sooner was he over it and out of the water, than Tom was pressing him on to the zigzag rails. Chancey tore over them, straining at the bit as he surged on to the low gate.

Sam clicked his stop watch as they cleared the stone wall.

"Good." He beamed as Tom returned to the group.

Good! Rosie couldn't believe her ears. It had been bordering on dangerous. And, as she had volunteered to go last, she would have to watch another four of her friends ride madly around the course before it was even her turn.

She turned Pepper away from the group, trying to keep her cool. She tried to relax as she loosened him up, but all she could hear were the words 'speed, speed, speed,' ringing in her ears. She knew she wasn't going to have a good round... knew that by going fast, she would jeopardize her style. She couldn't bring herself to watch the others. When eventually it was her turn to ride the course, she had no idea how they had done. She circled Pepper, waiting for Sam to indicate that she should start, watching him for a flicker of movement. Then Sam nodded his head and she nudged the little pony forward. She turned him to the start and pushed him on into a canter.

"Faster."

Rosie heard the roar from behind her and tried to lengthen Pepper's stride. Pepper tried to put in an extra stride as he headed for the tiger trap and stumbled over the fence. Rosie knew she had completely misdirected the little pony. Her arms and legs were all over the place as she tugged at Pepper's reins in an effort to slow him down. Hurtling over the brush hurdle, they bounded on to the hayrack.

Pepper was excited now and he snorted impatiently. Rolling his eyes, enthralled by the speed, he surged ahead and for the next two jumps, Rosie found herself hanging behind. They thundered into the woods.

Rosie felt the panic rising in her throat as the low-hanging branches brushed against her clothes. She was slipping in the saddle. She didn't know how she managed to stay on over the tyres. And when the little pony checked himself at the water jump, Rosie almost flew over his head. Splashing on through the water, Rosie lost a stirrup. Desperately trying to regain her seat, she found herself completely off-balance for the next two fences and was shaking when she joined the rest of the group. It had been a terrible round.

"Not bad," said Sam, clicking his stop watch.

Rosie stopped for a minute to catch her breath. Her heart was pounding and her arms ached. She had been frightened, actually frightened. Everyone must have seen that.

"Good pace, Rosie," said Jess. "If we all go that speed at Tentenden, we'll be in with a real chance."

Rosie didn't know what to say to her friend. She turned away, disgusted with herself. Hadn't Jess seen how badly she had ridden? Nothing had been said about her place on the team and her time was still the third fastest. But she didn't feel happy with the way she had ridden.

Turning back to the yard, Rosie led Pepper back into his stable. She tied him to the ring and closed the door behind her. Relieved to be alone at last, she untacked the pony.

"I won't let Sam spoil Tentenden for us, Pepper," she whispered to the little horse. As soon as she'd finished sponging him down, she went to complete the Tentenden application.

Adding the last finishing touches to the form, Rosie

fished out a stamp from her pocket and attached it to the envelope. Then she hurried to find Sam. Knocking at the door of the cottage, she waited patiently.

"Sam," Rosie said hesitantly as he answered the door. "I've got the entry form for Tentenden here. Do you think you could sign it before I post it? It should really go off today to make sure it gets there for Friday."

"Just leave it there Rosie. I'll sign it and send it myself," Sam said.

But he wouldn't meet her eyes and Rosie felt uneasy. Sam hadn't said anything more about a change of team, but Rosie didn't trust him an inch. Would he actually leave her name on the form, or would he substitute someone else's? She hesitated. She couldn't bring herself to ask him. She just wasn't sure she wanted to hear the answer.

7

FROM BAD TO WORSE

Sleep didn't come easily to Rosie that night and when it did, it was disturbed by dreams... dreams of horses falling at open ditches and thrashing about in icy water. Tossing and turning, she woke in a cold sweat. She looked at her watch. Six o'clock. There wasn't any point in trying to get back to sleep, she'd have to be up in half an hour anyway.

Drawing back the curtains, she looked out of the window and sighed. It was just getting light and an eerie mist hung over the fields. Rosie felt uneasy as she remembered yesterday's events. Sam really shouldn't have given Whisp such a hard ride. She hoped the horse would be all right. As for her riding, it had been appalling.

Reaching to her bedside chair, she grabbed her clothes and pulled them under her duvet. They were cold to the touch as she struggled to put them on.

On the count of three, Rosie threw back the covers and jumped out of bed. Picking up her waterproof jacket, she tiptoed down the stairs and grabbed a piece of bread from the kitchen before making her way outside to her bike. The air felt heavy with rain. All was still and silent as she cycled to Sandy Lane. She passed no one on the empty country roads.

Turning into the drive, she rode into the yard and hopped off her bike, propping it up against the water trough as she walked over to Whisp's stable.

At first Rosie couldn't see anything when she looked over the door, but once her eyes had grown accustomed to the dark, she could see the shape of the horse lying down on the floor. Whisp looked up and struggled to her feet. Rosie grimaced as she realized that the horse's back offside leg was swollen. Whisp's head hung low and she teetered painfully on three legs.

"Damn you, Sam," Rosie muttered through gritted teeth.

Drawing back the bolt on the door, she entered the box, talking sweetly to the horse all the time.

"It's OK Whisp. You're going to be all right, poor old lady," she crooned. Whisp turned her face towards her and snickered softly. Swiftly, Rosie ran her hand down the horse's leg and felt the heat.

"I think we'll have to have the vet called out for you," she said, fondly patting the grey neck.

Rosie hurried over to the tack room and dialled the vet's number. When he heard what was wrong, he promised to come straight away. For the moment, there was nothing more Rosie could do, so she waited anxiously by the gate.

Soon the others arrived at Sandy Lane. Rosie was

gloomy as she told them what had happened.

"Oh," said Tom sheepishly. "Poor Whisp. Sam did take her round pretty fast. I suppose we'd better cancel her rides."

Rosie headed off to check the bookings. Slipping into the tack room, she opened up the appointments book. That was strange – today's page seemed to have been torn out. Rosie flicked through the book. Even stranger – all the other days were there, but today's was clearly missing.

"Tom," she called. "Tom, do you know anything about this?"

Tom hurried into the tack room as Rosie held up the book with the ripped page.

"Where can it have gone?" he puzzled. "Who can have taken that page? It's our only record of who's riding who. How will we ever work it out? Can you remember?"

"Not really. I know that Melissa White's on Pepper at some time but that's about it. Vanessa's the only person who might know," she said.

"What might I know?" a voice called.

Rosie saw Vanessa leaning in the doorway of the tack room.

"Something about this?" Tom held up the diary. "Today's page is missing. It's been torn out."

"Maybe someone tore it out by mistake," she said, looking away rather too quickly.

"Well, we need to try and work out the bookings pretty fast," Rosie said frostily, "or we won't be ready for the day."

"Let me see then," said Vanessa. "I might be able to remember. Give me ten minutes. I'll sit down and try to put a list together. Yes, I think I'll be able to do it."

"Great," said Tom. "And that must be the vet now," he said as a car pulled up in the yard.

"The vet? What's going on?" Vanessa asked.

"Don't you know Whisp is ill?" Rosie bridled, angrily striding off to meet the vet before Vanessa had a chance to answer. Tom hurried over to join her.

"Where's the patient then?" the vet asked in a friendly voice.

"In here," said Tom, drawing back the bolt to Whisp's box.

The two friends poked their heads anxiously over the stable door as the vet looked at Whisp's leg.

"Poor old lady. She's taken a bit of a knock. There's a small cut above the fetlock. It's nothing serious, but she must rest." He patted her neck. "I'll bandage it up," he said, setting to work. "And I'll leave you some gamgee bandages to keep it clean. Make sure she isn't ridden," he said. And, as quickly as he had arrived, the vet put his car into reverse and backed out of the drive.

"Here we are," said Vanessa stepping out of the tack room and waving a piece of paper. "All sorted out?"

"As sorted out as it can be for the moment anyway. Whisp is lame and she can't be ridden – another cost the stable could have done without," Rosie muttered. "But apart from that, things are just fine," she said sarcastically.

Vanessa smiled, seemingly ignoring Rosie's words. "Well, I've put a list together," she went on. "It's all hacks today and no lessons, so you should be all right."

"*We* should be all right?" Tom asked questioningly.

"Didn't Sam tell you he was away today? He's got things to sort out. And I'm off shopping," said Vanessa. "I can trust you two to look after the yard though, can't I?"

"Sure," Tom sighed, giving the list a cursory glance before handing it on to Rosie. Rosie glanced down the names. It was a lot of work. She shrugged her shoulders. Storm Cloud, Feather, Napoleon and Minstrel had to be ready in a quarter of an hour for the ten o'clock hack for experienced riders.

"Are you listening everyone?" Rosie called as Vanessa drove out of the yard. "We haven't got much time – fifteen minutes to get four horses ready – so let's make it snappy."

By two minutes to ten, the four horses were tacked up and waiting, eager and ready for the hack.

Ten o'clock came and no one arrived. They waited and waited. After all, people were sometimes late. But by ten thirty there was still no sign of anyone. Rosie was fuming.

At eleven o'clock the riders eventually turned up for their hack. Rosie's heart sank when she saw them. They were all novices, and none of the ponies waiting were novice mounts.

"Is Blackjack ready?" Mrs. Taylor asked, surprised to see Jess lead Storm Cloud out from her stable for David to ride.

"Er, I'm afraid we're a little behind this morning," said Rosie, playing for time. "We had a bit of an accident. Whisp's lame and there seems to be a bit of a mix-up with mounts."

"Not another double booking!" Mrs. Taylor groaned. "This is getting ridiculous. Where's Sam this morning? Does he know how often this keeps on happening?"

"I should think so, he is to blame for it,' Rosie muttered through gritted teeth. She turned back to Mrs. Taylor.

"If you could give us another five minutes," she said, smiling sweetly. "We're almost there."

The regulars converged in the tack room and quickly decided what to do. Breathlessly, Jess led the unwanted ponies back to their stables while the others hurried to get the novice mounts ready.

Rosie hurried off to Blackjack's stable. There wasn't enough time to give him a thorough grooming, a quick going-over would have to do. Dashing to collect his saddle, she was puzzled to find it wasn't in its correct place.

"Tom, have you seen Blackjack's saddle?" she called across the yard.

"No," said Tom, swooping into the tack room and picking up Horace's tack.

"Jess, am I being stupid or something?" Rosie said turning to her friend. "I can't find Blackjack's saddle anywhere. It's not on his peg."

The two friends hunted high and low, but it was nowhere to be found.

"What are we going to do?" said Rosie. "We can't put Blackjack in another saddle. It'll rub him raw with his hollow back. That saddle was made especially for him. It cost a fortune. Nick will go spare if it's lost."

"It's got to be here somewhere," said Jess. "A saddle can't get mislaid!"

"Come on you two. What are you up to?" Tom called into the tack room.

"Blackjack's saddle has disappeared," Jess cried.

"It can't have done," Tom said. "It was there yesterday. It can't have vanished."

"Well it has," said Rosie. "David will have to ride Horace. Who's going to be the one to break the news to his mother?"

"I will," Tom groaned, when no one answered.

Swiftly crossing the yard, he tried to explain things.

"I'm really sorry, Mrs. Taylor, but I'm afraid that Blackjack's saddle has gone missing. If David wouldn't mind riding Horace."

"Where's Blackjack?" the little boy wailed. "I always ride Blackjack. Where is he?" he cried. "I want to ride Blackjack!"

"I'm sorry," his mother apologized. "But David only has one riding lesson a week and he looks forward to it so much. He adores that pony."

"I do understand," said Tom sympathetically, as Mrs. Taylor led David to the car. Tom was glad when they were gone. David's mother had been very understanding, but Tom knew it was terribly unprofessional. She had every right to complain.

Things got no better as the day progressed. Vanessa's list turned out to be worse than no list at all. There were mix-ups everywhere. Pupils booked in for private lessons were down for hacks, horses had been double-booked, rides had been mysteriously cancelled. The day ended up a catalogue of disasters. As the last hack drew to a close and the horses were bolted into their stables with their evening feeds, Rosie breathed a sigh of relief. She hoped she would never have another day like it.

Despondently, the Sandy Lane friends met in the

tack room. They still hadn't found Blackjack's saddle. If it didn't turn up by the morning, they'd have to order another one. They couldn't have him missing lessons.

They counted their takings, which were lower than usual for the third day in a row. Rosie didn't like to voice her doubts but the sooner Nick and Sarah got back the better, as far as she was concerned.

* * * * * * * * * * * * * * * * *

Three days had passed since the dreadful ride over the cross-country before Rosie finally plucked up courage to call the Tentenden office. She wanted to find out which riders Sam had actually entered on the team. He couldn't drop her now, could he? Phoning from the tack room, she felt strangely nervous.

"Hello... yes... er... I wonder if you can help me," she said nervously, as she slotted her money into the pay phone.

"I hope so," a voice answered.

Rosie swallowed hard. "I just wanted to check the names on the entry form for Sandy Lane Stables."

"Sure, hang on a minute," the voice at the other end answered.

Rosie waited patiently, shifting her weight from one foot to the other. The phone was eating her change. It seemed ages before the voice returned.

"What was the name again?" asked the voice.

"Sandy Lane." Rosie took a deep breath.

"I'm afraid I don't seem to have an entry for that name."

"What?" Rosie gulped. "Are you quite sure?"

"Positive," the voice answered quickly. "There's nothing here under Sandy Lane. I've gone through them all."

"But the form was posted three days ago. It should be with you by now."

"Well I don't have it."

"But what can we do?" Rosie said quietly.

"There's not a lot you can do," the voice answered sympathetically. "I'm sorry, but I'm afraid it's too late to send in another one. You'll just have to apply earlier next year."

As Rosie put the phone down, her head was swimming. She had to sit down for a few moments for it all to sink in. What had happened? Was it lost in the post? Or... a dreadful thought dawned on Rosie. Maybe Sam hadn't posted it after all.

Disappointment turned to rage. What had he done with it? No Tentenden Team Chase for any of them this year! Well, Sam couldn't wriggle out of this one that easily.

Rushing out of the tack room, she called all of her friends over.

"You're never going to believe this," she spluttered. "Who do you think I've just phoned?"

Everyone looked blankly at her.

"The Tentenden Office, that's who. And they've no record of our entry," Rosie shouted. "They say they've never received it," she said triumphantly. "And now we can't enter. It's too late."

"What?" Tom jumped to his feet. "There must be

some kind of mistake."

"The only mistake was letting Sam post the entry form for us!" Rosie snapped.

"I think we'd better go and find Sam," Tom said getting up quietly. "See what he has to say. Come on everyone."

The team trooped out of the tack room and hurried over to the cottage. Four faces waited for Sam to appear as Tom knocked on the back door.

"Hello, well it's the whole team," Sam said, smiling as he came to the door. "What do you want?"

Rosie stepped to the front of her friends and, before Tom could stop her, the words had spilled out in full torrent.

"You never sent it did you?" she shouted angrily. "The Tentenden form... they've never received it. All you had to do was post it. I'm going to phone Nick," she yelled, her voice getting louder and louder.

"Now, hold on a minute, Rosie," said Sam. "What are you talking about? Of course I posted the form," he said smoothly. "Do you mean to say they haven't received it? Look I'll give them a ring now and clear things up," he said in a charming voice. "I'll be with you in a minute."

"Rosie, what do you think you're playing at?" Tom said angrily, as Sam walked back into the cottage. "You can't go round making accusations till we find out more. You must calm down."

Rosie didn't answer him.

Impatiently, everyone stood around waiting until, moments later, Sam appeared.

"It seems Rosie's right," he said. "They never received the form. It must have got lost in the post. I explained the situation and said how hard we'd all been working, but they've already sorted out starting times. They just wouldn't listen. I'm sorry. I thought I'd be able to pull a few strings."

Rosie's face was black as thunder as she listened to Sam's words. Before he had a chance to finish, she had turned on her heels and was striding off towards Pepper's stable. Tom hurried to catch her up.

"*Lost in the post* – what rubbish," she muttered, angrily. "All he had to do was put it in a post box and he couldn't even manage that."

"Look Rosie, we're all disappointed," Tom said, grabbing her arm. "But I'm sure Sam wouldn't say he'd posted the form if he hadn't."

"Why not?" Rosie shrugged Tom off angrily. "How do we know what lies he's been telling to cover his mistakes. They're useless... so inefficient. We've got to phone Nick and Sarah and tell them what a mess things are in here. School starts on Monday – Sam and Vanessa won't even have us to help them then. Nick and Sarah might not even have a Sandy Lane to come back to if we leave it any longer!"

"Oh come on," said Tom, trying to get her to listen to him as she stomped across the gravel. "Aren't you just being a little over-dramatic?"

"No," said Rosie determinedly. "I don't care what you say. My mind's made up. I'm phoning them. *You* may not care, but I'd set my heart on Tentenden."

"We'd all set our hearts on Tentenden, Rosie, but if we're not entered, there's nothing we can do about it," Tom snapped. "I'm going to be setting off for home in a minute. Have you nearly finished here?"

"Yes," Rosie said, her jaw jutting out defiantly. "I'll

just go round the yard once more and then I'll be off too. See you tomorrow Tom."

"See you tomorrow," he answered, shrugging his shoulders as he walked over to his bike.

All was quiet as Tom cycled out of the yard. Rosie felt a shiver run down her spine. It was creepy at the stables when there was no one else about. Shadows lurked everywhere. She must get Nick and Sarah's phone number from the notice board before she went home. Groping along the wall in the inky blackness of the tack room, she fumbled for the light switch.

It was very dark. Something brushed against her legs. She screamed as she flicked on the light switch to find Ebony looking up at her reproachfully.

"Silly dog," she said breathing a sigh of relief. "I thought you were someone else."

Leaning across to the notice board, she scrabbled around for the scrap of paper... taxi cards, old farriers' bills, a raffle ticket. It must be here somewhere. She'd seen it only yesterday. Pulling aside each of the pieces of paper, she started to panic. Where was it? She checked the floor, the desk, the appointments book. Her heart skipped a beat. It wasn't there. It had gone. There was no doubting it, Nick and Sarah's number had disappeared. It had vanished into thin air!

8

STARTLING NEWS

Rosie's head was still reeling from shock when she got home that evening. Someone must have removed that piece of paper. Someone who didn't want her phoning Nick and Sarah and telling them about all the mishaps at Sandy Lane. And Rosie could only think of one person who that might be... Sam!

She wanted to phone Tom immediately and tell him about the missing number but she couldn't bring herself to pick up the receiver – not when he already thought she was overreacting anyway. What could she do? Rosie thought carefully. There was only one other person who might know the number... Beth. After all, Beth had phoned Nick and Sarah after her accident.

Rosie made a mental note to ring her for the number in the morning. Rosie started to feel a whole lot better once she had made up her mind what to do. All right, so they had decided not to bother Nick and Sarah. But this was different. Sandy Lane was going downhill, and if she didn't do something about it, no one else would. It was only as Rosie undressed for bed that she realized how tired she was. She had been working so hard at the stables, that she had no difficulty in falling asleep that night.

When she awoke the next morning and looked at her bedside clock, she realized she had been asleep for ages. It was half past eight. *Half past eight*. She'd slept for ten solid hours. All thoughts of phoning Beth flew out of her mind as she hurried to get to the stables.

"Mum, Mum," she cried. "I'm late. Could you give me a lift to the stables? Please? Just this once?"

"I gave you a lift last week, Rosie," Mrs. Edwards groaned. "I don't want to make a habit of it... OK then," she sighed, seeing Rosie's despondent face. "Grab your things. I've got to go into Colcott anyway. I'll drop you there on the way."

Rosie waited patiently by the door, willing her mother to hurry up. At last Mrs. Edwards was ready. Rosie felt subdued as she did up her seat belt and gazed out of the window at the passing traffic. Her mother seemed to realize she didn't want to talk, and the journey passed silently.

"Thanks Mum." Rosie smiled weakly as she jumped out of the car at the bottom of Sandy Lane and walked up the drive. As she reached the corner of the yard, she was surprised to see everyone gathered in a group around Sam who was reading aloud from a piece of paper. Rosie just caught the end of what he was saying and the words froze her to the spot.

"...so please go ahead and sell Pepper for me."

Rosie approached the group.

"What's going on?" she said frostily, her heart beating faster as she saw Kate's tear-stained face.

"Rosie. It's too awful for words," Kate burst out.

"Nick's selling Pepper. Sam got the letter this morning. Sandy Lane desperately needs the money and someone's offered a good price for him," Kate wailed.

"What!" Rosie cried. She heard the words screaming in her head – *But he can't, he wouldn't, not Pepper.* Instead, she found herself answering in a calm and reasonable manner.

"That can't be right. Nick would never sell Pepper," she said. "He was one of their first ponies."

"It's true, Rosie," said Tom. "They have to. Nick and Sarah need the money. I can't quite believe it myself but..."

"But Nick doesn't care about money," Rosie interrupted coldly.

"No," said Tom softly, handing her the letter. "Not normally, but Sandy Lane hasn't been doing too well lately and there are vet's bills and fodder bills to pay and then there's all the extra expenses like the flight tickets. Not forgetting that Blackjack's saddle alone is going to cost two weeks' earnings. It's all there in the letter."

"When's he going then?" Rosie asked woodenly.

"Next Friday," Sam interrupted.

"Next Friday." Rosie repeated the words quietly. "But that's so soon."

Rosie turned away clutching the letter. She felt a lump rising in her throat, almost choking her. Nick had tried to justify his reasons, explained about the endless bills, the reduced takings, Blackjack's saddle.

The list went on and on. It was all very fair, but as Rosie read it over and over, the words seemed to get fainter and fainter. It all seemed so unreal.

"Well, work as usual," Tom said. "Try not to think about it everyone."

But as Rosie made her way over to Pepper's stable, she knew she couldn't possibly not think about it. No more Pepper...

"It seems you're off next week Pepper," she said, opening the door to his stable. "I know that you'll miss Sandy Lane, but you'll have a new owner who'll love you enormously, and your very own paddock and orchards full of apples to look out onto and... and..." The words choked in Rosie's throat and her lips quivered as she fought back the tears. She had to stop herself. Anyone would think Pepper was her own pony the way she was acting.

"I'm going to give you a good grooming, let everyone see how beautiful you are. Come on."

Rosie tried to put it out of her mind and, picking up a body brush, she began to make a start on Pepper's coat. Taking the worst of the dirt off with her dandy brush, she brushed him until he shone.

Putting on a brave face, she led him out of his stable.

"All ready for our hack, Rosie?" Jess called out.

"Yes, Jess," Rosie answered, despondently. "Who's taking it out?" she asked.

"Sam," Jess answered.

"Great," Rosie muttered under her breath. "Just the person I was trying to get away from." She shrugged her shoulders. "Oh well."

"Do you need any help?" she called to Susannah, the little girl struggling with Horace.

"No, I think I can manage," Susannah answered. "I tacked him up myself," she added proudly as she led the pony to the mounting block and scrambled on. Rosie smiled absently.

"All ready?" Sam called impatiently as Hector pawed the ground.

Rosie followed on at the back as Sam led the ride out through the gate into the fields. Pepper sniffed the air excitedly.

"OK Susannah?" she called to the little girl ahead of her.

"Fine," Susannah answered, bumping along on Horace as they trotted through the fields.

"Let's start with a canter," said Sam, turning round to face the group. "All meet up by the corner of that field," he pointed.

Rosie looked uncertainly at Susannah. She had thought it was supposed to be a gentle, leisurely hack.

"Are you OK for a canter Susannah?" Rosie asked.

"Yes," she cried. "Lovely."

"Well follow on after the others then," Rosie said. "I'll go last."

Susannah circled Horace and nudged him on with her heels.

"You'll have to give him a bit of a kick. Wake him up," Rosie shouted. Horace was liable to be a little sluggish if he wasn't pushed. Rosie had found that out the hard way. She'd learnt to ride on him herself and many times she had found herself defending him until she had been forced to admit that perhaps he was a little lazy.

Pepper was a much more responsive ride. He didn't even hesitate as Rosie asked him to canter. Rosie's eyes watered as the wind bit into her face. The horses ahead of her were a blur. Susannah looked as though she was sitting at an angle as they raced on.

Rosie gasped. Susannah *was* sitting at an angle – Horace's saddle was coming off! As Susannah slipped down his side, she clung onto his mane for dear life.

"Help, please help!" Susannah wailed pitifully.

Rosie didn't stop to think. All she knew was that they had to be stopped. Digging her heels into Pepper's side she pushed him forward, urging him on and on. The sweat rose on Pepper's neck as she pounded forward until they were neck and neck with the cantering horse. Leaning perilously out of the saddle, Rosie grabbed Horace's reins and they swerved to the right. It was too late. As Horace slowed to a trot, Susannah bounced to the ground in bumps. Rosie swung the pony round, drawing him to a halt as she made her way over to where Susannah was slowly scrambling to her feet. Unaware of the disturbance, Sam and the others had cantered on.

"Are you OK?" Rosie called.

"Yes Rosie," Susannah said weakly. "I'm all right really," she said bravely.

Rosie jumped off Pepper and walked over to the little girl. She was shaking from head to foot.

"You're not all right are you?" Rosie said stroking her shoulder. "You're a bit shaken aren't you?"

"A little," Susannah trembled.

"Try stretching your limbs. Do you hurt anywhere?" Rosie asked.

"No, I don't think so."

Rosie breathed a sigh of relief. No broken bones this time.

"Did you do the girth up properly?" she asked gently.

"Yes I did. I definitely did," Susannah protested. "I double checked it too. It was really tight. I don't know how it could have come undone."

"Don't worry," Rosie said, seeing Susannah's distress. She didn't want to press her. This was the sort of thing that could destroy someone's nerve and she was such a promising little rider.

"We'll collect the saddle and you can hop back on," Rosie said calmly. "We'll go to the yard, but we ought to wait for the others to turn back or they'll worry. There they are now."

In no time at all, Sam had thundered over to join the two of them.

"What on earth is going on?" he cried, seeing Rosie holding Horace's reins.

"The saddle came off, Sam," Rosie called.

"The saddle? You stupid girl," Sam shouted, turning to Susannah. "You can't have done the girth up properly, can you? I might have known you wouldn't be able to manage something on your own."

Rosie winced at his harsh words.

"I'm s-s-orry, Sam," Susannah whimpered. "I was so sure I had."

Rosie was furious. A reprimand was the last thing the little girl needed.

"Come on Susannah. I'll go back to the stables with you," she said, giving Sam a filthy look.

"Did you have to do that?" she said to Sam as Susannah turned away. "She took a heavy enough tumble as it was."

"I won't tolerate you talking to me like that, Rosie,"

Sam said in a harsh whisper. "She has to learn. Take her back to the yard and get her cleaned up. We don't want her mother seeing her like that. And I'll see *you* later." Without another word, he turned Hector in the direction they had just come from. "Come on everyone," he barked.

Jess looked embarrassed as she turned Minstrel to join the others. "Rosie, are you happy to go back with Susannah?" she asked her friend.

"I'll be fine," said Rosie. "You go on ahead. We'll manage. The ride's been spoiled for me anyway."

Jess smiled apologetically and turned to catch up with the others.

"Come on Susannah. Don't listen to that awful man," Rosie said, turning to the little girl. "When I had just started learning to ride, I put the saddle on the wrong way round, imagine that." It wasn't true, but at least it brought a smile to Susannah's face as they walked off in the direction of the saddle.

"There it is." Rosie pointed to where the saddle had landed. "Can you go and get it while I hold onto Horace and Pepper?"

"Sure." Susannah rushed over and picked it up as Rosie gazed into the distance. She could just see Minstrel's hindquarters as the last of the horses entered Larkfield Copse.

"Rosie, Rosie, quickly, come here."

Rosie's thoughts were disturbed by Susannah's pitiful cry.

"Look," Susannah cried, excitedly. "I knew it wasn't my fault. I knew I'd done it up properly. Look what I just found under the saddle flap."

Rosie looked at what Susannah was showing her

and gasped. The girth had snapped in two.

"It must have been a rotten girth if it broke this easily," Susannah was saying. "They're dangerous."

"You're right," said Rosie, edging over to where Susannah was standing. "Can I just take a look at that?"

"Of course," said Susannah.

"Well, we can't ride back to the yard now," said Rosie, looking at the girth. "If you can hold the saddle in place on Horace's back, I'll lead the horses back."

"OK Rosie." The little girl chattered away, seemingly having forgotten her fall.

"Now, do you think you could groom Horace when we get back?" Rosie asked as they walked along.

"Of course I can," Susannah grinned.

Rosie smiled at her enthusiasm and, as they reached the last field, she opened the gate to let them through.

"If you could lead these two back to their stables, I'll take the saddle," Rosie said quickly.

"OK," said Susannah.

Rosie took the saddle and hurried into the tack room. Once alone, she closed the door and examined the girth properly. It was as she thought, although she hadn't liked to admit it in front of Susannah. Girths didn't just snap in two. This one had been cut... and very deliberately cut. It must have been hanging by a thread when Susannah tacked up. But who could have done it? Rosie felt the hairs rising on the back of her neck. Her tummy was tying itself in knots.

Thoughts jostled around in her mind as she crossed the yard. She couldn't believe how many things had gone wrong in the couple of weeks that Nick and Sarah had been gone. She needed time to think. But time was the one thing she didn't have at the moment. There was something niggling her, right at the back of her mind. Something that held the key to it all. Something to do with the letter. But what was it?

And then it came to her, as clear as crystal. Rosie stopped in her tracks. Why hadn't any of them thought of it before? She could save Pepper yet. She smiled to herself. She had to speak to Beth.

"Hey, what are you doing back so early?" Alex called, appearing from Hector's box.

"Susannah took a tumble. Do you think you could see to her?" Rosie said, speeding off down the drive.

"Sure," said Alex. "But where are you going?"

"I'll tell you when I get back," Rosie said mysteriously. " Just tell Sam that I've gone home for lunch. Cover for me if you can."

"OK," Alex said and, before he could stop her, Rosie had done a quick about turn.

"Rosie." Alex's voice rang out hollowly.

But Rosie didn't reply. She didn't want to tell Alex what she was doing. She didn't want to tell him where she was going. This was something she wanted to do by herself... something she had to do alone.

9

A CHILLING DISCOVERY

Rosie's tummy rumbled as she jogged up the drive to Beth's house. It was the first time she had felt hungry in days. It must be a good sign.

Rosie gulped as she stood on the doorstep. It was vital that she explain everything properly and she wasn't sure she knew where to begin.

"Double bookings, reduced takings, Whisp's lameness, the missing saddle, the Tentenden entry form, the letter, the severed girth." Rosie said it all aloud, counting the points off on her fingers. It was all there. There was only one thing she couldn't explain – the reason why.

Beth would know what they should do, how to go about things. Rosie took a deep breath and reached out for the brass door knocker, rapping it hard against the old oak door. Clank!

Rosie waited patiently. For a moment, she was

worried there wouldn't be anyone at home, but then she heard the sound of feet padding along carpet. Rosie breathed a sigh of relief as Beth's mother answered the door.

"Hello, Mrs. Wilson. Is Beth in please?"

"Oh Rosie, it's you." Beth's mother smiled. "Beth was wondering when you'd come to see her."

"How is she?" Rosie asked quietly.

"Oh, much better. Another few weeks and she'll be back with you," said Mrs. Wilson, leading the way into the sitting room where Beth was sitting on the sofa.

"Rosie." Beth grinned warmly. "At last. I thought you'd forgotten me. Hang on a minute. I'll turn off the video."

Beth was right. It was the first time that any of them had visited her. Rosie felt embarrassed. She hadn't even come to ask Beth about her leg either.

"You look worried," said Beth. "Come and sit down and tell me your news. How are things at the stables? How are the new people fitting in?"

"That's sort of what I've come to talk to you about," Rosie said desperately. "It's not good. I need your help."

"Why, what is it?" Beth asked, concerned. "There isn't anything wrong is there?"

"I'm not sure." Rosie took a deep breath. "I think I'd better start at the beginning."

Beth propped herself up as Rosie started to go through everything that had happened, trying to explain it all as clearly as possible, until she came to the letter.

"And when I got to Sandy Lane this morning there

was a letter from Nick and Sarah asking Sam to sell Pepper," she said breathlessly.

"What?" Beth gasped. "Nick would never sell him, not Pepper."

"I know, and that's when I started thinking... I don't think the letter's from Nick at all," Rosie continued excitedly.

"Well, who's it from then?" Beth asked, bemused.

Rosie stopped to draw breath.

"Well, I think Sam might have sent it himself. You see, it's typewritten for starters. Why would Nick have typed a letter to Sam? It doesn't make any sense." Rosie didn't wait for an answer before she went on.

"That set me thinking. The letter said that Pepper had to be sold to cover all of the extra costs at the yard... fodder bills, vets bills, farrier bills – that sort of thing. Fair enough. But one thing that was included as an added expense was Blackjack's saddle – the one I told you about."

"Yes," said Beth. "I bet it's going to be really expensive."

"It is," said Rosie. "But don't you see, Beth? Nick and Sarah couldn't have known about it. We only ordered it two days ago and a letter takes more than two days to arrive from Kentucky!"

Beth let out a low whistle.

"So even if Sam and Vanessa *had* phoned Nick about the saddle, a letter still couldn't have got here in that time. So the letter can't be genuine, can it?" she said, slowly rising to her feet. "I think I'd better come to the stables with you and find out what's going on." She reached for her crutches. "I'll see if Mum will drive us there. Where did Sam and Vanessa come from anyway? And whatever happened to Dick Bryant? What did Nick tell you about them?" Beth's questions tumbled out one after the other.

"I don't know," said Rosie. "We haven't spoken to Nick since he left. In fact, you're the only one who has."

"I haven't spoken to Nick," said Beth.

"Yes you have," said Rosie, "when you phoned and told him about your accident."

"But I didn't phone, *you lot* did," said Beth.

"We... we didn't phone." Rosie's cry was strangled in her throat and her face drained of all colour as she grasped the enormity of what they were saying. The two girls looked at each other in shock. If none of them had phoned Nick and Sarah, then who had? Unless... unless Sam and Vanessa hadn't been sent by Nick and Sarah at all.

Rosie felt a shiver run down her spine.

* * * * * * * * * * * * * * * *

Beth and Rosie discussed how to play things on the car journey to Sandy Lane and began to make a plan.

"I'd better arrive after you, Rosie. I've got to appear to be calling on the off-chance – just to see how things are going," said Beth.

"OK. I'll go on ahead of you when we get there," said Rosie. "And we really must phone Nick and Sarah tonight."

"But how can we get hold of them?" said Beth. "You said the number had gone."

"You must have a copy of it though, haven't you?" Rosie said pleadingly.

"Well, no... I don't, Rosie," Beth said sheepishly. "I never jotted it down from the notice board. I didn't think I'd need it."

"Oh Beth," Rosie wailed. "What are we going to do? We can't ask Sam and Vanessa for the number. Even if they've got it, they'll never give it to us. Should we go to the police?"

"No, we've got to find out what they're up to for ourselves first," said Beth. "Who's going to believe us when we don't even know that?"

"You're right," said Rosie.

Mrs. Wilson dropped the girls at the bottom of Sandy Lane and Rosie set off up the drive. A few minutes later, Beth hobbled into the yard, where she was immediately surrounded by excited faces and greeted with question after question.

"Beth, how's your leg?"

"Have you missed us?"

"Are you back for good?"

Beth smiled wearily. "Not exactly," she said. "I'd be a bit useless with this thing, wouldn't I?" she said, pointing to the white plaster cast on her leg. "I've just come to see how you're getting on."

"Not that great," said Kate, gloomily. "The takings have been down all this week."

"Where are Sam and Vanessa?" Rosie interrupted.

"Away again," Tom said gloomily. "There was a telephone call. They had to rush off... said they'd be back in an hour."

"I wonder where they've gone," Rosie said.

"Does it matter?" asked Jess.

"It might do," Rosie said mysteriously.

"Rosie and I have got something to tell you about our friends Sam and Vanessa," Beth explained.

"Something important?" Tom asked.

"Well." Rosie took a deep breath. "I think we'd better go somewhere more private. Just in case they should arrive back."

"Don't keep us in suspense," said Tom. "Tell us."

Quickly, they all hurried to the tack room.

"I don't know where to begin," Rosie said, looking at the faces turned towards her.

"Start at the beginning... like you did with me," Beth said encouragingly.

"OK," said Rosie.

And she took a deep breath and began the story at the very beginning... starting with her misgivings about Sam and Vanessa, glossing over the incidents they all knew about already, right through to the letter.

There was a great deal of commotion as her story unfolded.

"Go on Rosie," said Beth. "Tell them about the significance of the phone call, or rather the non-phone call."

Amid gasps of horror, Rosie told them how Beth hadn't phoned Nick and Sarah.

"But neither did we," Tom gasped.

"Then where have Sam and Vanessa come from?" Kate burst out.

"That's what we've got to find out," Beth said in a calm voice.

"I think we should phone Nick and Sarah," Tom

said sensibly.

Rosie and Beth exchanged nervous glances.

"We can't, Tom," said Rosie.

"Of course we can, Rosie. I know we decided not to bother them before, but this is an emergency. They'd want to know."

"You don't understand, Tom," said Rosie. "There's something I haven't told you... last night, after you left, I was going to phone them. Do you remember?"

"Of course I do," said Tom.

"Well, I couldn't," Rosie said gloomily. "When I got to the tack room, the number had gone and Beth hasn't got a copy of it."

"Oh no," said Tom, holding his head in his hands. "What can we do? Who can we tell?"

"We should go to the police," said Kate.

"And say what?" said Rosie. The others all looked worried.

"Look everyone," said Beth. "Rosie and I have thought all this through. If you'd just give us a chance to explain, we'll tell you our plan."

The others all nodded in agreement.

"Well," said Beth. "We don't have any answers at the moment, so we have to tread very carefully to get them. We don't want Sam and Vanessa getting wind that something's up and we can't go around accusing them of anything until we know what's going on."

"But we're back at school Monday," Tom said. "Who'll look after the yard? Nick and Sarah aren't back until Saturday. Who knows what could happen in a week!"

"I don't propose that we sit tight for long," said Beth. "Just until we can find out what they're up to.

And if you introduce me to them, I'll offer to help out while you're all at school. I know I won't be much good around the yard, but they'll need someone to take bookings. I can keep an eye on things then."

"But what if they don't agree to it?" said Jess.

Beth laughed grimly. "By the sound of it, I don't think they're going to turn down the offer of free help, do you?"

"You're right," said Tom.

"OK then. So that's decided. Are we all agreed?" Beth asked, turning to the group.

"Yes," everyone answered.

"But what about Pepper?" Rosie asked. "He's supposed to be sold on Friday. If we don't put a stop to Sam and Vanessa soon, he'll be gone before we know it."

"We'll just have to take him ourselves and hide him somewhere," said Beth.

"Where?" asked Rosie.

"There's Mr. Green's pig farm?" Tom suggested. "It's near enough to the stables, but no one would think to look in one of those crumbly, old outbuildings at the back."

"Good idea," Kate and Alex said in unison.

"But what if Sam and Vanessa call the police?" said Tom. "What if they report Pepper as stolen?"

"I don't think they'll do that Tom, do you?" said Beth. "I think they'll want to avoid the police at all costs. But it's a gamble we'll have to take. Now, isn't that a car? We'd better break this up. And remember everyone, try to behave as normally as possible." Slowly, everyone filed out of the tack room.

"Hi Sam, hi Vanessa," Tom called, trying to act

cheerfully. "We've got a visitor."

Sam stepped out of the car to face him, looking puzzled.

"Meet Beth, our stable girl," Tom said, as Beth stepped out of the tack room. Rosie watched Sam's face for a reaction. He must be a better actor than she thought for, although he looked surprised, he was quick to collect his composure and stretched out his hand.

"Hi Beth," he said, stepping out of the car. "Pleased to meet you. Heard all about your terrible accident. How's the leg then?" he asked.

"Oh fine. N-n-not bad," she stuttered.

Rosie watched the colour drain from Beth's face. If she wasn't careful she'd be the one to give the game away. They were all supposed to act as though nothing was wrong and Beth was being all jumpy.

As if able to read Rosie's thoughts, Beth managed to regain her composure in time to make her offer of organizing the bookings.

"That's very kind of you," said Sam. "We could do with some help around here too. We'll be rushed off our feet with our regulars back at school." He grinned.

"Well, I am getting a little bored at home too," Beth smiled weakly. "I can't stand being away from the stables."

"That's settled then," said Sam. "Now, what have we got on this afternoon?" he asked.

"You're giving a lesson at three, Sam," Tom answered. "I'll make a start on getting the horses tacked up."

"Fine. Well, I'll get a cup of tea at the cottage and then I'll join you."

"And I'll help you with Pepper, Rosie," said Beth,

forcing a frozen smile in Sam's direction.

"You don't have to," Rosie said surprised. "Why don't you sit down and rest your leg? You look tired."

"No, I'd like to," Beth said forcefully, following her over to his stable.

Rosie drew back the bolt and let them inside. Beth closed the door behind her and let out a huge sigh. Leaning against the wall, she looked as though she'd had the wind knocked out of her.

"What's up? What is it Beth? You look like you've seen a ghost," Rosie said. "You've gone quite pale. You almost gave the game away out there. Are you sure you're going to be all right here on your own next week?"

"Yes, I'll be fine. It's not that, Rosie. I've just had a bit of a shock that's all. You see, I recognize Sam."

Rosie frowned. "Where from?" she asked.

Beth took a deep breath. "If I'm not mistaken, Sam was the driver of that car... the one that almost ran me down."

"What!" Rosie gasped. "The red sports car? Are you sure?"

"Quite sure," said Beth. "There's no doubt about it. Sam was definitely driving. Rosie, he could have killed me!"

10

MIDNIGHT RIDE

Rosie stared at Beth in horror. If Sam had no qualms about running someone down, then just what would he stop at? Rosie shuddered. Things were slowly starting to fall into place – Sam and Vanessa knowing so much about the accident; the way they had arrived so promptly; all of the disasters that had struck. The pieces of the jigsaw were beginning to come together. And Rosie wasn't too sure she liked the picture.

"All right in here girls?" Rosie jumped as Sam's face loomed over the stable door.

"Yes, fine," she said returning his clear, calculated gaze.

Beth couldn't bring herself to look at him.

"Beth, we've got to get Pepper out of here straight away," Rosie whispered urgently once Sam had walked away.

"We'll have to be careful, Rosie," Beth breathed.

"We can't take him too soon or we won't find out what they're up to and we won't stand a chance with the police. Who's going to believe us? It all sounds so ridiculous."

"But can't you tell them that Sam was driving that car?" Rosie said desperately.

"But I said in my statement that I couldn't remember what the man looked like. And it was true. It was only seeing him today that jogged my memory. It's going to look very strange if I suddenly come up with the perfect photofit."

"It certainly doesn't look that good," Rosie said thoughtfully. "But we can't hang on for much longer."

"No," said Beth. "But we have to try to get some evidence... see if Sam and Vanessa let anything slip. After all, at the moment, we don't even know what they're up to. It's probably best if you take Pepper on Thursday evening."

Rosie gulped. "Isn't that cutting it a bit fine? Someone's coming to collect him on Friday."

"No," said Beth firmly, "not if I keep an eye on things here. And I'll phone you if there's any news."

"OK," said Rosie hesitantly. "Thursday it is, then."

* * * * * * * * * * * * * * * *

Beth was as good as her word and kept everyone informed about the goings-on at the yard, but there wasn't a great deal to report and the next few days passed slowly for Rosie. Concentrating on school lessons was near impossible. She couldn't help worrying that something terrible was happening in her absence. She was sure that Sam and Vanessa must be planning some grand finale before Nick and Sarah returned.

When Beth phoned on Thursday evening, Rosie was shaking so much she could hardly hold the receiver.

"All set Rosie?" Beth whispered. "I can't talk very loudly. My mother's lurking in the background. Have you got it all mapped out for tonight?"

"Yes," Rosie answered. "Yes, I've set my alarm for eleven thirty."

"And you know exactly where you're taking Pepper?"

"Yes, the old shed to the right of the huge barn. It's all sorted out," said Rosie.

"Well, good luck then."

Rosie put down the phone and looked at her watch. Nine o'clock. Eleven thirty seemed like an eternity.

"Are you all right, Rosie?" her mother asked. "You look a little peaky. You're not about to come down with something are you?"

"No Mum," Rosie said. "But I think I'll go off to bed and get an early night."

"OK." Rosie's mother smiled. "Good night then."

Rosie padded up the stairs and closed the door behind her. Quickly, she double-checked she had everything: torch, pony nuts, riding hat. Yes, that was the lot.

Pacing up and down the room, she set her alarm clock and pulled out her jodhpurs from the cupboard. Climbing into bed, Rosie turned on the bedside lamp and picked up her latest pony book. But five pages later, she realized she hadn't taken in any of the story. It was no good. Turning out the lamp, she snuggled under her duvet.

Drifting in and out of sleep, she woke up to see the luminous hands on her alarm clock at twenty past eleven. Swiftly, she turned it off before it could make a noise. Creeping out of bed, she threw off her night clothes and pulled a jumper on over her head as she gathered up her things. Stopping for a moment to plump up her pillows and put them under her duvet, she tiptoed out onto the landing. Her heart was racing and her legs felt like jelly. Easing her way down to the hallway, careful to avoid the creaky stair, she drew back the bolt on the front door and stepped outside.

The cold was the first thing that hit her as she hurried over to her bike. It was a clear night and there wasn't anyone in sight. Nimbly, she cycled out of the drive, and down the dimly-lit roads. As she headed into the dead of the night, the trees cast their shadowy silhouettes on the ground. Rosie reached Sandy Lane in no time at all.

Jumping to the ground, she wheeled her bike off the drive and hid it in the hedgerow. Taking a quick glance up the drive, she was surprised to see the cottage all lit up. A hazy yellow glow surrounded it. She knew she should go straight to Pepper's stable but she found herself inextricably drawn towards the light in the cottage. She couldn't stop herself. What would Sam and Vanessa do if they caught her? Rosie shuddered at the thought.

Ducking down, she stole up on the cottage, like a lion stalking its prey, and peered into the sitting room.

Inside, Sam sat twirling a silver cigarette lighter in his fingers. The smoke from his cigarette spiralled out of the open window. Rosie strained her ears to hear what they were saying.

"I should never have listened to this mad scheme. You're taking things too far, Ralph." It was Vanessa's voice.

What were they talking about? Rosie froze to the spot. She took a long look through the window. She could only see Sam and Vanessa inside, so where was Ralph? Unless...

Rosie strained her ears to listen to the continuing conversation. The words that followed sent shivers down her spine. Her heart began to palpitate.

"...I haven't gone far enough, that's the problem," Sam was saying. "I told you we wouldn't be able to ruin Sandy Lane's reputation with double bookings and cancelled rides. Nick Brooks – damn him – he's back on Saturday and time's running out. I've got to do something serious... something to destroy Sandy Lane, once and for all."

Rosie staggered back, stumbling into the bush behind her.

"Who's that, who's there?" Sam called, opening the door to the cottage.

Rosie felt the hairs rising on the back of her neck. Could he see her? He seemed to be looking straight through her. Her pulse was racing. She couldn't breathe. She felt herself burning up.

"There's no one there. You're imagining things," Vanessa's voice whined. "Come on back inside. We ought to get some sleep. We've got a lot to do over the next couple of days. Pepper's being collected tomorrow isn't he? What have you done about payment?"

"Cash on delivery, that was the deal," said Sam, walking into the kitchen and out of earshot.

Rosie was chilled to the spot. Scrunching herself up into a ball, she sat tight. What did it all mean? What terrible thing did they have planned for Sandy Lane?

She looked at her watch. Half past twelve. How long would she have to wait until the coast was clear to get Pepper? Gingerly, she stood up and looked inside the cottage. Sam was sitting up poring over some papers. Would he never go to bed? She was starting to feel the cold now and the night air was numbing her fingers. She settled herself down again.

It was a good ten minutes before she saw one of the lights flicker off. Her heart leapt and slowly she raised herself to her feet. Vanessa was wandering around the room, switching the lamps off as she went. They must be going to bed. Rosie breathed a sigh of relief. She had made it undetected. She waited a few more minutes to give them time to get up the stairs and into bed, then stealthily she crept into the yard.

Pepper looked wide-eyed as Rosie drew back the bolt and stepped inside his stable.

"Ssh, ssh my boy. We've got to get you away from here quickly," she said, holding out the handful of pony nuts she had brought with her.

Pepper munched contentedly as Rosie shone her light around the stable. Beth had been as good as her word and left the tack out for her. Deftly, Rosie put the bridle on over Pepper's head.

"Easy now," she whispered as she grabbed a haynet and slung it over her shoulder. There wasn't time for a saddle. She'd have to ride bareback.

Leading Pepper out of the stable, she turned him to the gate at the back of the yard. She was going to have to ride him to Mr. Green's pig farm across the fields, to avoid passing the cottage. With a quick backwards glance, Rosie vaulted onto the little pony's back. She half-expected to hear an angry yell as she nudged Pepper forward into a trot. But all was quiet.

The further Rosie rode from Sandy Lane, the more confident she felt. Cantering through the fields, they crossed the old coastal track and headed into Bucknell Woods.

It was dark, but Rosie could vaguely see her way by the light of the moon. The sound of a hooting owl stopped Pepper in his tracks, but Rosie was quick to nudge him on. The smell of pine clung in the air as they picked their way through the trees.

"We're nearly there, Pepper," she said, more to reassure herself than anything else.

All was quiet as they walked out of the woods and crossed the road. This was the bit where they had to be careful. If Sam had heard them leave the yard, he would be bound to come searching by car. But Rosie could hear neither the sound of a car engine nor see the flash of headlights. She started to relax as they trotted across the tarmac.

Taking the back route into Mr. Green's pig farm, she headed straight for the shed.

"No one will think to look for you here, Pepper," she whispered, jumping to the ground. "I know it's not what you're used to, but you'll be safe," she went on, as she took off his bridle and shut the little pony in. "I'm going to have to leave you now – before anyone notices that I'm missing. You'll be all right, really you will." She scattered the last of the pony nuts on the floor and attached the haynet to a ring. "And Jess is going to come and see you tomorrow morning before school, with your breakfast." She patted his speckled shoulder fondly.

Pepper snickered softly as Rosie filled the trough with water. She wished she could stay all night to keep guard over him. But there were other things she had to do. She must be up early to phone everyone and tell them her awful discovery. They needed to make plans. With a heavy heart, Rosie turned for home.

11

PLANS

"Sam's furious. He's been running around cursing, accusing everyone imaginable of taking Pepper." Beth laughed down the phone. "You should have seen his face. He looked absolutely livid. You're top on his list of suspects by the way."

"Beth," Rosie said quietly.

"And I double-bluffed him too," Beth continued, not stopping to listen. "Asked him why he didn't call the police. But it's as we thought. He didn't want to."

"*Beth*," Rosie pleaded urgently. "Would you just stop and listen. You're not going to believe it. I overheard Sam and Vanessa talking at the cottage last night... the double bookings, the cancelled rides... they planned it all. It was all done on purpose, to ruin Sandy Lane's reputation," she said breathlessly.

There was no answer from the other end as Beth listened to what Rosie was saying.

"Beth... can you hear me? Are you still there?"

"Yes, yes," Beth said. "I'm still here. But why? Why would they want to ruin Sandy Lane's reputation? It doesn't make any sense."

"I don't know why, Beth," Rosie said. "But from the way they were talking they're certainly not friends of Nick and Sarah's." Rosie took a deep breath. "It gets worse. They know that Nick and Sarah are back on Saturday, and they're planning to do something else... something more serious. Sam talked about destroying Sandy Lane once and for all. What can he mean?"

"I don't know," Beth said hesitantly. "I daren't think. Rosie, are you sure you heard things right?"

"Quite sure," said Rosie. "We've got to go to the police, Beth. Now... this is getting out of control."

"But what do we tell them, Rosie? What do we say? That you overheard a conversation at the cottage in the middle of the night? They'll never believe us. We need proof of exactly what Sam and Vanessa are up to. Look, Nick and Sarah are due back tomorrow aren't they?

"Yes," Rosie said slowly.

"Then we'll just have to sit tight and keep watch. Whatever Sam and Vanessa have got planned, they've got to do it soon. And we must be there to stop them. If we can get firm evidence, then we can go to the police. Listen, you go to school and I'll think of a plan. Do you think you can get everyone to meet me at eight this evening at the bottom of the drive?" Beth said quickly. "We can't leave Sandy Lane unguarded for a moment.

"Yes," said Rosie. "I'm sure I can slip word to

everyone at school."

"Good," Beth said.

"But Beth," Rosie said uncertainly. "What if we can't stop them?"

There was no answer, as Beth stopped to think.

"We will, Rosie," she answered grimly. "We just have to."

* * * * * * * * * * * * * * * *

It was dusk when everyone met up at the bottom of the drive and the twilight cast an eerie haze around the group of figures. Alex and Kate stood huddled up inside their anoraks as Charlie shuffled his feet. Tom held a torch, lighting up Jess's pinched features. They had been horrified when Rosie had told them what she had overheard.

"Is everyone here?" Beth asked, looking around her. They all nodded.

"OK," she went on. "We've got to decide on a plan of action. We don't know exactly what Sam and Vanessa are going to do, but whatever it is, we've got to catch them red-handed. We'll have to keep an eye on them every minute of the day until Nick and Sarah get back... that means we can't leave Sandy Lane unguarded at any time, starting with tonight."

"But what do we tell our parents?" Rosie said, worried.

Beth bit her lip nervously. "I don't think we should

tell our parents anything – not yet."

Rosie looked anxious. "OK then," she said slowly.

"I think we should make the tack room, the barn, the cottage, the outdoor school and three separate stables all look-out points," said Beth. "Is everyone happy with that?"

"Yes," they all answered.

"Well, there are seven of us," Beth went on. "At the first sign of trouble, we have to hold them and call the police. Is everyone agreed?"

Everyone nodded in acceptance.

"Now," said Beth. "Remember, no one is to raise the alarm until they are absolutely certain Sam and Vanessa are up to something. They should have finished the evening feeds by now. My guess is that they'll be in the cottage clearing out their stuff, so make sure you get to your positions without being seen."

Beth was right. As Rosie crept behind the stables, she could see the silhouetted figures of Sam and Vanessa moving around inside the cottage. Their Range Rover was parked close to the cottage, its boot wide open as they stacked their stuff in for their getaway. Rosie was furious to see Nick's silver racing trophies piled up with all the other things in the back, but something told her that this wasn't the worst they could expect. She couldn't resist pausing by the cottage to listen to Sam and Vanessa's conversation as she made her way to the barn. They were arguing. Rosie felt pleased when she realized that her handiwork was the cause of their distress.

"We can't wait any longer for Pepper to show up," Sam was saying. "It's a nuisance. We desperately needed that money. I'm sure those wretched children must have taken him. If only I could think where." He scratched his head.

"We can't worry about that now," said Vanessa. "It's more important that we clear out of here quickly. Things are starting to get a little uncomfortable for my liking."

As much as she would have liked to have stayed and listened, Rosie dragged herself along to the big barn. As she crept along the path, she heard Feather let out a loud whinny, but apart from that, all was quiet.

Climbing on top of the hay bales, she settled herself down. She knew she was in for a long wait and she was tired. She hadn't got to bed until two in the morning and she'd been up at seven for school. She had to stay awake. Desperately, she tried to keep her eyes open, but her head kept lolling back. What had Beth said? No one was to raise the alarm until they were certain... absolutely certain. Rosie yawned. The light wasn't good in the yard at the moment. She was losing her concentration.

Rosie looked at her watch. Eight thirty. She shifted her body as she cast her mind back to all that had happened. There was something bothering her. If only she could think straight...

Rosie leant back, the words from last night ringing in her ears. Ralph... Ralph... Ralph.

She must have dozed off because, when she awoke, there was a loud commotion going on in the yard. A strong acrid smell permeated the air. She drew her breath in sharply. What was it ? It smelt like a garage... It was petrol, that's what it was! Peering over the top of the hay bales, she saw Sam and Vanessa carrying large cans across the yard. Rosie started to panic as she scrambled out of the hay. Fire! They had meant exactly what they had said. They did mean to destroy Sandy Lane once and for all – Sam and Vanessa planned to raze the stables to the ground. Rosie's heart sank. Had she and her friends arrived too late?

Rosie felt sickened. What did Sam and Vanessa think would happen to all of the horses? Did they plan to let them go up in smoke? Rosie went hot and cold at the thought. She was rooted to the spot. Her feet felt like leaden weights.

"What can I do?" she croaked.

But before she had time to do anything at all, she saw Tom step out from the shadows and shout across the yard.

"Just stop right there." His voice echoed around the stables.

* * * * * * * * * * * * * * * *

Sam seemed startled for a moment and then he saw who it was and started to laugh.

"So you think you're going to stop me do you, Tom?" he jeered.

Rosie grimaced as beams of light bounced off the silver object in Sam's hand. It was the cigarette lighter she had seen him playing with before. One flick of the wrist was all that was needed to destroy Sandy Lane. With all the petrol Sam and Vanessa had used to lace the stables, Sandy Lane wouldn't stand a chance. Sam smiled sneeringly, flicking the lid of the lighter up and down whilst he waited for Tom's next move.

Rosie held her breath. If Tom didn't act quickly, Sandy Lane would go up in smoke. She had to do something herself.

"Yes, we can put a stop to you," Rosie called from her hiding place. "We know what your game is. Deliberate sabotage... isn't that what it's called? I think the police will be very interested in what we have to say."

Sam laughed a low, menacing laugh.

"So you think the police will believe you lot do you? By the time they've heard your version of events, Sandy Lane will be history and we'll be out of here without trace."

"You may be out of here, but we'll know where to find you, Ralph... Ralph Winterson," Rosie said bravely.

Sam looked startled.

"Isn't that your real name, Sam?" Rosie went on, stronger now. "You're nothing but an imposter – Ralph Winterson of the Clarendon Equestrian Centre, although you never do any work there either. Been had up for cruelty to horses as well, haven't you?"

Tom let out a loud gasp. For a moment there was silence. And then the stillness of the yard was broken by a loud clapping sound.

"Very good, my dear."

Sneeringly, Sam clapped his hands together in mock applause.

"You've certainly done your homework. But you can't prove a word of it. Can you?" he challenged.

"Can't I?" Rosie said calmly. "But I can. You see, I have evidence to prove it – a taped conversation between you and Vanessa about twelve thirty last night, talking about the double bookings and cancelled rides. Does it ring any bells?" she demanded. "I think the police will believe us then."

"You're bluffing," said Sam. But from the look on his face, Rosie knew that he wasn't sure.

"OK," he said, changing his tactics. "What do you want? Money?"

Rosie looked at him disgusted.

"The only thing we want is to get you away from here before Nick and Sarah come back. Did you really think you could ruin Sandy Lane's reputation so easily? Did you really think everyone would flock to your lousy stables?"

"Well, if we do as you say, what will you do with the tape?" Sam's voice reverberated around the yard.

"Nothing," said Rosie calmly, "on one condition..."

The others all looked at her in amazement.

Tom seemed about to say something, but Rosie held up her hand to silence him and swallowed hard.

"We won't do anything, so long as you agree to close down the Clarendon Equestrian Centre without any fuss. Pack your bags and disappear out of this neighbourhood for good."

Sam opened his mouth to speak and closed it again. Realizing he was beaten, he shut up his lighter with a final snap and turned to go.

"And one more thing," Rosie called sharply. "You can put Nick's racing trophies back in the cottage where you found them."

Sam shot her an angry glance and turned to Vanessa.

"Come on," he growled. "We're out of here. We've got better things to do."

Everything had happened so quickly. One minute, Sam held the future of Sandy Lane in his hand, the next, he and Vanessa had shut up the boot of their Range Rover and were speeding out of the yard.

"I hope that's the last we'll see of them," said Rosie.

No one knew what to say and for a moment there was an uncomfortable silence until Jess burst out.

"Rosie, you were brilliant," she said. "I can't believe you worked all that out for yourself."

"It wasn't that hard," Rosie said blushing graciously. "Just a bit of detective work."

"But to get it all on tape," Tom said admiringly.

"Well actually, I didn't." Rosie reddened and laughed. "I couldn't possibly have got anything clearly on tape from that distance. That was just a bluff."

12

ALL IS WELL

"So when Sam, or should I say Ralph, realized that he couldn't destroy Sandy Lane's reputation so easily, he turned to more drastic measures."

It was Saturday at Sandy Lane and the regulars had spent the morning hard at work, getting rid of all the petrol-soaked straw. Susannah was listening to Rosie's story.

"So, that explains the '*For Sale*' board outside the Clarendon Equestrian Centre," said Susannah. "Everyone's been talking about it."

Rosie smiled thoughtfully.

"But there's one thing I don't understand," Susannah went on. "Why didn't you go straight to the police when you found out what they were up to?"

"Well," Rosie hesitated. "First, we didn't really know what they were up to until the very last minute, and secondly, I didn't have any evidence anyway. It would have been my word against theirs."

"You're right," said Susannah.

"And what's more," Rosie said proudly, "I've just had some amazing news."

Rosie bent down and whispered something in the little girl's ear.

"Wow," said Susannah. "Tentenden! Wait till the others hear."

"What are you two gassing about?" asked Jess, coming up behind them. "Did I hear the word Tentenden mentioned?"

"You certainly did," said Rosie. "Guess what?" she said proudly, as everyone gathered round. "I can't keep it a secret any longer. We'll be riding in the Tentenden Team Chase next weekend after all. I phoned them this morning, just in time it appears." She grinned mischievously. "It seems one of the teams have dropped out, the Clarendon Equestrian Centre, no less." Her eyes sparkled. "And we can take their place."

"What?" shrieked Tom.

"But that's fantastic, Rosie," Jess whooped, throwing her riding hat in the air.

Rosie beamed as she looked around at the delighted faces of her friends. In her dreams, the Tentenden trophy had long been theirs. She could almost see it now, the silver cup shimmering in the tack room.

But at that moment, everyone's excited chatter was silenced as a car rounded the corner and pulled up in the yard. Then there were voices. Voices they all recognized. Nick and Sarah had returned from America! Ebony went quite wild and hurled himself upon them as they stepped out of the taxi and everyone gathered round.

"Whoa boy, now calm down," Nick laughed. "Hi everyone," he said looking around him at the welcoming faces. "Phew. It's good to be home," he grinned. "I don't suppose much has happened here while we've been away, but have we got some stories for you."

Rosie looked at the others and smiled.